DANCES WITH RAPTORS

A DINOVERSE NOVEL

POPPY WOODS

Dances with Raptors

POPPY WOODS

For all the nerds like us
Keep it up, you clever girls.

CONTENTS

COPYRIGHT

Cover art by Rabbit Hole Graphics
Formatting by The Swamp Goddess

A WORD FROM THE AUTHOR

Dear Reader,

Thank you, firstly, for taking the time to give this book a chance. Kendra and I know that this universe is a little different than the shifter books you are used to reading and our inner nerds are *so* excited that you have decided to come on this ride with us!

The Dinoverse was born before my first book in *The Unsung Veil* series was even published, way back in November 2018. I met Kendra during her release party for *Clockwork Butterfly* and we hit it off *instantly*. She's my nerd bestie and I couldn't do any of this without her. We were rambling—I was probably drunk, but she definitely wasn't—about all the nerdy things we like and started talking about dinosaurs and, "Why aren't there any dinosaur shifter books?! There's dragons!"

That lead to us both admitting we had ideas on the back burner for a dino-shifter novel. *And that lead* to us combining our ideas into one shared universe for you guys to devour and fall in love with! Okay, maybe that last part is wishful thinking, but I'm an optimist. We started world building and talking about cover designs—our covers are made by Kendra, aren't they gorgeous?—and what we could do with this amazing sub-genre that hasn't really been touched on yet.

What you can expect from The Dinoverse: We are going to be doing dual releases for the entirety of this series. They will be listed in 'chronological order' meaning whichever story takes place the farthest in the past will be listed as the first/next in series, but there will always be two at a time and the stories themselves are not connected by characters or plot. The theme for book one and book two in The Dinoverse is 'past.'

And so I give you *Dances with Raptors*. I hope you enjoy Sage as much as I enjoyed writing her and her boys.

Poppy Woods

Chapter
1

Sage

I stared up at the rafters of the home I'd lived in most of my life. We'd had to rebuild after a big storm felled a tree when I was ten. Luckily, it had missed everyone inside. Mom had thanked the tree repeatedly for not harming her children. My little brother had only been a toddler when we had to rebuild the chickee. The small, open-sided homes didn't take long to build, but they still required a lot of effort and energy.

Stop procrastinating.

I groaned at the guilty voice inside my head, ignoring the wind whipping the tapestry that separated my parents' space from the rest of our home. Today was the day. Today, I would go out in search of my ancestors so I could become the next matriarch, the next leader of my people. Women had always been the natural born leaders of our people because they were natural born caretakers, and my people understood that a good leader should be concerned with the welfare of their people. For example, it would bother a leader when a warrior was lost in a battle, so much so that they were willing to dismiss their own pride and avoid a battle altogether. Matriarchs were those things and more. They were the people that bound us together. They were peace bringers, mediators, leaders, and war-makers when necessary.

1

"Are you ready?" Chayton whispered from across the room.

I sat up and stretched my arms, while looking across the space separating us. My little brother was growing up. He was twelve now and had already begun going on hunts with the other boys in our village. I smiled at him and nodded my head.

"I'm ready," I lied. I didn't want to disappoint my family. I didn't want to shame my mother. As the current matriarch, she was tasked with finding the spirit of the next one—the next leader of our people. I swallowed and tried to hold the smile on my face.

"Liar!" Chayton teased from his bed on the floor. I reached for my comb and tossed it at him.

"Shut up," I sighed. "Are they awake yet?"

"They're not even here. Mom is already in the village with the elders, preparing everything for your walk." Chayton reached his arms over his head, mirroring my own wake up ritual. "They'll be ready for you soon."

I bit my lip and narrowed my eyes on my annoying little brother. It wasn't *actually* his fault that today was the biggest day of my life, and I still wasn't sure why my mother seemed to think I was worthy of leading our people.

I'd never done anything remarkable. Ever. I spent most of my time outside the village, exploring the peninsula, instead of mirroring my mother and caring for our people. I had always explored and my parents had always called me their curious child. My name, Sage, even meant knowledge. I guess it was fitting. I scratched my nose and rose from my bed on the floor. I needed to make myself look presentable for the elders. Today was going to happen no matter how much I wanted to avoid it.

No one had ever refused the position of matriarch. Our history goes back generations, and the elders had never mentioned a matriarch who didn't rise to the challenge. Our tribe hadn't been at war in a long time, thanks to the treaties our ancestors had secured. The closest tribes were allies, often coming to seek medicine for their sick, and our healers were renowned for their skills. An old, deep magic ran through the blood of our people.

According to the shaman, one of our tribe members had been there to help the world's first panther when it emerged from the Shell of Life. The panther is the creator's favorite animal, since they are cunning, wise, and quiet unless there's a need to not be. When it first came out of the Shell of Life, the panther tripped on a rock. There aren't rocks above the arch—the place where the Spirits lived—so it made sense that he wouldn't know he could stumble on them. The panther broke his ankle, and one of our ancestors found him laying at the bottom of the hill.

The hunter took out his bow and aimed, but couldn't bring himself to kill the injured animal. Instead, he took the panther to his village and nursed it back to health. Weeks later, when the cat could finally walk on all four paws, it left the chickee village. The shamans claimed that night, the man went to sleep and dreamed of the creator, and awoke the next morning as the world's first healer. He had the power to set bones so accurately they healed much faster than normal, and for as long as the man lived in the chickee village, sickness never claimed a life. When he realized he was growing old and would soon die, he begged the creator to share his gifts with his people so that they could continue to prosper.

I shook my head and pulled myself out of my thoughts, blinking at my reflection in the bowl of water. Of all the stories that our people kept alive, that one had stood out to me the most as a child. I swept my long, dark hair back and braided it until it fell over my shoulder in a uniformed cord. I pulled my beaded bone necklace on over my head, and smiled when it fell into the hollow between my breasts.

"I can't believe you still wear that thing," Chayton called, as he jumped from the chickee to the ground.

"Why wouldn't I wear it?" I followed him toward the center of the village, elbowing his ribs as we walked.

"You're just so sentimental about the strangest things." He shrugged, waving to a group of men as we passed them. "And not others." His voice was lower now, his eyebrows wiggling suggestively as we passed the last man in the group.

"Hello, Sage," Rain murmured.

"Hi." My pace picked up and I stared at my feet as I hurried toward the center of the village. Rain had made his intentions for me known, but I didn't return his affections. I wasn't sure why I wasn't attracted to him, except something about the man set my teeth on edge. He wasn't a bad man, I didn't sense any evil from him, but Rain was probably too good, if I was honest.

Rain was the healer's apprentice. He was absolutely brilliant and had healed several wounds for me over the years so that my mother wouldn't find out the kind of stuff I'd gotten up to when I'd snuck out of the village. His mother's husbands were all different kinds of men, but every single one of them were mild-mannered, as was Rain. Whenever he pursued me, tried courting me, I couldn't help but crave *more*. More adventure, more romance, more excitement . . . more than Rain.

"Why do you do that?" Chayton mumbled, once we were far enough away where Rain couldn't overhear us.

"Do what?"

"Why do you dismiss him? He's a good man, Sage. He'd be a good husband for a matriarch." Chayton pointed to where my mother stood next to our father. My mom, Ayasha, had only one husband. My father was fierce though, and he had won my mother's heart when traders tried to raid the village. He'd taken an arrow in his chest defending her mother, and they'd been inseparable ever since. I sighed as I watched how my dad doted on her. He tucked a stray piece of hair behind her ear, and whispered something that made her blush, and the fact that he could make her blush after so many years together amazed me.

"Because of that." I waved in the same direction he was pointing. "They're perfect for one another. There's a spark between them, Chayton. I don't expect you to understand, you're just a kid—"

"I am not!"

"You are," I grumbled, walking closer to the crowd gathering around my parents. The elders were lined up to the side, and in front of each woman sat a small bowl. I glanced at my brother and he smiled grimly at me.

"It's going to be fine, *ervhv*," he whispered, reaching out to cup my shoulder.

I smiled at him and turned to face the people gathered in front of my mother and the elders. I threw my shoulders back and walked proudly between my people toward the matriarch. Even if I was unsure why the Spirits thought I'd make a good matriarch, I owed it to my people to act like one until they rejected me.

And they will reject me, because there must have been some kind of mistake.

"Approach, future matriarch!" my mom called out. I walked up to her and waited. Her face didn't match her formal tone at all. She was all smiles, her light brown eyes shining in the morning light.

"Matriarch," I murmured, and bowed my head respectfully.

My mother smoothed my hair down, her hand trailing down to my cheek as she lifted my chin up. I gazed up at her and was awestruck again. Paint clung to her skin along her cheekbones and her forehead, and holy designs swirled down her arms and her tawny legs. The beautiful colors of the symbols stood out bright against her skin and I swallowed. They'd be painting me any moment now. As the future matriarch, I'd be painted in white, but other than that they'd be identical to my mother's.

If I managed to pass whatever test the ancestors set out for me, I'd return home and begin studying under the current matriarch, my mother. As time moved on—and I learned how to be a good matriarch —the white symbols would be replaced with colored ones until they matched hers. On that day, the Matriarch Ayasha would step aside and take her place as an elder, while I'll lead our people.

I gulped as my mother waved her hand toward the line of elders waiting with bowls in their hands. I moved to the first woman, who was the matriarch who had trained my mother. Her weathered, wrinkled face greeted me with a knowing smirk. Nova had been a trouble-maker in her own day. My mom had told us stories about the time they'd almost been taken hostage by a neighboring tribe, but Nova seduced the warriors and escaped.

Those three warriors had found their way to our village and begged to marry Nova. She finally accepted them after they refused to leave for an entire moon cycle. Her dark green eyes twinkled with mirth as she raised her hand and began drawing the symbols on my forehead.

"May the ancestors see your soul for what it is," she murmured.

My eyes snapped to hers, a gasp slipping from my lips. The old woman only chuckled and patted me on the arm before she stepped back. My mother tossed me an encouraging smile from beside her mentor. I bit my lip and moved on to the next elder, and she was not much older than my mother.

One by one the women whispered their words of encouragement and smudged the cold, white paint across my skin until I was complete. My mom walked down to the end of the line where I stood and clasped my face in her hands.

"I am so proud of you, Sage," she murmured. "You will do your ancestors justice, my curious one."

I choked back tears and nodded. She had so much faith in me—so much misplaced faith. I forced my lips to smile, even though my heart was heavy with the knowledge that I'd fail whatever test awaited me.

There must have been some kind of mistake.

"Here," she began, in a louder voice for everyone to hear. "Your supplies for your journey." I took the satchel she handed me and glanced inside. A large bone knife clinked against some smaller bones, which had been painted in the colors of the matriarch.

"What am I supposed to do with these?" I asked, glancing from woman to woman.

"You'll know when the time comes." Nova winked and I sighed, looking through the rest of the items in the satchel. There was some dried meat, bound together with twine, along with a fire rock.

I slid the knife into the belt around my hips and nodded. I couldn't argue with them. Skepticism had always been a part of my nature, but the people around me tended to believe whatever they were told. It bothered me.

There were things in the world that couldn't be explained with our eyes—like my people's affinity for healing—but that didn't mean there was divine intervention lurking around every bend.

You're blasphemous, that's the entire problem. Do you even believe in the creator?

I ignored the doubt and guilt that was rambling around inside my head and turned to face the crowd, holding my arms up above my head. My mother did the same, and one by one the elders followed suit. Pretty soon the crowd was cheering. Off to the side stood Rain and Chayton, their heads inclined toward one another as they pointed at me.

The feel of so many eyes on me had my skin crawling. If this was a lot of attention, though, I couldn't *wait* to see what would happen once I returned as a failure. I tilted my chin up, gazing out into faces that were depending on me. Young and old villagers alike stood there, smiling and cheering for their future matriarch—they believed in me. A young mother balanced her baby boy on her hip and waved, and the gesture had a rock forming in my stomach... they needed so much more than I could give them, didn't they?

"You're not going to find your place in the history of our people by comparing yourself to others, Sage," a male voice whispered by my ear.

I jumped and spun around to face the offender. My father cracked a wide grin and held his hands up in mock defense. I narrowed my eyes on him before I laughed, and let him pull me into a hug.

"How did you know?" I peered up at him, wondering for the millionth time in my life how he always seemed to know what I was up to.

"Can't tell you that, little one." He tapped his finger to his temple and winked. I shook my head and glanced out at the edge of the water. Our village was at the edge of a river, close enough that we could get water. It's one of the reasons our chickees were raised off the ground, since flooding was a regular occurrence here and some of the water animals could be testy. No one wanted to wake up to an angry alligator in their home. We hardly ever found snakes in the chickees either, thankfully, as they just slithered right by on the ground.

"When Mom was confirmed as the matriarch, she stopped a scaly from ripping the village apart. She calmed him down and convinced him to shift back to his human form and he left. That took so much bravery, I don't—"

"You do, Sage. You're your mother's daughter." My dad stared back at me with sad eyes. He was disappointed in me, I guess, and just couldn't admit it to me. I shrugged my shoulder before I put my public face back on, turned toward the people who believed in me, and waved goodbye.

"Until we meet again," I called out, placing my fist over my heart.

"Until we meet again!" a cacophony of voices responded. I searched the crowd for Chayton, but he was nowhere to be found. I didn't like that, I wished I could tell him goodbye properly. I spun around and marched out into the brush that began on the other side of our village, away from the river.

Chapter 2

Sage

I dug my toes into the sand and stared out at the big water. I came here sometimes when I needed to think. I was supposed to be out on some big spiritual journey, but I had no idea where to begin. I wasn't given a map or any kind of direction. My mother had handed me some basic survival tools, a spiritual totem for our people, and sent me on my way.

"Where the fuck do I even go from here?" I groaned, and tossed a rock out into the surf.

Caw!

Caw!

I glanced up, shielding my eyes from the sun as I searched for the source of the shrieking. High above me, a hawk chased a smaller bird. I gulped, watching the chase. Every time the bird of prey got close, the smaller bird—a swallow, I think—would dart in a new direction. I curled my fingers into the sand, praying for the little guy's escape.

The small bird swooped lower and I was finally able to make it out, and my earlier assessment had been wrong. It was a mockingbird, which dove down and zipped to the right, narrowly avoiding the hawk's talons before it fluttered safely into the cover of the thickening brush behind me. A small smile curved my lips. For some reason, that tiny bird's survival felt like a small, personal victory for me.

I rose to my feet, dusting the sand from my butt, and began walking along the shore, waiting for some kind of sign from the ancestors.

"Oh, divine intervention?" I called out to the empty shoreline. The only answer was the soft whisper of the waves and the screeching of a hungry hawk above. I shrugged my shoulders up to my ears, listening to the comforting clink of my beaded necklace as it followed the movement.

"Ow!" I howled, stopping in my tracks and lifting my foot up from the sand. I bent my knee, and balanced precariously on one leg as I investigated my left foot. I winced when I saw the culprit. I'd stepped on the wrong end of a shell. My right eye closed as I focused on the thing sticking out of the bottom of my foot, before I pulled it out with a yelp and a string of curses that would have made my father blush.

I wiped the blood away from my sole, peering warily at the wound. It didn't seem very deep, so it would be fine. I placed my foot back in the sand, bracing myself for the sharp pain that accompanied the movement, and then examined the shell I still held in my hand. It was beautiful and an almost completely intact curved nautilus. The shell was only broken at the very end where it had lodged in my poor foot. My thumb swiped away the red staining at the end of the white and pink seashell, but the blood wouldn't wipe away from the ivory end. It had stained the shell a dark crimson already.

A shiver wound up my spine and I glanced around, trying to shake the feeling of being watched. I studied the thickets that lead up to the sand, which grew sparser the closer you got to the sea. There didn't *seem* to be anyone out there, but I knew from experience how misleading appearances could be.

Warriors were especially skilled at hiding in plain sight. My father had once painted darker lines along his body so he blended in with the trees he was hunting in. The flexibility that our hunters and warriors had never ceased to amaze me. Asha, my mother's sister, was one of our finest warriors. She'd never lost a fight to anyone, not even my father.

I squinted my eyes, trying to be one-hundred-percent sure I wasn't being watched. I swished my mouth from side to side and tucked the shell into my satchel before I began walking again, waiting for some kind of sign that I was worthy—or unworthy—of returning home a matriarch. I turned toward the brush and decided to head inland. There was nothing out here on this beach but my loud thoughts and me.

I PADDED THROUGH THE TREES ON SILENT FEET, CONCENTRATING on the world around me. The woods were filled with the sounds of birds. I'd been walking for hours and there was still no sign of a test from the ancestors. I stretched my arms over my head and listened. There was a stream nearby. Moving toward the sound of trickling water, I licked my lips. I was thirsty. I pulled the empty bladder from my belt as I approached the edge of the water.

Glancing around, ensuring I was alone, I bent to fill it with water for my trip. When it was filled, I slid the bladder into the satchel on my side and crouched, cupping water in my hands to wet my face. The cool water was refreshing. The hot day had crept up on me quickly, and even among the trees, the heat was sweltering. I rinsed my face a few more times, dabbing water on my throat and the back of my neck. Some water seeped into the roots of my braid and I shivered at the cooling effect on my scalp.

I looked at the water and pulled my satchel over my head. Since the water had felt so amazing against my skin, I was going to take a dip in the stream while I could. I pulled my top over my head and untied my skirt—the pieces of fabric and animal hide were something I'd made earlier in the year. It was different, and I liked that. I rolled my clothes up and placed them over my satchel, in case anyone happened by, and tiptoed into the cool water.

My toes dug into the smooth rocks for purchase as I waded out into the middle of the stream as it gradually grew deeper. The river was shallow and clear, barely reaching my waist at the deepest point, where I sank down into the water, and dipped my head under. I unfastened the end of my braid, letting the cool liquid saturate my hair. I shot out of the water, wiping my eyes before I blinked them open again.

I gasped for air as I surfaced, spitting water out of my mouth. That water was colder than I'd anticipated against my hot skin. The sun always felt hotter after a storm blew through and it had taken its toll on me at the beach. I splashed some water against the heated flesh of my arms, as goosebumps rose against the fresh intrusion of cold water.

Crack!

My body went completely still, my heart thundering away inside my chest. I cut my eyes in the direction the noise had come from while remaining as still as possible. I didn't want whoever or what-ever was watching me to know I'd noticed them. Slowly, my hands slid down to the water and cupped some, as I pretended to bathe my arms. My quick fingers rebraided my now soaking wet locks and I turned casually toward the shore, and my clothes and weapon.

I didn't dare look in the direction the noise had come from. If it was a predator, then making eye contact would only make the attack come faster and I wasn't near my weapon. If it was a person, the moment they knew I'd caught them they'd act on whatever their intentions were. I was alone in the woods, and currently nude, so their intentions couldn't be that great and I'd rather not confront them until I was armed.

I stepped from the water and onto uneven ground, pulling myself up by a small sapling as I climbed the tiny embankment. My eyes lifted from the ground to the spot where I'd left my pile of things and my blood ran cold.

They were gone.

My clothes, my satchel, everything was missing. I glanced down at my body, covered only by the paint that still clung to my skin—the pigments were strong, they wore down over time but a special soap had to be used to remove them early—and then into the tall grass and thin trees.

"Looking for something?" a familiar voice called out from the other side of the stream. I spun around and glared at Rain, crossing my arms over my breasts.

"How in the Great Mother's name did you get there so fast?" I picked up a small rock, ready to throw it at him if he didn't bring me my things.

Rain patted the satchel at his side and grinned. My clothes were layered over the top of it, tucked between the leather and his hip. I ground my teeth at the sight. I wanted to scream at him, but if having a little brother had taught me anything, it was that reacting too soon was never a good thing.

"I have my secrets," he taunted, pulling his own satchel over his shoulder.

"What are you doing out here? Are you following me?" My posture relaxed the tiniest bit as I watched Rain pause.

"No, young matriarch, I'm not following you. It's you who were looking for me, were you not?"

I opened my mouth to chastise him for being odd, but my tongue went numb as I watched Rain's face shift into someone different. I gasped, holding the rock back, preparing to throw it if this creature came closer.

"Who are you?" I stepped backward, my heartbeat thudding in my ears like a war drum. I didn't recognize the face staring back at me. He could be any man in any village. His wide-set eyes stared back at me, reflecting nothing. I swallowed, my eyes roaming the man's chest for any identifying marks.

Most tribes used paint or tattoos, like we did, to mark their members. My eyes frantically searched for anything that I could use to my advantage, but this man was plain. No tattoos or markings were anywhere to be found on the parts of his body I could see. The strange man smiled wider and turned, raising his hands as he spun around in a full circle.

"Find anything interesting?" he asked. I wanted to wipe the smug smile off his face.

"Give me my things back," I demanded, my free hand braced on my hip. A small bird flew dangerously close to my face and I swatted it away, blinking as the wings careened by my eye. Laughter boomed around me, as loud as the furious flapping of wings too close to my head.

"Why were you looking for me, young matriarch?" a voice whispered by my ear.

I squealed and spun around, throwing my hands out wildly. My fingers barely caught the silky black hair hanging from the mystery man. I forced my eyes open and stared into the gleaming black depths of the man before me.

He wore a different face now. The face of my father. My eyes widened and I took a step back, gripping the rock tight in my hand. "Stay back," I warned. The man's face slowly morphed into the same, unknown face he'd worn moments before. "Who are you?"

"I have a lot of names." He pulled my satchel over his shoulder and tossed it at me. I grasped the bundle, eyeing him with suspicion. Quickly, I pulled my top over my head, along with my satchel, and then stepped into my skirt.

"Why don't you tell me one of them?" I swallowed, pulling the lace tight against my hip for a snug fit.

"You know the answer," he replied, appearing bored. I peered into his obsidian eyes again and blinked.

Are those stars?

"Yes, young matriarch. You can see the night sky in my eyes. The Great Mother gave me these as a gift when she saved me."

I backed away until my back met a tree. There was no way I was talking to *the* Mockingbird, the Great Mother's chosen. There were many spirits that my people believed in, revered, but this was the Mockingbird. My hand flew to my necklace and I bowed my head. There was a small chance this was just some man who was crazy... but he had heard my thoughts, hadn't he?

"You doubt the Spirits, even in the presence of one?"

"I don't mean to," I whispered. I stared at the long knife that hung from his belt. It was carved from a large bone, a scaly maybe. The stories mentioned the large knife that had clipped his wings before the Great Mother found the Mockingbird and restored him to his glory.

"I know, it's in your nature, and it's the way the Great Mother made you." He held a hand out to me and I slid mine into his, wary of touching a Spirit.

"How is this possible?" I tried to be careful with my words, because I didn't want to offend the Spirits anymore than I had already.

"This is what happens, Sage. Every matriarch has to meet a Spirit. Sometimes it's the Great Mother, sometimes it's an ancestor, and sometimes the Great Mother sends me," he grinned down at me. "Or one of the others."

I shuddered as I imagined meeting the Bear in the middle of the woods. The Mockingbird was a trickster—or so I'd been told by the shamans since I was a little girl—but he wasn't nearly as intimidating as a bear the size of a tree.

"I'm pretty intimidating," he huffed.

"Stop that!" I cried out in frustration. "Please, stay out of my head. I can't think properly if I know you're listening to me," I mumbled.

"You're just like she said you'd be."

"Who?" My brows cinched down as I pondered his words.

The Mockingbird blinked his starry eyes and shook his head, wagging a finger at me. "No, no, young matriarch. There's a time and a place for that. Why did you seek me out? I've asked you over and over and you still haven't told me."

"I didn't—" I clamped my mouth shut and narrowed my eyes on the man in front of me. I *had* been looking for something, I just didn't know what. "I didn't know what I was looking for. I'm supposed to pass a test and become a matriarch." I shrugged. This was the strangest encounter I'd ever experienced. I had so many questions to ask him.

"So, you were wondering about your test then." The Mockingbird tilted his head to the side. It wasn't lost on me that it was a very bird-like gesture. His lips stretched into a smile and he jiggled my hand a little with his excitement. "I can't tell you what your test will be, young matriarch. You are responsible for that. The Creator and the Great Mother only intervene so much."

I bit my lip, sucking on the skin loudly—it was a nervous habit, something I did when I was thinking or upset. His words actually matched my own thoughts about the Spirits. I didn't *not* believe in them before now, I just didn't believe quite as thoroughly as most of my people.

"Can you tell me anything?" I squeezed his hand, pleading with him. I didn't *want* to fail my people, I just didn't think I deserved this position.

"Trust your instincts, in all things. You will do fine, young matriarch. Your ancestors believe in you more than you believe in yourself," he whispered. The edges of his face blurred and I blinked my eyes again, trying to focus. I pulled my hand from his and reached out for his face, but when my fingers reached his skin, he shrank down into a mockingbird. The ends of his grey feathers—stark against his white ones—looked like they'd been dipped in ink. I peered closer at the bird hovering in front of me.

No, I thought, *they look like they've been dipped into the night sky.*

Sure enough, when I looked at the creature's eyes, the same starry black orbs that had been staring out of a man's face only moments before, gazed back at me. I shook my head, dropping my hand as the creature flitted away.

The edges of the world went fuzzy again and I turned around, trying to gain my bearings. Everything shifted and fell away to reveal a deep, endless darkness. I tried to call out for the Mockingbird, but no sound came from my lips. It was as if the darkness sucked the sound from my mouth before it even formed. My heart hammered against my chest. I'd never been scared of the dark before. I'd snuck out of the village many times in the quiet of the night, but this was different. Absolute darkness was the most hollow thing I'd ever experienced.

I sat up quickly, with a scream clawing its way out of my throat. My hands went to my face, dabbing at the sweat beading on my brow. I smoothed my hair away from my face and glanced around, taking in my surroundings. A soft bed of animal skins lay beneath me, and the elders were gathered around the bed in a circle. The moon was hung high in the sky, a stark contrast to the blazing fire a few feet away. I scrambled onto my knees, rising slowly as I stared at the women around me.

"What is this?" I demanded.

"Calm down, Sage." My mother's voice drifted into the circle from behind Nova.

I held my head high, my eyes narrowed, as I waited for someone to explain what was going on.

"You're confused right now. It's a common reaction to the tea. Calm down, Sage, please." Mom's eyes glistened with emotion and I raked my fingers through my long dark hair. She was right, I *was* confused. I'd left for my Spirit Walk already. I was just talking to the Mockingbird...

"How did I get here, Mom?" I sounded panicked, even to myself. I searched frantically for the man—er, Spirit—I'd only just been with. "Where is he?"

"Where is who?" Mom asked me, arching her eyebrow. "What did you see in the other world?" Her hand came down on my shoulder and I shook my head, before pressing my palm to my forehead as I tried to make sense of things. The other world. The tea.

"You gave me a potion at dinner?" My voice went up an octave and she winced, nodding.

"It's the way of things, curious one. The same happened to me, and to Nova before me." She waved to the old woman crouching against her walking stick.

"Stop asking her what she saw." Nova clicked her tongue against her teeth, chiding my mother. It was an odd occurrence to witness.

"She's my daught—"

"No," Nova interrupted. "She's the future matriarch. She's your daughter *second*, Ayasha. It's hard to let go, I know, but she has to figure these things out for herself if she is going to lead our people." With that, Nova turned to me and nodded. "Yes, you were given a sacred tea last night with your dinner instead of that swill you usually drink. You'd drank enough that you didn't even notice the difference in taste," she sighed. "Whatever is confusing you right now, hold on to it, girl. You were in the spirit world for but a few hours. Whatever and whoever you saw there, was meant to help you on your journey. Your journey begins now."

"I believe in you, Sage," Mom whispered.

The rest of the elders nodded their agreement and rose to their feet from the ground. The grass sprang back to life beneath them, relieved to be free of the pressure their bodies created. I winced, rubbing my temples. My head pounded like I'd knocked it on a tree. "Everything was a dream?" I whispered to their backs. My mother paused, glancing over her shoulder to say something, but Nova grasped her arm and pulled her along, murmuring something to her that I couldn't hear.

I looked from the fire to the pile of skins I was crouched on. Beside me lay a pile of things. I pulled it toward me and stared at the satchel from my dreams. I rummaged through it to find the same knife, the same bone totems, and... I pulled something hard and smooth out of the bag. I dropped it immediately, scrambling backward until a bush scratched my shoulders. On the animal skin blanket lay the seashell I'd stepped on at the beach. I pressed my eyes shut, wishing it away. When I opened them again, it was still there. The moonlight and firelight warred against the soft hue of the shell, but I was almost certain if I picked the small thing up again, the darker shade at the bottom would be crimson. I was almost certain it would be stained by my blood from when it'd stabbed my foot.

I rose to my feet, struggling to stand straight thanks to the pain in my foot. In the distance, something roared and whatever made that noise was big, probably a scaly. I shuddered at the thought of running into one by myself. They didn't usually bother our people—they had their own tribes to worry about—but on occasion, the really feral ones could be problematic. I swallowed and quickly began kicking dirt and mud into the fire. Soon, the flames were low and smoke clouded my vision. I covered my mouth and nose, before swiftly rolling the blanket up and tying it to the satchel they had left for me.

I threw the satchel over my shoulder and began walking toward the forest. I wanted to be under the cover of the high grass and trees, not out in the open. Stepping forward, I bit back a scream when something pierced my foot. I held it off the ground gingerly and felt along the bottom of my sole for the thing that had nearly caused me to cry out.

Standing there on one foot, my toes digging into the damp earth, I sucked in a breath as a thought entered my mind—this felt familiar. My eyes fell to my hand as I pulled the offending object free from my skin.

I gulped and rolled the seashell between my fingers, examining it. I fisted my hand around it and closed my eyes. *There has to be a good explanation for this.* I slid my hand into the satchel at my side and let the shell drop inside, clinking against something as I hurried toward the trees.

Chapter
3

Kishil

I snapped at the tyrannosaurus' leg. My teeth sliced through the hard scales, meeting soft muscle, as blood poured from the wound, coating my snout. If this asshole didn't change back soon, we were going to end up ripping one another apart. Elu limped toward a tree, favoring his left leg, and a snarl rose from my throat as I barely avoided the large gnashing jaws again.

The clicks behind me let me know that Talon was still in the fight, at least. We hadn't meant to trespass into his territory. We were out hunting and crossed paths—all of this was *really* unnecessary.

"Stop!" a human voice I knew as well as my own called out. I canted my head to the side, watching Elu stumble toward us in his human form. He held his hands out above his head, waving at the tyrannosaurus like an idiot. "Change and talk to us, please."

The tyrannosaurus snorted, bending its head down again. I took full advantage of my raptor vision, eyeing the angry shifter with my left eye, and my vulnerable pack mate with my right. I blinked, trying to focus on both of them. The tyrannosaurus seemed to be calming, now that he saw a human, since most dino-shifters didn't interfere with humans. Of course, there were always rogues. They were usually sick, feral from letting their animal rule them for too long.

20

The large dinosaur shimmered for a moment, and he snorted before the sound of breaking bones and ripping flesh tore through the night. I focused my attention away from him as a courtesy. It wasn't polite to watch another man's shift, because shifters were at their most vulnerable in that moment. When the grunts sounded more human than dinosaur, I snapped my head back toward the man. Beside me, Talon shifted as well and I chuffed, lingering back. They could shift and talk to the territorial prick, I wasn't going to leave us vulnerable. Our human bodies stood zero chance against a pissed off rex, and they knew that.

Idiots.

"Why in the Great Mother's name are you in my woods?" He pushed his long black hair out of his face, tying it in a knot at the base of his skull. "Are you stupid? I could have hurt you." His eyes weren't quite right, even in his human form his eyes were amber and his pupils slitted. There was something wrong with him. Three clicks sounded from my throat before I could stop myself. The signal for danger.

"What's your friend doing?" He backed away, his eyes shooting from Elu and Talon to me. I chuffed and shook my head.

"Your eyes are probably making him nervous. Why haven't they shifted back?" Talon prodded. It was probably a rude question, but something we needed to know if we lived this close to another predator.

"Heh," the man laughed. I focused on him, noting he was older than the three of us. He had snowy white hair growing in at his temples, so he *must* be older than I even thought. Our people didn't age as fast as humans. "I don't even know what they look like anymore. Haven't been in this body in..." His voice trailed off as he tried to remember when he'd last taken his human form.

Elu glanced to me and I chuffed again. He wasn't a territorial asshole, he was a confused old shifter who lost himself to his animal. I looked at my pack mates and shook my head. If I was ever that far gone, I'd want someone to put me out of my misery. It wasn't safe for shifters to lose control, it put other people in danger. We'd had an unspoken treaty with the human tribes for a long time, at least in the Plains Nation. I missed the plains. The land here was taking me far longer than I'd like to get used to. Where I was used to running on flat, uninterrupted ground, there were countless swamps, bogs, rivers, streams, and *trees* here. I'd ran into a few trees when I wasn't paying attention—that shit stung.

"It's alright, brother," Talon murmured. His father was feral, still running somewhere on the plains we'd left behind.

A noise behind us caught my attention and I bayed out a warning to my pack mates, turning around to face the new threat. I canted my head to the side, studying the trees and bushy undergrowth. I didn't see anything. I could smell something different though. I scented the air again, stepping toward the tree line as Elu and Talon hushed the older man behind me.

An arrow flew past my head and I crouched low on instinct.

A loud roar vibrated my skull and I bared my teeth, trying to discern which direction the arrow had come from. A shout sounded behind me and I knew the old man had been shot. The scent of blood was growing stronger. Behind me, Elu and Talon snarled frantically. The last thing we needed was an injured rex running wild, it would take The Creator himself to settle the damn beast.

I leaned my head low, darting into the brush as I looked for the source of the attack, and the wilderness came alive around me. Shouts rang out behind me and a man jumped into my field of vision, waving a metallic weapon. I tilted my head, staring at the fool, before I lashed out with a claw. He fell to his knees, slashing about with his strange spear. It pierced my left flank and I let loose a high-pitched shriek. I bent forward, swaying my tail back and forth for balance while I recovered from the blow. The pale man turned his hand, trying to get a better angle with his weapon, and that's when I struck. I darted in close and clamped my jaws around his arm, severing it. The weapon fell to the ground as I swallowed the arm down, baying loudly for my pack mates and letting them know I was okay. I waited to hear the call back from them, but instead all I heard was the yelling of men. I turned in a circle, and everywhere I looked stood a human, a trader. I snarled, a low sound that tore a few clicks out of my throat. My tail twitched from side to side as I eyed the man who I considered the biggest threat.

I leapt on him, my talons digging into his throat as I pushed off his body and darted back toward my pack mates. I rushed into the clearing, skidding to a stop. Before me lay the old man, his clear, green human eyes wide open, looking back at me, lifeless. I bayed out, searching for Elu and Talon. *Where are they?* The wound in my side burned. It would heal if I could just shift, but I was stronger as a raptor than I was as a man—at least against this many enemies.

In the distance, I heard the sound I'd been waiting for. A loud, repetitive bay. I clicked as I turned in a circle, eyeing the humans that were closing in around me. The strange clothes they wore were familiar to me, identifying them as the traders that had chased tribe after tribe from the plains. Any tribe unlucky enough to be settled in their trade route, had been raided and enslaved over and over until eventually the tribes resettled elsewhere. Why had they come this far south? I lowered my snout, snorting as the first man rushed me. Something sharp tore into my thigh and I let loose a snarl that rattled my bones.

The humans were closing in. Prodding me with the ends of their weapons. Some poked me with sticks while others rushed in, leaving shallow wounds in their wake. They weren't trying to kill me, they were trying to weaken me.

I lashed out with a claw, before darting in to snap a hand off a man wielding a knife. The edges of my vision blurred and I stumbled into a group of humans. Something coarse came around my scales and I chuffed, trying to breathe through the dizziness.

I have to hold on to my form.

Something told me that I didn't want these traders to see what I really was.

Chapter 4

Sage

I stepped gingerly between the overgrown tree roots sticking up out of the boggy reeds. I was almost to the wide oak tree. There was a hollow in it where I'd hid my boots. Seasons ago, I'd traded a neighboring village two whole alligator hides for those boots. I still shuddered when I remembered trying to catch and kill those alligators—it hadn't been easy, for lots of reasons. I wasn't a hunter by nature and it wasn't what I wanted to do with my life. I wasn't sure *what* I wanted to do with my life, but that option wasn't even on the list.

The boots had been worth it though. The seamstress had made buckskin boots with alligator hide bottoms. They had traction where my bare feet—or even plain, flat shoes—didn't. I stepped through the soggy ground and sighed when my feet hit solid dirt once again. The soil was still soft compared to the hard packed earth just off the beach, but it was a huge improvement to the swampy shallows I'd been trudging through. I picked up my pace, jogging through the brush, and dipping around trees. An owl called out in the distance and a chill blasted across the back of my neck.

Owls bring omens.

The shaman's words bounced around in my head again. It was

one of the many lessons that had been drilled into all of the children in the village during our education. My mind drifted back to the strange dream I'd had. I couldn't believe my mother had let me be dosed with sacred tea and slip into the spirit world unprepared—if that was actually the spirit world.

I wasn't completely convinced that it wasn't just a really strange dream. There were definitely some things that didn't add up—like the seashell, and even thinking about that small totem made my skin crawl. How could it have been in my dream, in the exact same condition as it was when I saw it for the first time with my own eyes?

The vegetation had slowly changed from reeds to tall ferns as I neared the hiding place. I ran the rest of the way to the tree, tapped the side of it to scare out any snakes that might be hiding inside the hollow, and then reached my hand inside. My fingers brushed against the buckskin and I pulled out the boots. The canopy was thick here, there was barely any moonlight to see by, but I managed to wipe off the bottoms of my feet on some moss before I shoved them inside the boots.

I sighed. These were truly a luxury, something I'd kept hidden even from my little brother. I padded over the ground much more comfortably than I had only moments before, while reaching into my satchel for a piece of dried meat. It had been a long time since I'd actually eaten, I realized. They'd drugged me at dinner, and then I'd woken up with the moon high in the sky. Despite what they'd said, it felt like I'd been in that dream state for well over a day. I shook my head, trying to dismiss the unease in the pit of my stomach. That dream had felt entirely too real for me to just dismiss it.

What are the odds that the Mockingbird had come to me in a dream? I chewed on the dried meat and picked my way between ferns and trees, heading... I had no idea where.

"What am I supposed to do?" I mumbled to no one in particular. I didn't expect anyone to reply. I knew better than to wait around for the Spirits to tell me what to do with my life. I'd been agonizing over becoming the next matriarch for months. No one had magically appeared to save me from embarrassing myself. Nope, here I was, wandering through the wilderness alone, not being tested.

A series of whistles and chirps sounded above me, but I ignored them and kept walking. I wasn't going to acknowledge the fact that the bird singing in the middle of the night was probably a mockingbird. It wasn't odd at all that there was a mockingbird out here, since they were everywhere. Denial was my friend, my near and dear friend. I swallowed and pushed a leafy plant out of my way, but it promptly snapped back and slapped me in the face.

"Great Mother!" I hissed, wiping the sticky wetness off my cheek.

Behind me, someone cleared their throat and I whipped around, my hand dipping to the bone knife I'd slid into my skirt belt.

"Who's there?" I called out. I searched the dark path behind me, but could see nothing. It was dark in this part of the wood. I walked backward, scanning the area. I didn't like feeling like prey. I'd been in the wilderness enough as a child—I'd even seen a panther kill a fawn firsthand and had almost gotten mauled for daring to watch—so I knew when I was being hunted.

The hair on the back of my neck prickled and I turned around, slamming into a hard chest. I instantly backed up, trying to right myself. I didn't scream—oddly enough—I just stared at the pale-skinned man watching me. I pulled the knife from my belt and waved it between us. His mouth curled into a wicked smile as he took a step toward me.

My heart thundered in my chest, and I looked around for an escape route. I could dart into the trees and disappear into the brush. This man didn't look like he belonged to any of the tribes I recognized, and I could easily lose him, especially if I ran until I reached the swamps. My mind made up, I feigned right, and when the man reached for me, I pulled to the left and ran. Pushing my legs as fast as they could run and holding the knife in my palm, I zigged through the trees and zagged around overgrown ferns. I ducked a low-hanging branch and took a hard right, heading west toward the swamps. There was usually a small canoe tucked beneath a certain tree—I'd helped a young hunter mend the oar and he'd promised me I could use it whenever I needed to—and now seemed like the perfect time to borrow it.

Behind me, voices shouted. There was more than one person chasing me. Of course there was. *Why can't anything go right?* I pushed myself harder, and I could feel the change in the soil beneath my feet as my boots began to lose traction, but I could also hear the voices getting closer. They yelled in a language I wasn't familiar with. I cast a glance over my shoulder, seeing yellow hair whip around the man's head as he ran after me. He was the closest pursuer. I focused on the path ahead, cutting around a fallen tree and darting between two large bushes. I quickly turned around, bending to cover my tracks with leaf litter, and stepped lightly behind a bush.

I held my breath as the crunch of footsteps grew closer. Two men talked to each other in hushed tones as they peered down at the where my trail had ended. I gripped the knife tight in my hand, turning the handle until it was in the perfect position. I knew what happened to women caught by men like these... I absolutely would *not* be taken prisoner without a fight.

Just walk by. Look elsewhere.

I bit my lip, willing them to move on to another area. I could double back around whatever camp they had and continue on my journey to wherever on Gaia I was going. I still had no idea.

Snap!

I stiffened at the sound of a twig cracking behind me. I slowly glanced over my shoulder, knife held at the ready, and my eyes went round.

The man with the long, yellow hair sat behind me with a cocky grin on his face.

I lunged at him, digging my fingers into his scalp as I tried to push the knife toward his throat. I was a quick little demon, according to my father, but this man was faster. He grabbed my arms and wrenched them to the side, then wrapped me in his arms until I was unable to move. My fingers still clung to the knife and I bent my

27

wrist, a desperate attempt to cut him—any distraction could be used to my advantage. The blade slipped against his skin and he winced, hissing out a breath. He muttered something I couldn't understand and I glared at him.

"Let me go!" I screeched in his face. Spittle covered his nose, which he wrinkled before glaring back at me.

"Well, now I know what language ya speak at least," he replied in a heavy accent. My eyes went wide.

"You know the Language of the Sun?" I don't know why that mattered right then, when I was being kidnapped, but it seemed interesting that this man who clearly wasn't from the peninsula—or anywhere near it, from what I knew—could speak our language. He nodded and adjusted his grip on me, grabbing me firmly by my upper arms. I held the knife tightly until someone ripped it from my hand.

"This one is feisty," the new man muttered. He slid my knife into his belt and leaned in close to my face. The stench of his breath was unbearable and I looked away. He must have mistaken my disgust for fear, because he laughed.

I quickly whipped my head back and spat in his face. "You have no idea," I growled at him. I'm sure I didn't look very intimidating to these men, but they didn't know me. I didn't fight back when the man holding me raised us both to our feet. I didn't try to wiggle free. Instead, I stared blankly at the fuming man wiping his face. His hand fell against my cheek with a loud crack.

I stumbled backward, aware that the first man had let me go. Covering my face with my hand, I turned to run, my right eye squinting closed through the pain. I bumped into another man and blew out a breath, my heart hammering against my chest. I didn't have the knife anymore, I was weaponless and surrounded.

The small man said something in the language I didn't understand. I shook my head and rubbed my cheek. Hopefully, he knew I had no idea what he was asking of me. Behind us, the first two men argued. Loudly. I turned to watch the man with the long, yellow hair as he admonished the one who'd hit me. I didn't know what he was saying, but he didn't seem pleased. I couldn't imagine a simple slap would matter to these men if they were what I thought they were. I narrowed my eyes as I studied the exchange.

Finally, the man with the yellow hair turned toward me, pulling his hair back into a ponytail. "The man behind you is going to bring you to our camp, I don't suggest fighting him."

"You expect me to be kidnapped, willingly?" I gaped at him, crossing my arms over my chest.

"You can do what you want," he replied, "but you *will* be coming with us, woman. Please make it as easy on yourself as you can. I can't promise to be around to protect you from every fool you meet."

I opened my mouth to speak but thought better of it. I'd bide my time and escape. The man behind me nudged my back with something hard and sharp. I glanced to the man with the yellow hair and took note of their weapons. He had a large knife, as long as my arm, strapped to his back. The blade looked like metal, but it was more than I'd ever seen in one place in my entire life. Our people used what little metal we found for things like cooking, and making and repairing clothing, since bone weapons were plenty sharp anyway.

The man who'd struck me spat on the ground and glared at me. His face glowed a bright red, even in the darkness. He was clearly embarrassed by how his chieftain had handled the situation.

The one behind me poked my back again and I narrowed my eyes, stepping forward. I took each step more deliberately than the last. If he was going to be rude, I could be annoying. I wasn't going to make this easy on them.

I TRUDGED ALONG BEHIND ONE OF MY CAPTORS AND IN FRONT OF another. They didn't trust that I wouldn't run, and they were smart for it. I wish they were a little less smart. I sucked my teeth as we came to an abrupt stop and I found my face smashed into the yellow ponytail and broad back I'd been following through the woods.

"Oaf," I mumbled, as I pushed off his back and righted myself. The idiot behind me poked me again with this strange knife. My lip curled up, but I swallowed the string of curses I had for him. I wasn't a warrior, and I had never strived to be the strongest woman in the village, but I was going to shove that knife up his rear end if he touched me again.

"Quiet," the man with the yellow hair hissed. I raised an eyebrow, opening my mouth to snap back when I heard it.

Loud, high-pitched shrieks followed by low, short bays. I shuddered and tried to peer around the man in front of me. There was a scaly somewhere ahead. I leaned farther to the side, glimpsing a large wooden cage. Several men pulled on ropes that were tied around the poor thing. They were trying to push and pull him into the cage. It looked sturdy enough, with each piece of wood was as thick around as any man here. The raptor shook his head back and forth, refusing to enter the tiny prison.

Why doesn't he just shift into his human form and explain he's not an animal?

I glanced around at the men surrounding me, realizing they weren't from around here. Maybe they didn't know what scalies were... I pondered the thought. Did they not have shifters where they lived?

"Wait here until they get the beast in the cage. We've been trying to catch one of these dragons since we found this land, and now we have!" He grinned from ear to ear. I stared at him with wide eyes.

"Dragon?"

"The beast in the cage, it's some kind of dragon. Our people have tales about them, what do you lot call them?"

I glanced nervously at the raptor and toyed with my necklace. I didn't want to answer him. If the scaly hadn't shifted in front of these men, there had to be a reason. I wasn't going to share his business with them. In the distance, a mockingbird sang a mixed tune. I shivered and turned back toward my captor.

"We call them dinosaurs, that's the name for the kind of beast they are."

"Well," he mumbled, narrowing his eyes on me. "Our people have always talked about dragons. Large, scaled beasts that kidnap women, and hoard gold. Do you think it has gold?"

I snorted and shook my head. I could definitely picture a dino-shifter running off with a woman, but I wasn't about to say that to this man. He thought they were dragons—whatever those were.

"Come on," he huffed, wrapping a hand around my arm and pulling me into the camp. The door to the cage swung shut as the raptor rushed it, his snout sliding through the bars as he tried to snap at the men closest to him. I kept an eye on the raptor as we walked through the camp. He led me to the fire and pushed me down on the ground with a grunt.

"What's your name?" I raised an eyebrow and waited for his response. I couldn't stand to continue thinking of him as the man with the long yellow hair. The moniker was too long, even worse than some of the elders' names in my village.

"My name is Gunner," he sang out, as he moved away from me to a large pot. The man brought me a wooden cup full of some sort of stew. I smelled it and wrinkled my nose. It might be rabbit, based on the stringy texture of the meat I was staring at, but it smelled atro-cious. I winced and turned the cup to my lip, taking a small sip of the broth. It didn't taste as bad as it smelled, at least there was that.

"Don't like the cooking, aye?" Gunner's lips curled in a smile as he glanced toward a group of men sitting around another fire. They seemed to be enjoying their meal, judging by the empty cups laying on the ground by their feet. I scanned the area, trying to get a head count for the camp. I could see at least twenty men. There were prob-ably more somewhere, based on how many tents there were spaced between the trees. I swallowed some more of the stringy stew and shook my head, placing the cup by my feet.

"You don't know how to cook a rabbit properly," I accused.

"What's this?" His laugh boomed through the camp and several men looked our way.

I glanced warily around at the men staring at us. They were all similar in their odd coloring, but their hair was different shades. Some had blue eyes, others green, and some had the brown I was most used to seeing. Their hair was the most interesting feature though. While Gunner's hair was straight and yellow, a few of them had curly hair that was as red as a flame. Others had brown hair, or a sandy combination between brown and yellow. I shrugged my shoulder up to my ear and nudged the cup away.

"It tastes like boar piss. I can show you how to cook rabbit, if you'd like. There's no need to kidnap me for the recipe, I'd gladly share it for free." I stared blankly at him as the words rolled from my tongue.

The camp erupted in laughter and soon the men went back to their meals and individual conversations. I pulled my knees up to my chest and wrapped my arms around them, laying my head on my arms.

"It'll be dawn soon. We don't usually hunt at night," he admitted. "We heard the dragon in the wood and ran off to find it. Some of us went one direction and some the other, and my men found the dragon and I found you." His eyes drifted from mine to my legs and I pulled my feet tighter to my body. "What is *your* name?"

"I won't tell you." I bit my lip to keep my mouth shut.

"Because names have power." He squatted down in front of me, resting his elbows on his knees. "Keep your secrets, woman. I don't need to know your name. You can help us with any other locals we capture."

"I absolutely will not." I recoiled from him, disgusted. Did he think I had no pride at all? Behind us the raptor bayed, pacing in his cage. He was calling out to his pack. Only the biggest predators were solitary animals, which I'd learned at a young age. The dino-shifters tended to stick to their own kind, and although we had a tentative peace with them, we weren't allies. They simply stayed away from us and we kept away from them. This fire was the closest to the cage that held the raptor. I looked over at the shifter, noticing the wounds that still oozed blood. His brownish-green scales glinted in the firelight, highlighting the dark red gashes along his thighs and shoulders.

"I'm here to do a job." Gunner reached his hand out to my cheek, caressing it. My skin crawled under his touch and I twisted my head away from him, curling my lip.

"If you touch me again, I'll bite your finger off." My voice was cold, devoid of emotion. I wouldn't be treated as a plaything by these strange men.

Gunner rocked back on his heels and shook his head before rising. "The best thing you could do is show me some respect, woman. I'm the only man in this camp who can keep the rest of them away from you," he whispered. "You'd be smart to help me with the locals. I speak the language, but they respect their own."

My eyes widened. Was he really threatening me with rape? I swallowed as I recounted how many men I thought were in this camp. I opened my mouth to speak, but the raptor threw himself against the side of his cage, chuffing. Gunner jumped back, obviously frightened by the erratic behavior.

"Crazy beast!" he spat. I turned my full attention to the dino-shifter, watching his eyes. His slitted pupils tracked Gunner as he walked away from the fire and toward a group of his men, huddled around their own roaring flames. My shoulders relaxed once he was a safe distance away.

"Won't you heal if you shift?" I whispered, low enough that only the raptor would hear me.

The animal went completely still, canting its head to the side. Clicks rattled out from its throat as it stared at me. Its head bobbed up toward the ceiling of his small prison.

"They don't know what you are," I breathed.

The raptor bayed out a short, hollow call. I was going to take that as a yes.

"Your secret is safe with me." I wrapped my arms tighter around my knees and laid my head down, facing the fire.

"There were people with him?" Gunner asked one of his men. The group around their fire had thinned out as men ambled to their tents or into the woods. I closed my eyes and pretended not to listen.

"Aye, there were three men. The old one died in the battle. We lost nine," the man growled. "That beast in the cage took an arm from one and he died before we could staunch the wound. It took my left hand, but I can still swing a sword." He seemed to be hurrying at this point in his story. "I won't slow you down, on my honor."

"You don't *have* any honor, Erik." Loud laughter boomed through the camp. I was convinced there was a thundercloud living inside that man. His voice was obnoxiously loud for a single man, even one of his size. "So, what about the other two men?" His laughter trailed off. "Were they hunting the dragon?"

"No." The other man's voice wavered. "They were fighting to get to it. Maybe the locals keep them as pets or livestock?"

"A dragon plowing a field," Gunner mocked. "That'd be an interesting sight." The other man, Erik, clapped his hand down on Gunner's shoulder with a loud smack.

"It looks nothing like the dragons we've heard of. Maybe this is the, er, domesticated version?"

I could feel eyes on me, but I refused to acknowledge Gunner's stare. He wouldn't get any information from me and I'd be surprised if he tried again. Whoever taught him the Language of the Sun would have taught him our principles as well. I'd never betray someone for my own gain, not even to live. Our people were faithful to the end.

And that's when it hit me... *Why can I understand what they're saying right now?* I lifted my head from my arms, glancing around me nervously. The words sounded different than my native tongue, but I understood them nonetheless.

Dawn painted the sky in light pinks and blues as the sun rose to meet the day. I ran my fingers through my hair, rebraiding it as I worried over my current dilemma. A small grey and white bird flitted down to the ground in front of me. My fingers stilled and I studied the creature. A mockingbird. I glanced over its feathers and stopped when I reached the black tips at the end of the grey... they shone in the low light of the new morning like stars. I gasped and leaned back, falling on my hands.

Understanding is important, young matriarch.

The voice in my head wasn't my own. I swirled a finger inside my ear, chasing the sound. What in the Great Mother's name was happening to me? Behind me the sounds of the camp coming alive distracted me. Men were arriving from the wood.

They have horses.

I glanced at the large animals as they shied away from my side of the camp. The raptor clicked at them and they whinnied, carrying their riders to the farthest end of the small area. I narrowed my eyes on the dino-shifter, wishing he could speak to me. He was as close to *one of my people* as I could get at the moment. I stretched my arms over my head and yawned. I'd been up for a while, and been through a lot in that period of time. I'd somehow managed to get kidnapped, I was hearing voices in my head, and imagining Spirits, mockingbirds, and the Mockingbird. There was an injured dino-shifter being caged like a wild animal—though it seemed he wanted them to think he *was* a wild animal—and the leader of the expedition was... interested in me. I shuddered at the thought.

He was an attractive man, but he wasn't meant for me. I wasn't Nova and I wouldn't be seducing my way out of this camp. I bit back another yawn as the men tied the horses to carts I hadn't noticed before, and began loading the broken down tents into the back. Another set of horses was led slowly toward the cage and I raised my eyebrow.

There were wheels on the bottom of the cage. I doubted the horses would allow a predator to be behind them for long without spooking. Horses were noble creatures, but they were also extremely intelligent. No prey animal would want a predator breathing down the back of their neck. I sighed and rose to my feet, hoping I could sneak away while they were distracted. I stepped forward, not bothering to look behind me, since acting guilty would only draw attention. I made it a few more steps before a firm hand came down on my shoulder.

"Where are you going, woman?"

"Um." I turned around, searching for a lie. I didn't have one so I simply shrugged and waited for what was going to come next.

"Don't do that," Gunner warned. He pulled me along behind him toward the center of the camp, and then went to work trying to secure the horses to the rolling cage. The raptor was suspiciously quiet. I drew my brows down and crossed my arms over my chest. A small bird flitted through the camp and I groaned inwardly. I wasn't mentally prepared to deal with any more mockingbirds at the moment. Maybe I was still experiencing side effects from the sacred tea my mother drugged me with. I was going to have a serious conversation with her and the elders about that when I got back. That was *not* okay. I would have drank the tea gladly, I just wanted some kind of heads up that I was going to go into a sleep like death.

Gunner wiped his hands on his pants and strolled toward me. He waved his hand toward the setup attached to the raptor cage. "The horses will pull the cart, the cart will pull the dragon. You can ride in the cart... here." The next thing I knew, I was being lifted off the ground and placed into an almost empty wooden cart, also save for a few rolled up tents and blankets. I hoped he didn't expect me to drive this thing. As if answering my silent question, Gunner climbed into the cart sitting down on a raised portion in the front and took the reins. I was closer to the ground where I sat, and from there I was staring directly into the cage where the raptor sat. His strange eyes met mine and I couldn't look away. The colors around the pupil varied in hue. They were amber, brown, and gold, with blue mixed in as well. They were beautiful.

We stayed like that for a long while, staring at one another, neither one of us making a sound. The cart bounced leisurely, lulling me closer to sleep. The terrain in this part of the peninsula was rough, so we were moving slowly. My head bobbed forward and I caught myself, snapping my head back up. The raptor still stared at me, and when I caught his eye, he chuffed and turned around, lying down in his cell. I yawned and untied the animal skin blanket from my satchel. I pulled it around my shoulders and followed the dino-shifter's lead. It was as good a time as any to take a nap. I'd need to be well rested to make an escape.

Chapter 5

Elu

I pressed my hands to the fallen man's wound, trying desperately to staunch the bleeding, but the arrow was a kill shot. There was no saving him. The older man coughed blood and reached out for my arm. His amber eyes slowly faded to a more human green as he tried to speak.

"Run," he rasped out between coughs.

I glanced frantically at Talon, he stood to the side, eyes wide, as he watched the old man die. I turned, searching for Kishil where he'd ran into the woods without a second thought. I could hear him in the forest nearby, but I couldn't see through the thickets separating us. The crunch of twigs and leaf litter drew my attention. Five men ran at us with weapons drawn, and I held my arm out, pushing Talon behind me.

"Get to the woods," I whispered. These were traders, like the ones who'd chased tribe after tribe and pack after pack from our homeland in the plains. A snarl rattled my chest. My raptor wanted to rip out of me and tear these men to shreds, but there were too many of them to risk it. If even one got away, he'd know there were more prizes to hunt for in this land than the crops and supplies they'd been stealing from innocents. One man reached me as we backed toward the cover of the brush.

He yelled something in words I couldn't understand, his weapon pointed at my chest. I held my hands in the air and continued backing away. Talon was close behind me, I could feel his presence in the hairs on the back of my neck. The man yelled something again, raising his weapon above his head. A snarl ripped from Talon behind me and I shook my head.

"Don't shift," I murmured.

"Where's Kishil?" Talon sounded frantic. This was shaping up to be a really terrible day. A tyrannosaurus shifter had tried to *eat* us, and now the traders we thought we'd left behind in the plains had shown up on the peninsula.

"Kishil will make it to us, or we will go find him. We can't shift here. Run!" We turned in unison and tore into the crowded woods. The trees and shrubs were overgrown and crowding one another. Each thin branch and leaf whipped at my skin as I ran, stinging my exposed flesh. I could smell my own blood mixing with the scent of Talon's. We'd just changed, and running naked through the woods wasn't something I'd usually recommend. Sometimes, I really regretted agreeing to come here... especially if the traders were moving in on this territory too. I could hear the humans crashing through the forest behind us. The soil beneath my feet had changed, it was no longer hard packed, and instead it gave way to soggy, damp earth.

"We can't change in front of them."

"Why?" Talon hissed. I glanced at him as we wove through the skinny trees toward the swamp up ahead.

"They're traders, Talon!" I snarled. His eyes had already gone full raptor. There was no human white left in them. I'd be surprised if he was able to hold himself together until we reached the other end of the wetlands. We could lose the humans in the swamp if we were careful. Or at least get far enough away that they wouldn't be able to make it back to their camp.

"Traders? Like back home?" His voice rose an octave as he glanced over his shoulder.

"Same clothes as the ones we ran into on the plains," I huffed. My legs had grown tired from running through the soft ground. Every step meant I had to pull my foot out of the wet soil and bring it back down just to sink again.

"Great Mother," he growled, coming to a stop. I slowed a few yards ahead of him and turned around, watching for the humans. They wouldn't give up easily. The traders we'd encountered were willing to sell anything—livestock, food, goods, people... it didn't matter to them.

Entire villages had disappeared from the plains. Some had moved to avoid the traders, but others were simply *gone*. Everyone knew what happened to them, except no one liked to talk about it.

"What are you doing?" I demanded. The humans were getting close, I could smell them.

"My damned foot is stuck!" he roared, twisting his leg again and again. I rushed to his side, looking at the ground where his foot was buried to mid-calf in some kind of gunk. I shook my head, muttering under my breath. There wasn't time for this.

My fingers dug into his skin and I pulled on his leg, but it didn't budge. "What have you gotten into?" I shrieked at him. They were closing in on us. I turned to face the first man as he came to a stop a few feet away. He brandished his oversized knife in my direction, with a cruel smile stretching his lips.

I held my hands out, waiting for the attack. We were unarmed men—as far as they knew—and they still chased us. These men had no honor. They came to our land every year and did whatever they wanted before they disappeared again.

"Elu!" Talon yelled. His words ended on a click and I knew he was close to changing. I could hear the other humans approaching, but they weren't within eyeshot yet.

I nodded my head, "Do it."

My raptor exploded from my body, and the world shifted around me, coming into focus as I stared at the man with the weapon. Elu changed, falling on his side as his leg came free from the pit he was stuck in. He bayed out, panicked until he righted himself. I charged the human. He stood there, clutching his weapon above his shoulder, his eyes wide as if he couldn't believe what he'd seen. I darted in and bit into his side, pushing him over with my momentum as my talons dug into flesh. His screams pierced my ears and all I could focus on was making him be quiet. I needed the screaming to stop.

I snarled when I felt something slice my side. It was only then that I realized the other humans had finally reached us. I leapt to the side, facing my attackers. A burly man sneered at me, pacing to the side away from me—it was like a dance between us. Blood dripped from the end of his weapon, my blood. A high-pitched shriek tore from my throat, my snout darting in close to grip his arm. My teeth slid through his skin like butter but he yanked back, muscle shredding in my mouth. Somewhere to my right, Talon clicked happily as another scream tore through the night.

The trader shouted something that I couldn't understand. The other men inched closer and I lowered my snout, daring them to approach me. I'd take every limb from their bodies if they were dumb enough to get too close. A loud shriek pulled their attention away as Talon landed on one man, knocking him to the ground. His claws tore into the body beneath him as he snapped at the men left standing.

I stalked toward the men Talon couldn't reach. Their weapons lowered, pointing toward me. The man with a fire red beard stumbled over in the muddy ground and fell backward, reaching for his companion. The dark-haired man stared down at his friend, then glanced at me before he mumbled something and began running. I leapt at my prey, gnashing at his tender flesh. These men had hunted us like animals, like trophies. They had no honor and they didn't deserve mercy.

When the man beneath me stopped twitching, I bayed for Talon. We had things to do. I rose up, extending my neck as I bayed louder. I could hear Kishil's reply, but it seemed far away already. I shook my head and lowered myself back down, running in the direction the human had ran. Talon ran to my side and we sprinted into the woods. The earth beneath our feet became harder and we picked up speed. His scent trail was easy to follow, as he reeked of fear and blood. He must be injured. I glanced at Talon out of the corner of my eye as we wove through the trees. He must have been the one to land a blow, I hadn't touched that human.

Talon was wild. The males in his family were predisposed to going feral, but he'd never given me any reason to think he was capable of it until now. He'd just decimated those humans without any hesitation. It was worrisome.

The loud crunch of clumsy footsteps rang out in my skull. Talon and I clicked at the same time, turning toward the noise. We ran for him. The human's dark hair bounced behind him as he glanced over his shoulder.

"Aaaah!" he shrieked, looking forward again and running harder. He was panting. He probably hadn't ran this far or this long in years, based on his size. It didn't take long before we were nipping at his heels. I stretched my neck out, clamping down on the back of his thigh.

Talon leapt on top of him, ripping into his throat for a quick kill. I couldn't shudder in this skin, but if I could, I would have. I backed away from the body and chuffed at my pack mate. I crouched low to the ground, my tail swaying as I watched him tear into the dead human. He wasn't paying attention to me.

I looked around us, trying to tell if there were any more threats in the area. Slowly backing away several feet away—I didn't want to do this too close to Talon—I called the change. My scales receded into soft human skin and I grunted as my bones popped back into place. I dug my fingers into the earth to ground myself against the sensation.

"Talon," I called out on a hoarse whisper. He turned to face me, blood gleaming on his teeth. I held out my hands in an attempt to calm him. "You need to shift back. You're not yourself right now, brother."

Talon's nostrils flared and he looked from me to the human he'd mauled. He chuffed low in his throat and backed away from the corpse. A piercing shriek tore from his throat before he turned and ran through the woods, away from me. He was heading toward our camp. I sighed and shook my head as I turned to go search for Kishil.

"He probably headed back to camp already too," I sighed. I trudged through the woods, alone, looking for my pack mate. I'd make sure he wasn't injured out here somewhere before I returned home. And when the three of us were all back at camp, we were going to have a serious discussion about Talon's raptor. His ferocity was concerning... and I'd promised him I'd never let what happened to his father, happen to him. I swallowed the emotion and peered into the woods. There could be more traders lurking, I'd need to be careful.

I hope Talon makes it home safely.

Chapter 6

Sage

I came awake in a rush, lurching to the side. Panic set in fast and I turned this way and that, trying to figure out what was going on. I blinked, clearing my eyes as I searched for answers. Near me, a strange low chuffing sound caught my attention and I whipped around to face the source.

The raptor... That's right, I got kidnapped.

I groaned, rubbing my bleary eyes. The scaly stared at me, but his eyes were unreadable. A shiver ran down my spine as I could finally see him clearly in the daylight. The noon sun beating down on us highlighted the blues in his scales. He was mostly a dark brownish-green, but the striations in his scales were blue and a lighter shade of green that caught the eye. Truth be told, he was beautiful. I glanced away from the scaly and peered out at the area we had come to. They must have been traveling all day while I slept, because the land had changed drastically. I rose to my knees in the cart and tried to get a look behind us, to see where we'd come from.

I was pretty sure we were traveling north, but I couldn't be certain. I'd have to wait until the sun moved again to be sure. Gunner cleared his throat and I turned to face him, narrowing my eyes.

The scaly snarled and reached a claw through the cage in our direction. I resisted the urge to jump, I wouldn't give him the satis-faction.

"We'll be stopping soon, woman." He didn't turn his head or acknowledge my presence other than speaking. Maybe he had heard me moving in the cart. I hadn't woken up gracefully at all.

"Stopping for what?" I pinched the bridge of my nose and sighed. "Did you finally see the error of your ways and decide to let me go?"

Gunner snorted and shook his head. The horses trudged along through the large, open field we'd found ourselves in. We must be farther from peninsula than I'd thought. There weren't many fields near the village and I didn't know this one. I bit the inside of my cheek and tried to remain calm. How far had we traveled? Once I made my escape—and I would escape—how long would it take to get back to the village?

"There's a small village up ahead, along the river. We're going to *trade* with them." The way he emphasized the word trade sent chills down my spine. The scaly let out a hollow shriek, and I turned to face him. He must have felt the same way, considering the way his eyes bored into the back of Gunner's head.

"Trade what, exactly? Do you have any real trade, or do you just kidnap young women and wild animals as you see fit?"

The scaly snarled again and Gunner glanced over his shoulder, pulling on the horses' reins just as a small village came into view. Once the horses came to a complete stop, he dropped the reins onto the floor, and turned toward me and the cage, pointing at the vicious animal inside.

"I swear that *thing* understands us," he muttered. "It's almost like it's responding."

"Some animals are smarter than others. Horses, for example," I supplied in a rush. Behind me, the scaly snorted. The sound of his claws clicking against the wooden bottom of the cage was distracting.

"What do you know about them?"

"Ah... well," I began, searching for a lie. I'd never been a good liar.

Gunner raised an eyebrow, eyeing me with suspicion. I shrugged my shoulders. "I have to pee."

"If this is some escape attempt—"

"I have to pee. I just got kidnapped, and then shoved into a cart where I slept till midday. I need to relieve myself, unless you'd rather I did it right here?" I made a show of beginning to squat in the cart, my chin held high in challenge.

"No, no, stop." Gunner's face burned red and he called out to a man passing by. "Please escort the lady. Dinnae touch her, or I'll cut your fingers off." He swapped to his native tongue for the last, his accent coming through strong as his agitation grew. I shook my head, still unsure what the Mockingbird had done to make me understand these strange men.

Or why he would want me to understand them.

Do I even believe the Mockingbird spoke to me? Maybe I'm losing my mind...

I blew out a breath and moved to the edge of the cart. The young man waiting for me held out a hand, but I raised my eyebrow at the gesture and braced my palm on the edge of the cart, quickly hopping over. My feet hit the grass with a thud and I looked from Gunner to his companion with narrowed eyes.

"Tell your friend I'm not in need of his *help*," I muttered. Gunner relayed the message with a laugh. The younger man blushed and waved a hand toward the woods at the edge of the clearing. Apparently, he wanted me to lead the way. I sucked air through my teeth and marched toward the tree line. I was annoyed. I was a little frightened, but above all else I was annoyed. These oafs were interfering with whatever it was that I was supposed to be doing. I just wanted to get back to my people. I glanced at the village just past the field where the river began. A group of the traders stood with a group of local men. I tried to staunch my curiosity, because I really *did* have to pee.

"Please don't try to run away," the boy whispered as we grew close to the edge of the field.

I looked at him and then focused on walking once more. I didn't want them to know I understood their native tongue, regardless of how that had come about.

"You can't understand a word I'm saying, can you?" He shoved a hand in his hair. It was curly and dark, and his eyes were as blue as the sky. I paused at the edge of the tree line and pointed to the ground. He needed to stay here.

"No, I can't let you go in there alone. You'd never come back and Gunner'd have my ass for it."

I crossed my arms and stared at him, waiting. He was *young*, he had to be about five summers younger than me. He would give in, I was certain of it.

The young man cursed under his breath and pointed into the woods, making a show of looking at the ground as I walked by him. I hurried to a tree big enough to provide some privacy and relieved myself. When I was done, I eyed my surroundings. I could run. I could probably make it with this much of a head start. The boy wouldn't be much of a hardship to get rid of if he pursued me, and if he went back to the camp to get assistance, I'd be long gone. I bit my lip, weighing my options.

There are no guarantees in this life, young matriarch...

I spun around, looking for the source of the voice. It had sounded as clear as my own thoughts. I tilted my head to the sky, ready to let loose a cry of frustration, when I saw him. The mockingbird... or the Mockingbird? I pointed at the bird and whisper-screamed, "You!"

The creature spread its wings then retucked them against its sides, cocking its head to the side and staring at me. The black-tipped feathers coated in stardust told me I wasn't losing my mind.

"You're driving me crazy, are you real? Why can I understand the travelers?" I was moments away from deeming this entire experience a hallucination. I was probably still asleep somewhere near the village, my body working through whatever was in the sacred tea. The mockingbird only whistled and flew away. I sighed. I was talking to birds now. I turned to check and see what my guard was

47

doing, only to run smack into him. The young man raised an eyebrow at me.

"Who were you talking to?" he demanded, looking around us. I tried to keep my face blank when he focused back on me. He looked so very serious.

"The bird," I replied in my own tongue. The boy stood there, frustrated, with his hands on his hips.

"Is. There. Someone. Else. Here?" He enunciated each word so carefully I couldn't help but laugh. I covered my mouth when his eyes widened. "You understand me don't you?"

"I just want you to let me go home," I told him. "Maybe the Mockingbird knew what he was doing giving me this power—or mental breakdown—this is hilarious." I covered my mouth, hiding my grin.

"Ahhh! Go back to the cart before Gunner kicks my ass!" he shouted. Above us, the song of a mockingbird rang out in the canopy and I couldn't help but look up with a smile.

Once again, I found myself crouched beside a low burning fire next to the cage holding the raptor shifter. The hot night air clung to my skin, amplified by the heat radiating from the fire. I turned the spit that held the rabbit Gunner had brought me and glanced at the cage for the millionth time. I didn't know much about scalies—they kept a lot of their own secrets—but it couldn't be easy for him to have stayed in his raptor form for so long.

"Has anyone fed the scaly?" I asked Gunner. He stirred from his place across the fire and raised an eyebrow.

"Do you have any virgins on hand?" His eyebrow cocked at the same time his mouth curved in a wicked smile, and my fingers itched to slap it off his face. I wiped my hands along my skirt and smirked at him.

"In my culture, virgins are unlucky. Why would you want one of those?" I blinked innocently as he sputtered. I probably shouldn't tease the man holding me captive, but he was just *too* smug.

"I—"

"Gunner!" someone called from the edge of the camp. Gunner looked over and nodded, then rose to his feet.

"I'll be back, woman. Try not to do anything stupid while I'm gone."

"Did you just call me stupid?" I growled, staring at him. I was a lot of things—impulsive being one of them—but I wasn't stupid.

"You did try to escape once already, and my man told me you were up to something in the woods this afternoon too." Gunner winked and my skin crawled. Thankfully he turned around and jogged out of sight, toward whoever had called him away.

I needed to be careful. My need to argue was often mistaken by men as flirting, and the last thing I needed was for Gunner to think I was interested. He'd kidnapped and threatened me. There was no way I could forgive that, not in a million years. In my culture, women were leaders or considered equal to men. We were respected. There were almost never rapes in my society—like Gunner had threatened me with—and when there were, the offenders were dealt with swiftly and publicly. The man would be held down and the woman would carve his cock from his body. I'd never had to witness this ritual though, since apparently castration is enough of a deterrent for men who simply didn't *understand* the laws of our people.

More than that, beyond the harsh—but deserved—justice, our people knew that without women the world would be barren. The Creator made this world but he couldn't fill it on his own, he had to turn to the Great Mother for help. There had been whispers for the past few years about traders who were invading the lands to the north and the west. Pale men, like these ones, who spoke a strange language and thought they were leaders. I shook my head.

I wasn't sexist, I respected men, but everyone had a place in life. Leadership simply requires more skills than the average male possesses.

I turned the rabbit once again, and stared into the flames. My thoughts spun like a hurricane through my mind, ricocheting off one another. In the past twenty-four hours I'd been drugged, had an excruciatingly strange dream experience—that may or may not have been more real than dream—gotten kidnapped, heard birds talk to me, and was worried about the welfare of a scaly who I hadn't seen take human form yet.

"Maybe you're not human anymore," I whispered. "Maybe I'm losing my fucking mind." I pulled the spit from the flames and tore a few pieces of meat from the side before I walked toward the cage with my offering. The raptor stared at me—he was always staring at me, it seemed—and his nostrils flared as I approached. He glanced down at the rabbit, a low chuffing sound coming from his throat that ended on a click.

I held the stick I'd been using as a spit closer to the cage, hesitating to push it through the bars. What if he attacked me somehow? I glanced down at the rabbit and then back to the scaly, forcing my heartbeat to slow. "If you bite me, I'll let these idiots starve you until you decide to show yourself. Understand?"

The raptor clicked over and over, and if I didn't know any better, I'd say he was laughing at me. Maybe he was. I pushed the rabbit through the bars and waited. The scaly angled his head to the side, blinking. His eyes didn't shut when he blinked, in fact I wasn't sure he'd moved a muscle, other than the fast, thin membrane I saw slide horizontally across his eye and then back again.

"Wow," I murmured. He tilted his head up, staring me directly in the eye, and I pushed the rabbit farther in. "Go on, take it."

He closed his jaws gently around the small meal and pulled back until the meat slipped from the stick. One quick chomp as he tossed his head back, and the meat disappeared behind rows of razor sharp teeth. A series of clicks rattled out of him and I smiled. He must have been hungry. Goosebumps broke out across the back of my neck a moment before the scaly snarled and paced toward the bars. I backed away, confused, and hit something hard. I turned to see Gunner glaring at the dino-shifter.

"I think he likes you."

"I think he likes you more, you should go pet him," I purred, as I took a step away from my kidnapper. His mouth screwed up to the side and he pointed to the stick in my hand.

"Did you feed that beast our dinner?"

"Our dinner? No, I fed him some of *my* dinner. You have all these men, go find yourself some food." *Our dinner,* I scoffed to myself. *He's lost his mind.*

"Woman—"

"No," I interrupted. "You speak my language. I know you know better than this, even if you were raised somewhere barbaric—and you probably were—whoever taught you the Language of the Sun had to have taught you manners as well. You *kidnapped* me and you're *starving* an animal because you think it reminds you of something from your own folklore. I won't be having dinner with you." I swallowed when I was done and turned to face the cage head on. I tried really hard to be a logical woman, but my patience was gone. Did I need this man to escape? Maybe, I wasn't sure. Was I willing to be his plaything in the meantime? No.

I never saw whatever hit me. I blinked through the pain assaulting my temple, but even the dim light of the fire was too bright. I blinked again, my fingers digging into the dirt. I could just barely make out the scaly as he slammed into the side of his cage, before darkness crept in from the edges of my vision.

Chapter 7

Kishil

My talons dug into the wooden floor beneath my feet, as I tracked the human as he came up behind her. This woman was a matriarch. I knew what the symbols on her skin meant, I'd learned about the Sun Tribes as a boy. My mother had wanted me to know the people responsible for raising her, even if they'd cast her out for falling in love with a *scaly*. I blinked, clearing my thoughts.

As much as I hated my mother's people for everything they'd put her through, this woman was important. Matriarchs were queens to them. They believed the Spirits chose them to lead their people, and communicate with the matriarchs of neighboring tribes to keep the peace. This woman would lead her people some day soon. She was their alpha and they needed her.

"I won't be having dinner with you." She visibly swallowed when she finished speaking, waiting for the tongue-lashing she knew would come. She was brave to stand up to this man.

Of course she's brave, she's a matriarch.

The sound of skin cracking skin rang through the night. The matriarch fell to her knees on the ground, as a dark red mark covered her face from her temple to her eye. The trader stood there with his fist still curled, glaring at the woman. I leapt toward the bars as she fell over into the dirt, my body slamming into them.

He hit an unarmed woman, a matriarch!

I snarled, reaching my claws through the bars toward the man. He stared at me, before glancing between me and the matriarch with a confused expression. I couldn't reach him, my talons just barely grazed the woman's shirt, and he was too far away. Anger swelled inside me. She was unconscious on the ground, why wasn't anyone doing anything? I slammed my body against the side of the cage, baying out for my pack mates once again. If I'd ever needed them to find me, it was now.

I hadn't given much thought to what would happen to me once I'd been taken. I'd either escape, or I'd die one death or another. When I'd seen the woman they'd captured was from the Sun Tribes —when I'd noticed *what* she was—I'd been watching. These men didn't have honor. They could hurt her, possibly more than what she knew was possible. Her people didn't participate in the kind of evil these men frequented in. I worked the tip of my snout between the bars, snarling at the human as he took a step toward the unconscious woman.

"You don't want me touching her, do you, dragon?" The man— Gunner, she called him—ran his hand over his mouth as he crouched down and surveyed his work. Two men walked over, murmuring low amongst themselves. "I'm fine," he snapped.

One man glared at his leader, his lip curling up over his teeth. I thrashed against the cage again, trying to force myself through the bars. I'd rip these idiots to shreds for hurting her. There was right and there was wrong.

This definitely fell under the latter category.

I pushed forward, trying desperately to squeeze my head through the bars. She wasn't that far away. If I could get to her, I could keep these animals away from her. *Humans,* another snarl tore from my throat. *Disgusting, fucking humans.*

A ruckus rose to the west. Shouts filled the night and the humans all turned toward the river, toward the village. The faintest scent of smoke irritated my nostrils, telling me there was a fire starting somewhere down there.

"Shit! Go see what's happened," Gunner snapped, running after his men as they scrambled to see what was going on. Several men ran through the camp toward the village, nearly trampling the matriarch.

Please wake up. If only I could speak in this form. Unfortunately, humans didn't understand the meaning of different sounds... clicks, chuffs, bays, and shrieks all had meaning to my people. The subtle differences were lost to human ears though. It all sounded the same to them.

"Mmm," a groggy, feminine voice moaned from the ground. My eyes snapped back to the matriarch as she slowly rolled to her side and then her back. Her hand came up to her eyebrow and she hissed in a breath, staring up at the sky. I let out a quiet chuff, sticking the end of my snout between the bars once again. She sat up slowly, blinking at me.

"Why won't you change?" The matriarch looked over her shoulder and gazed at the commotion by the river. Slowly, she rose to her feet, wobbling. The scent of her blood hit me all at once. Where was she bleeding? I focused on her brow and noticed how the dark hair looked the tiniest bit wet... he'd really injured her. "There's no one here to see you, scaly. Tell me what happened to you and what you know about these people." She nearly fell over as she finished speaking and I took a few steps back.

Nervous clicks bubbled out of my throat as I looked around the camp, making sure no one was watching. The only noises that reached my ears were the humans yelling from the river. I pictured my human body in my mind—less scales, more copper skin. My grunt came out a snarl as my bones popped and my scales shrank into the brassy skin I usually wore. My fingers curled against the wooden bottom to the cage and I rasped in a breath, trying to get my bearings.

Holding my raptor for that long had been tiring. I ran a hand through my hair, combing it back from my face as I stood. The matriarch's eyes widened, causing me to pause. I didn't trust her people. I'd been worried when she was being beaten, but I didn't *like* her kind. I glanced away from her light brown eyes shining in the firelight.

"What do you want?" I ground out.

Chapter 8

Sage

"What do I want?" I shrieked. The scaly's eyes widened and he looked around. I covered my mouth and followed suit, waiting for a herd of pale men to come thundering into the camp at any second.

When no one came, I glanced back to the man and lowered my voice. "Why do you not want them to know what you are?" I asked, pressing a finger to the growing knot on my forehead. My vision swam as I stared at the scaly, and he rushed to the edge of the cage, sticking his arm out. I reached for his hand and steadied myself.

"Are you okay? He hit you." His tight, clipped words warred with the soft eyes staring back at me. They were brown—like my own—but blue around the center. They were beautiful. I shook my head and instantly regretted it. My stomach rolled and I gripped onto the cage with my free hand.

"Everything is a little off right now," I murmured, squinting my eyes closed.

"Are you going to puke?" He sounded mortified. I snorted and ignored him, trying to focus on the questions I wanted to ask him. I'd been wondering things since the moment I saw him being forced into this cage. Of course I'd have the opportunity to speak to him and then be *unable* to do so.

"Why don't you want them to know what you are?" I repeated my earlier question, focusing on something other than the world spinning around me.

"They're traders," he replied. He pulled his hand back from mine and dragged it to the cage. I guess he wanted me to support myself. "They're why the raptors left the plains. They're why *everyone* has left the plains, or moved far enough north that they feel safe."

"I didn't know the raptors came from the plains," I whispered. I don't know why that was important, but for some reason I'd always pictured scalies like this one running over hills in large packs.

"What?" His eyebrows drew down close to his nose.

"Nothing," I sighed, dismissing the silly thought. "Who are you? What's your name?"

The scaly narrowed his eyes on me, crossing his arms over his chest. I tried—and failed—not to notice his muscled arms and sculpted stomach. My eyes wandered lower and lower, chasing the slim patch of hair that crept from his bellybutton down to his...

My eyes rocketed back up to his face and my cheeks burned as I tried to stare at anything other than the massive swinging *log* between his legs. He wasn't even erect! *Great Mother*... I groaned inwardly.

"Is there a problem, matriarch?" The grin he wore was cocky and any attraction I'd felt quickly fled.

"I asked your name," I snapped.

"Kishil," he laughed. "My name is Kishil Quick." He leaned against the bars of the cage with confidence, like he wasn't worried about being a prisoner at all.

"You have two names?" I pressed my palm to my head, muttering under my breath. "Never mind. That's not important. I'm Sage. How were you captured? Aren't scalies supposed to be stronger than us *mere mortals*?" My mouth quirked to the side, even through my pain, when I saw this strange man swallow a smile. There was something about him, this dino-shifter. And it wasn't the giant dick dangling between his legs... At least I didn't think it was.

"Sage. You're a clever girl, huh? Then how'd *you* end up a prisoner?" Kishil arched a brow, mocking me.

"I was on my Spirit Walk, to become the matriarch—"

"Aren't you already a matriarch? The symbols..." He waved his hand down, gesturing to the paint on my skin.

"I have to pass a test before it's official. These guys interrupted," I grumbled.

"Or this is your test."

I swallowed. That hadn't occurred to me. *Great Mother... Sage, you are an idiot.*

"This is my test," I repeated back to him, blandly. I was still absorbing his revelation.

"If you believe in that sort of thing." Kishil's head snapped up and he sank to the floor quickly. "I have to change back, Clever Girl. My pack will come for me, and when they do, be ready. If you can get away before then, do it. But by the Creator, please don't get caught trying to escape. I think the big, dumb, yellow one is growing tired of your mouth." He began to crouch down but paused.

"Don't go to that village. Someone's coming, please promise me you won't go to see the River People tonight. It doesn't sound good down there." His face grew grim until I nodded. With that, Kishil crumpled in on himself, a groan escaping his lips as his skin stretched.

The sound of bones creaking sent a shiver down my spine as I watched him shift into a raptor. I covered my mouth to keep a gasp from escaping. I'd never seen a scaly change before now. I knew what they were, knew that they shifted from man to beast, but seeing it in person was an entirely different thing. The raptor—Kishil—stepped toward me, his talons clicking on the wooden floor of the cage as he stepped closer. His nostrils flared and his pupils constricted into a thinner line, revealing more of the swirled amber and blue eyes.

He slid his snout through the bars, a low noise emanating from him. I laid my hand on his nose, a little scared he might bite, even though I knew, logically, that this wasn't a wild animal. Those teeth were intimidating however. His scales were smoother than I'd expected. The striations on them made him appear rough—and the texture of each individual scale added to that—but the scales themselves were smooth. The breath hitting my hand was so warm compared to the cool skin.

"What the hell are ya' doing, woman?" I flinched at the sound of Gunner's voice, before snatching my hand away quickly. Kishil snarled as Gunner approached. "Get back before the dragon takes your hand off!"

I stepped away from the cage, reluctant to follow any *orders* from Gunner. I clasped my hands at my waist and waited for him to reach the cage. My temple throbbed and I tried not to sway where I stood. Showing weakness to men like this could be my undoing. I wouldn't do it.

"What were you thinking?" he snapped in my face. He was much too close. The stench of alcohol on his breath was strong, and I winced.

Turning from him to take a deep breath, I smiled and replied, "I probably wasn't thinking clearly. I have a swimming head, thanks to this very *polite* man I know." I stepped back—closer to the raptor—and tilted my chin up, meeting his gaze as I repeated the words he'd spoken to me when we first met.

"Aye." Gunner rubbed his hand across his bearded chin and nodded. "Fair point, woman. I apologize for striking you. It wasn't right to do. I hope you'll forgive me for acting out of anger."

I gaped at him, ignoring the snarls echoing in the cage behind me. Apparently, Kishil believed this apology about as much as I did. He didn't seem conflicted, he was just using pretty words to cover up his own cruelty. I shook my head and waved a hand at him.

"Leave me alone, Gunner."

"I apologized," he growled.

"You're an ass. I don't want to be in your company. I'm a prisoner here, so I may not have any say in whose company I keep, but I *will* keep reminding you how much I despise your companionship until you finally leave me alone. I'd rather be anywhere on Gaia than near you." I chewed my lip, fighting back tears at the embarrassment this situation brought me. "You hit me. That's a grave crime amongst my people, know that. Now leave me."

His eyes widened a moment before they narrowed to slits, glaring at me. He mumbled something under his breath I couldn't quite catch, and threw his hands in the air. I stared at his back as he tramped off toward the river village, yet again. I worried for the people in that settlement.

Your mother would be proud. You sound like a true leader, young matriarch. Regal, demanding, but not selfish.

I wheeled around, searching the night for the source of the voice. My stomach roiled once again from all the sudden movement. I pressed my eyes shut, ignoring the chirping clicks coming from the cage.

"Do you hear that voice?" I focused on my breathing to combat the nausea. "This damn bird has been following me," I mumbled. "By the Great Mother's name, I swear I'm losing my mind."

Kishil bayed out, a strong but short sound that grabbed my attention. I opened my eyes to see him crouched low to the ground, eyes on me. He shook his head decidedly from left to right. So, that was a no then. He couldn't hear the Mockingbird.

I'm losing my mind.

A sweet tune sang from somewhere in the camp. The tune switched to another, faster whistle and I groaned. A mockingbird. The raptor chuffed, canting his head to the side.

"I've decided you're much nicer when you can't speak," I whispered.

Kishil snorted and moved away from the bars. I sank to the ground by the cage and leaned against it. I'd sleep here tonight instead of by the fire. Maybe the men would think twice about touching me if I was so close to something they feared so much.

"I'm going to lay here because they fear you." I kept my voice low, since I didn't want anyone in the camp to hear me speaking to a *dragon*. For some reason, I felt it was necessary to reiterate that I was staying close for safety. It was definitely for safety, not comfort. I glared at the sky for a moment, trying to figure out where that songbird was hiding. The Mockingbird—if he wasn't a figment of my imagination—was a pain.

I tipped my chin down to my chest, my eyes fluttering shut. How in the world had I ended up here? Behind me, Kishil made a noise I didn't have a word for. I resisted the urge—just barely—to look over my shoulder at him. The steady sound lured me to sleep.

I came awake to the sound of bustling movement. My eyes opened the tiniest bit, revealing the ruckus going on in camp. Everywhere I looked, there were traders hauling armfuls of goods. A few men even dragged people along behind them, tied together by a rope.

"Now, your treatment doesn't seem so bad, does it?"

I jumped at the intrusion. Turning to meet Gunner's gaze, I stared at him with sad eyes. Didn't he realize he was hurting innocent people? Didn't he care?

"Why do you do this? You honestly believe that you're a good person, I think. That fascinates me. How can you reconcile the way you're treating these people—the way you've treated me—with being a good man?" My voice hardened and I rose to my feet, dusting off the bottom of my skirt.

"You could have it worse," he reasoned.

"That doesn't make you a good man." I turned my back on him, digging in my satchel for the bone runes my mother had sent me with. I fingered them without pulling them out, since I didn't want these oafs taking them as well. They'd already taken my knife.

"Get ready to leave, woman," he sighed. "We'll push for the coast today, and then you'll have the whole trip home to think about the decisions you've made."

I didn't bother answering him. I didn't bother explaining that this was my home and always would be. I wouldn't be getting on that ship. I didn't know when Kishil's pack would come, but if they didn't come soon, I'd get myself out of here. I would have tried to escape last night, but I was injured and wouldn't have made it far. I bit my lip, ignoring the pain in my head. The throbbing in my temple had eased to a dull ache, and now I could feel the bruise above my eyebrow as well, as if thinking about it conjured the pain. I yawned and stretched my arms, trying to think of a plan.

I could seduce Gunner... I toyed with the idea in my head. I could make love to him and once he was sated, sneak out of his tent, then out of this encampment. My fingers drummed against my chin as I tracked Gunner across the camp. He was in charge. If I made him think I was giving into his wishes, I could possibly get away with a lot more.

No, I can't lay with that man. There was no way I'd be able to stomach having him inside me. He was vile. He was the worst kind of cruel. He thought he was a good person in spite of all the things he did to hurt innocent people. I shuddered at the thought of him being on top of me, rutting like some savage bull. *No thank you.*

Men came to hook the cart to the cage, and the horses were less wary of Kishil than they were the first time they met him. I walked over to them and ran a hand down the neck of a beautiful paint. She was gorgeous. Black, white, and grey splashes of color coated her body.

"Shhh, girl," I murmured. My fingers instinctively combed through the main hanging over her neck. They snagged on something and my eyebrows cinched together. I wrapped my hand around her mane closest to her skin and pulled the thing out of the rat's nest that had grown around it.

A feather.

These horses were stolen from a Sun Tribe. My fist balled around the feather as I looked over the camp once more, taking in all the new copper faces staring back at me. Varying shades of brown, brass, and wheat watched me. My throat tightened as I stared at the condition of them. There were few men, and most of the captives were women. I quickly searched for any matriarch markings. There wasn't a matriarch among them and that both calmed *and* bothered me.

On the one hand, I was glad that their leader hadn't been taken hostage. On the other, I was worried for her safety. No matriarch would let this sort of behavior go without retaliation. Was she somewhere with her warriors, planning to retaliate, or had something bad happened to her?

I quickly braided my hair and tossed it over my shoulder before marching across the camp to a group of women. Their wrists were bound, their clothes in disarray. My stomach clenched as the realization hit me. These women had been abused.

"Sisters," I murmured, approaching them carefully. If they had been through what I imagined they had, they may be timid at the moment. I looked around, waiting to see if any of the men would try to stop me from going to them, but no one intervened. The women held out their arms, beckoning me closer. I rushed into their embrace, inspecting them.

I didn't know these women. They weren't even from my tribe, but it didn't matter. All that mattered was that they'd been harmed. I brushed hair out of the first woman's face. Her deep green eyes watered as she looked back at me, her fingers dancing across the bruised on my temple.

"Matriarch, your head," she fretted. I pushed her hand down and shook my head.

"I'm fine," I mumbled, still uncomfortable with the term of respect. "Where is your matriarch?" I looked from the first woman to the other faces surrounding us. Their eyes hardened and my stomach dipped. I already knew the answer.

"She died defending the village," an older woman called out proudly. She must be an elder. I moved to her and bowed my head in respect. "She was murdered by these strange men. They told us they wanted pelts and we were glad to trade with them. Someone set fire to our village last night, and while we tried to put out the flames, they attacked."

I nodded and looked around at these people, looking to the west for the first time since I woke up. Where once I'd seen homes obscuring the river, now there were only a few structures still standing. Smoke hung where the village used to be. My arms wrapped tight around my middle and I resisted the urge to cry, these people didn't need my tears. They needed someone to look to. Their matriarch had been murdered.

Murdered—a matriarch! It was unheard of. I didn't ask them if the next had been chosen yet. If she had, I'd see her or they would have mentioned her. I didn't want to think about her. I closed my eyes, saying a silent prayer for the lost matriarch.

Who is going to help her people?

I stood to my feet and glared at the men securing the cart to the raptor cage. The dino-shifter inside caught my eye and lowered his head in some semblance of a bow. This was not the way of things. Searching for Gunner, their leader, I marched into the midst of a group of traders.

"Where is he?" I yelled. Several men stared at me like I'd grown three heads. I took a deep breath, praying for patience as I tried to think of how to convey my point. I could understand their language. I wondered, suddenly, if that meant I could also speak it. Now was as good a time as any to test the limits of my delusions.

"Where is he?" I tried again, focusing on the way their words sounded when they left their mouths.

"You can speak English?" a voice called out over the crowd. I narrowed my eyes, trying to find the man I was searching for. I caught a glimpse of yellow hair around a big man and I stomped through the men, pushing them out of my way one after the other.

"What is this?" I demanded.

"You can speak English?" Gunner repeated again, a grin spreading across his face. "That's wonderful!"

My fingers itched to slap the smile off his face. I rubbed them together, avoiding giving in to the temptation. It would feel fantastic to hit him, but then he'd probably kill me and that would help no one.

"What is this?" I screamed. I was trying to be calm and diplomatic, truly I was. That was apparently my role as the future matriarch, but these people had no matriarch and it was my responsibility to make sure they were taken care of before I left them.

"Their village burned overnight and they have nowhere to go. I've offered them a solution." Gunner combed through the beard on his chin with this fingers, eyeing me suspiciously. "I told you there would eventually be others."

"You call this a solution?" My voice grew louder with each word I spoke. My heart hammered against my chest as I pointed toward the women huddled together across the camp. "Someone harmed those women. Someone killed the matriarch of this village. I want them brought before me immediately and I will deal with them how I see fit." I tilted my chin, daring him to argue with me.

"Ah, well, you see..." Gunner began in a mocking tone.

My hand flew out before I could instruct it not to. My knuckles crashed into his face and he recoiled. Gunner stumbled and then glared at me, his skin glowing red where my fist had connected. I schooled the shock from my face and glared at him.

"I want the man, now. You wanted my 'help' with your captives? This is my role. I will see every one of you torn to pieces for disgracing these people this way."

"Restrain her," Gunner spat, and two men moved in on either side of me, reaching for my arms. I pulled away from them, kicking one in the groin as the other wrapped my braid around his hand and pulled me back.

"Stop fighting, princess," the man holding my hair muttered. My neck craned at an awkward angle. Kishil bayed from his cage, thrashing against the bars. I had a moment to worry that he was going to hurt himself before my leg caught fire.

I screamed, thrashing against the man who held me. I stared down at my thigh, which was weeping blood. It wasn't on fire. My eyes rose to Gunner's and he grinned, tightening his grip on the short piece of leather he carried. My eyes went wide as he reared back and I prepared myself for another blow.

Kishil bayed a hopeless sound and I winced before the lash even connected. I swallowed my scream as he marked my other thigh. Tears I refused to cry brimmed in the corners of my eyes. I turned my head away, focusing on the cage. The scaly threw himself against the bars over and over, and I couldn't stop myself from hoping that maybe they would break and he could eat these vicious men.

A bay caught my ear and my heart clenched. I'd been staring directly at Kishil, and he hadn't bayed, he'd been trying to chew on one of the bars. He released the wooden bar and tilted his head to the side before he rose up, letting out two quick bays. More bays came from a different direction. I looked to Gunner, who cast nervous glances around the clearing. A shriek cut through the silence that had fallen among us, followed by a high-pitched scream. I twisted my head, trying to see clearly, as yells rose from around the camp.

A blur of grey and green caught my eye behind Gunner. The man restraining me threw me to the ground, and I lifted my face out of the grass in time to see a raptor straddling a man not far behind where Gunner had stood. I pushed to my feet, looking around the camp. The cage. I needed the key for the cage. Men turned in circles, trying to track the raptors. From what I could see, there were two of them, but the way they were attacking made it hard to be sure. I moved slowly toward the closest body. On his waist was a knife, close to the size of the one that had been stolen from me. This one glinted more in the sun, but it would have to do. I scurried toward the prisoners, slashing the ropes that held their wrists together.

"Go, but don't run. These scalies are friends—I think—but they are still scalies. Running will trigger their predatory instincts. Be safe and start new."

"Matriarch!" someone called. I turned to face them, steeling myself. "What will we do with no matriarch?" The warrior's eyes were sad, his soot covered face tear streaked. My shoulders sagged and I pointed toward the river.

"You have to lead yourselves," I gritted out. "Until someone is chosen, you'll have to lead yourselves." I slid the knife into my belt, and wiped some sweat from my brow. The sun beat down on us without mercy, and the group I'd freed nodded, before moving to finish freeing the rest of their people. It wasn't long before they were heading to the edge of the clearing.

Another scream rose somewhere in the camp. I turned to the cage to see Kishil pacing back and forth. He stilled and chuffed. I felt the breath on the back of my neck a moment too late. I turned slowly, looking straight down the scaly's snout. The raptor was tall, as tall as me when he was bent forward like this, when he was in attack mode. I swallowed, focusing on the subtle differences between him and Kishil. His scales were grey and green with swirls of black throughout them. His eyes were more yellow than amber, with a puddle of green around the slanted pupil.

Scalies are not wild beasts. Scalies are not wild beasts.

The scaly chuffed once more and pushed his snout against my chest, inhaling. He was scenting me. Behind me, Kishil snarled and the new raptor's neck snapped in his direction. He snorted and padded off toward his kin.

I exhaled a breath I hadn't realized I'd been holding. My fingers curled around the hilt of the knife as the crack of bone rang out behind me. I whirled just in time to see a man on his knees in front of the cage, scales receding into his skin like they'd never been there. What had looked like swirls of black war paint in his scaly form, now revealed themselves to be tattoos. He was covered in them, from his neck down to his ankles. There was hardly any blank skin on his body. My eyes swept over the strange markings creeping across his skin. War paint covered many of the tattoos, and there was a hand-print across his heart. The dark marks graced his face, in addition to the red lines signifying he was battle ready. My eyes dipped to his arms. Beneath the bands painted for war, more dark tattoos swirled.

They weren't like any of the marks I'd seen in neighboring tribes. My people used paint to celebrate and tattoos to punish... tattoos couldn't be washed off. My mind whirled, wondering what this man had done to deserve such marks.

"Did he just—"

I wheeled around, pulling the knife from my hip as Gunner took a step toward me. His face was pale—even paler than usual—and his eyes wide. I brandished the knife between us, crouching in a defensive position.

"Don't come any closer," I growled, my eyes narrowed on him. The camp wasn't in chaos anymore. Several men surrounded a raptor, poking at it with their long knives.

"The dragon is a... a man?" Gunner shook his head, obviously trying to focus. He drew his long knife and twirled his arm, adjusting the position. "Get out of the way, woman." He grinned at me and chills blasted down my arms. I couldn't let him near the scaly. He'd just changed, he was vulnerable. Even I knew that.

"Are there really no shifters where you live?" I raised my eyebrow. Maybe talking to him would distract him from pursuing the dino-shifter for the moment. I could only hope he'd free Kishil before this got out of hand.

"What? Of course not," he sneered, rocking his head from side to side, and then he shrugged. "There are tales of men who can transform into wolves, but they're just fairy stories for the little runts in the village. There's no truth to them." His eyes flicked to mine with a question written across his face.

"Or maybe there is truth to them. I don't understand why you come to our lands to wreak havoc. Do you not have your own corn, your own furs and pelts?"

"Aye, but this land is so much more fertile than our own."

Gunner took a step toward me and I instinctively backed away from him. "And you have dragons. Our people used to worship dragons and the Dragon Gods. I'd love to take one home for my wife."

"*You* have a wife?" I laughed. "Is there a shortage of men in your homeland as well?" I smirked at him, tilting my chin up in defiance.

Gunner's lips twitched before he lunged. I dodged to the side, narrowly avoiding his attack. I wasn't as strong as him and I wouldn't be able to withstand another blow like the one I'd had the night before. I had to use my smaller size to my advantage. I sidestepped, watching behind him as he circled with me—this was the dance of war.

Behind the yellow-haired fool, the scaly pulled on the lock that held the door to the cage shut. It was made of metal and wouldn't be easily broken. I smiled at Gunner. I could distract him to buy them some time. The sounds coming from the fighting raptor were heart-wrenching alone. I tried not to look, but my curiosity won out. I glanced at the crowd surrounding the creature and my heart sank. Blood poured down his side as a weapon was pulled from his hide.

"You have sympathy for them. Why? They're beasts." Gunner stopped circling and I did as well.

"You've seen for yourself that they're not beasts," I spat. "And even beasts deserve dignity. What is wrong with you people?" I blocked out the screams of the scaly as Gunner's lip curled over his teeth and he began chasing me again. I stepped to the left every time he did. He leaned in with his weapon, swiping close to my body. I could tell he was hardly trying.

"I'm not sure if I should be grateful or insulted," I purred.

"Ah?" He twirled his weapon again, drawing it back toward his chest.

"I've never had a man let me win a fight before." I darted across the space between us and sliced at his thigh, pulling back out of his reach.

The fingers of his free hand dug into my arm as I pulled away. My heart hammered against my chest and my lungs screamed for air.

Time seemed to move so slowly as I watched his metal knife glint in the sun. I wrenched myself free from his grasp, my momentum carrying me in a circle to face him once again. My cheeks heated in the sunshine, my chest rose and fell as I stared at him. Gunner fingered the piece of cloth he'd torn from my shoulder before throwing it onto the ground. I glanced down at my arm. Red marks from his nails tore through my flesh, and blood beaded along one of them.

"You've drawn blood from me twice," I spat. His bright eyes bore into mine as I lunged at him. His eyes went wide the second before I landed on his chest. His long knife clambered to the ground beside us and his hand went to my waist, shoving at me. I screamed my war cry, shoving the dagger toward his chest. One of his arms snaked out, knocking my path astray as he wrapped his fingers around my wrist. The blade landed near his shoulder, lodged between his collarbone and the place the joint moved freely.

"Aaaah!" he bellowed. The sound was a shock to my system, enough to distract me. He shoved me from his body and rolled away. One hand wrapped around the knife sticking out of his skin and he braced himself on the other. "I'll kill ya' for this, woman," he growled.

I scurried to my feet and ran for the cage. The sound of metal snapping had my heart beating faster. Help was coming. Kishil would help me. The tattooed man wrenched the door to the cage open and Kishil shot past him.

He paused in front of me for a moment, his nostrils flaring as he ran his snout down my arm. I stood still, trying once again not to panic from being so close to a scaly. Gunner groaned and Kishil's head craned to the side, surveying the downed man behind me. I moved toward the tattooed man—he seemed much less threatening as a human—as Kishil lowered his snout toward the ground, stalking Gunner.

"Get back!" he shouted. "Help!"

The tattooed man pulled me behind him, and he didn't spare me a second glance otherwise. For some reason, that bothered me. I wasn't some obstruction in battle. I was a fucking *matriarch*.

I sucked in a breath.

When did I start thinking of myself as a matriarch?

"Stay behind me, matriarch." The man's voice was deep and rich. He sounded like honey tasted. I licked my lips and nodded. The adrenaline pumping through my body fueled bloodlust, which I had never experienced before. I'd been trained to fight, of course, but they were all sparring matches. I'd never seriously been in danger, since a true fight was an entirely different beast, and now I understood what all the old warriors were referring to. The bloodlust fueled your passions. My core was slick. Burying my blade in Gunner's shoulder had been *amazing*.

"Get back!" Gunner shouted again. I refocused my attention on the dino-shifter stalking toward him. Kishil's scales gleamed in the sun as he slowly stalked his prey. Several men rushed up behind Gunner, abandoning the raptor they'd been trying to wear down. I scrutinized the crowd brandishing weapons at the scaly. He had an opening...

He took it. As soon as the group of men darted for their leader, he slipped through the hole they'd created before it closed. A grey, almost yellow raptor ran toward us. He was light compared to the other two. Dried paint covered some of his scales, and he also had a handprint across his chest—they'd come out here searching for their pack mate. My eyes flew to the bright colors painted across his neck and around his snout. I knew those marks. These scalies were warriors in their tribe.

The raptor darted toward us. I could tell he was injured by the way he favored his right leg, but even injured he was faster than any horse. I sucked in a breath as he came to a stop near the tattooed man and me.

"Elu, you're hurt," the man whispered, quickly running a hand down his friend's flank. The raptor chuffed and chirped, while I studied them closely. The camaraderie between them was the same as it was with the warriors in my village. Our men and women who had fought beside one another against raiding parties were closer than blood relatives. They'd shared blood in a different, more important, way.

A scream tore my attention away from the sweet exchange and back to the raptor snarling in the middle of several armed men. My throat went dry as Kishil narrowly dodged a blow from one of the men. Gunner was somehow safe behind the line of weapons, holding his injured shoulder as he pointed toward the scaly.

"Kill the damn beast!" he roared.

"Kishil!" the tattooed man snapped. Beside us, the injured raptor bayed and Kishil's neck swiveled so he could peer in our direction. He turned his gaze back on the men in front of him, snapping his jaws at them as he backed away. His talons dug into the ground as he spun around in a semicircle and ran at full speed toward us.

"You're going to get on his back," the tattooed man explained.

"On *whose* back? I am perfectly capable of—" The breath rushed out of my mouth as his hands found my sides. Warmth spread along my skin where his palms lay and I stared up into his green eyes. A series of clicks had the hair raising on the back of my neck. The tattooed man's gaze seemed to heat as he stared at me and suddenly, my stomach dipped as I was lifted into the air. My bottom came down on the back of the raptor I'd been imprisoned with and my thighs clenched along his sides.

"Lean forward, hold on to his shoulders, not his neck. If you choke him, you'll never get where we're going." His words were rushed and I nodded, leaning forward. My chest pressed along the curve of Kishil's spine and my fingers clung to the rounded joint where his short arms connected to his body.

"Be careful, brother." The tattooed man nodded at me and I felt my stomach lurch once again as Kishil darted forward.

"Oh Great Mother," I whimpered as he beelined for the trees. I was certain we were going to run into the first one we came to. Shouts rose behind us, followed by snarls. Kishil bayed out, his body jerking beneath me. He didn't slow to check on his pack mates, he only called to them. My heart skipped until I heard the echoing call, closer than I'd imagined they'd be. These men were *fast*.

"Please, please, please stop doing that!" I clung to Kishil as we darted around another tree and between some bushes. A chirping click rattled through his chest. The bramble scraped at my legs, but I tried not to complain anymore. He was carrying me away from our kidnappers, which was more than I could ask for. I'd keep my complaints about scratches to myself. My right hand slipped along his scales and I pulled it up to see what was wet. Blood smeared my palm and I gasped.

"You're hurt!"

Kishil chuffed as he zigged through the trees. He hopped over a log and landed in what seemed to be a puddle. His pace began slowing, the terrain was changing and it was taking a toll on his efforts. Behind us the sound of two more raptors crashing through the woods interrupted the quiet of the forest.

"Stop and let me down. I can walk. We've made it far enough away that they shouldn't be able to catch up," I pleaded. I didn't enjoy this, not like I enjoyed riding a horse. Kishil's body moved in a completely different way and it was hard to hang on. His steps slowed to an even stride and I leaned up, glancing around us. A snout came into view on my left and I craned my neck to get a better view. The tattooed raptor pulled in close, his shoulder grazing my leg as he played with his pack mate. A look to my right revealed the greyish-yellow raptor coming up alongside us as well. Kishil came to a stop with a shriek and I hopped down from his back.

He twisted his neck around to look at me along his side. His swirling eyes drew my gaze once again and I ran my hand along his back as the sound of pops and snarls echoed around us. I supposed changing forms was painful. I couldn't imagine my body stretching into one of these creatures or shrinking back into a normal-sized human being.

"Are—are you petting him?" an unfamiliar voice huffed. I turned to face the newcomer. As soon as my back was turned, Kishil began shifting behind me. I peered curiously at the man who must have been the yellow raptor. His head was shaved and covered in tattoos I hadn't noticed on his raptor. I shrugged as my eyes traveled over his body.

"I didn't realize that was offensive."

"It's not," the tattooed man replied with a laugh, as he came toward me. He held my shoulders, causing me to flinch. Immediately, he stepped back and dropped his hands. "I'm sorry, matriarch. I didn't mean to offend you. I was only going to check you for injuries."

"You're a healer now, Talon?" Kishil groaned behind me. The tattooed man—Talon—smiled wide and shook his head.

"Shouldn't the yellow one get checked? He was injured pretty badly." I glanced back to the man with the shaved head. His eyebrows cinched together and he waved a hand down his abdomen as he turned to the side. The side view of his rear end was quite nice, actually... *Get it together, Sage!*

"I'm healed, as you probably noticed when you were ogling me," he snickered.

"I wasn't ogling."

"You were," two voices called out in unison. I glared at Kishil and his friend, Talon. I wasn't ogling anyone. I was acquainting myself with my surroundings—my very well sculpted surroundings. My eyes slid over Kishil's hard chest and I gulped. My heartbeat hummed in my ears and I pressed my hands to my cheeks. Was I blushing?

"I'm Elu," the bald man snickered as he reached out his arm. I clasped his forearm in my hand and nodded.

"I'm Sage." His eyes roamed down my body before meeting my gaze again. I released him from the handshake; I needed to be careful. These weren't my people and I couldn't be certain about scaly culture. I wasn't sure how far my position as a future matriarch would carry me around these three. I didn't want to end up in a similar position as I had been already. Though, I wasn't sure I'd mind either one of these warriors taking me. The adrenaline had run out and all that was left was need. I closed my eyes trying to push those thoughts to the side. I was supposed to be on a spiritual journey and instead I'd been kidnapped and now I was fantasizing about three scalies in the middle of a—I opened my eyes and searched my surroundings—a swamp. I was fantasizing about three scalies in the middle of a swamp.

"...smells amazing," one of them murmured. I wasn't sure which one had said it, and I wasn't sure what they were talking about, but it made me realize I was hungry.

"What does? Do you smell something we can eat?" I shifted on my feet, my thighs rubbing together. I really was going to have to scratch this itch later. I'd never been so damned turned on in my life.

"I don't know if you'd eat it but—" A loud *thwack* cut off Talon's words. Elu pulled his hand back and shook his head.

"Don't."

"Yeah," Talon's nostrils flared and Kishil backhanded him in the chest, mirroring Elu. "I'll go catch something."

"When you get back we need to move, I don't trust that they won't follow after us. Especially now that they know what we are," Kishil grumbled.

"Sorry about that," Talon winced.

Elu stood back, quietly observing the exchange. I fingered the end of my skirt, avoiding his gaze. He seemed intense. Kishil appeared to have a hair-trigger personality, where he was flirty one minute and angry the next. Talon, I wasn't sure about yet. Elu was reserved somehow. He had been a little forward with me when he first changed, but I think he was suffering from the adrenaline spike as well. He'd calmed down a great deal and clammed up.

I wandered backward, away from the scalies, and found a seat on a downed tree. My fingers traced the cuts on my thighs. I'd never been lashed before and I couldn't believe how much damage it did so quickly.

"Are you alright?" I wasn't sure which one was speaking. I only knew it wasn't Talon. His voice was so distinctive that I'd already recognize it.

"I'm fine," I murmured as I wiped the blood away with my hand. It smeared along my thighs, and I growled as I rubbed at it. I didn't want to be bloodied, it could attract predators, but my train of thought paused as I glanced around me again, and at the two dino-shifters staring at me. I was already surrounded by predators...

The question was—would they attack or protect me?

Chapter
9

Sage

I pulled my knees up to my chest as Kishil stoked the fire. He'd worn a grim look all night and I wasn't sure why. It was frustrating that he could go from flirty to distant in two seconds flat. He seemed interesting and I'd love to get to know him—out of curiosity, I'd never known a scaly before—but he wasn't making it easy.

"How's the snake?" Talon's voice called out across the fire. I tore into the chewy meat and smiled at him.

"It's good. My mother cooks it differently, but it's very good, thank you. Much better than the rabbit the traders tried to feed me." I covered my mouth as I spoke, since speaking with a mouthful was rude and I knew better, but these men didn't seem to care.

"You don't like rabbit? What's wrong with your kind," Kishil snorted.

"I never said I didn't *like* rabbit." I narrowed my eyes on him and finished swallowing the snake meat. "I love it, actually. They didn't know how to cook it so the meat was stringy." I searched beside me for a bladder of water. Elu passed it to me without a word, a soft smile on his lips.

"I usually just eat them when I catch them," Kishil shrugged and loaded more of the meat onto a spit over the small fire Talon had built. The firelight danced across his smooth skin and my fingers itched to touch it. I'd never touched him as a man. I'd petted him as a raptor, as embarrassing as that was. He'd never come close to me when he was in his human form though. In the camp, he'd only changed once, and only because he was worried about me after Gunner struck me. My stomach clenched at the thought of Gunner and I laid my meat down on my pouch, swallowing my panic.

"What's wrong?" Elu asked in a quiet voice. I shook my head and hugged my knees. "I'm just not very hungry anymore. You can have the rest if you want, or Kishil. I know he didn't get much food in the camp."

"Why do you smell scared?" Kishil spun on his heels by the fire, plopping the meat into his mouth without a second thought.

"I'm not scared," I snapped. I pulled my pouch over and dug through it for my runes. Pulling them out one by one, I laid them in a line in the dirt. The various colors told a story. My mother believed you could talk to the Spirits this way, or even see the future. I almost snorted at the thought—apparently the Spirits talked to me whether I wanted to talk or not.

I studied the colors, their progression, and location to each other. If I believed the lessons my mother and the shaman had been trying to teach me all my life, then these rune bones said that there was something coming.

Change?

"You are scared, I can smell it." Kishil's voice caught my attention and I cocked my head to the side, studying him.

"You can't smell emotions," I retorted. I scooped up the bones and slid them into the satchel again. My eyes flicked to the men around the fire and I paused as they all sat there, waiting for me to catch something. "Can you?"

A slow nod from Elu had me blushing. I pulled my braid over my shoulder and toyed with the end of it, making it more secure. Talon scratched his head, his hair flowing as he did. I loved the way his hair curled. It was different than most of our men. My people tended to have straight, maybe slightly wavy hair. Curls like his were rare in my culture and I couldn't stop looking at them. Everything about him was different—the tattoos that covered him from neck to ankle, his hair, even the fact that he was a scaly.

"Right now, for instance, you smell aroused," Elu murmured.

I blinked. The words set in and I looked away from Talon to Elu. "I smell... No, I don't." I clung to my satchel, refusing to look back to Talon. His eyes bore a hole into my skull but I refused to meet his gaze.

"Yeah, you do, matriarch." Kishil crouched down, his naked ass rested on the back of his ankles as he pulled some meat from the spit and handed a piece to Elu and then Talon. It seemed like they all deferred to Kishil and Kishil consulted Elu. I wondered if it was a dominance thing, like with other animals.

"That's not—" I bit back the lie that almost spilled from my lips. It wouldn't do any good to try and lie to them, because if they could smell me, they could smell me. All I could do was ignore it. My eyes dipped to the ground and I tried turning the conversation to something less embarrassing. "Tomorrow I'll leave for my village. Maybe this was the test." I waved my hands around at nothing. "Or maybe they'll tell me I failed. Who knows?"

"Well..." Talon cleared his throat and I glanced to him. His hands clasped in front of his waist, obscuring my view. I couldn't help but be curious. I'd seen Kishil's dick and it was *huge*. My curious nature had to know if that was a trait their race shared, or if it depended on the man as it did with humans.

"Our village isn't far from here," Elu finished for him, raising to his feet. My mouth nearly dropped. I was sitting down which meant I had an eyeful of huge, swinging, scaly—but not actually scaly—dick. I resisted the urge to cover my mouth, since it would only draw attention to my embarrassment—unless they could *smell* that too. "I think it'd be best if you came with us there, replenish yourself a little before you continue on whatever journey you're on."

I looked from man to man.

Kishil rose to his feet as well and nodded. "It's a good idea. If the traders tracked us, you'll be safer with us than on your own."

"You don't think I can defend myself?" I raised my eyebrow in challenge.

"I think you got yourself kidnapped," Kishil snarled, his hands on his hips.

"So did you," I pointed out, leaning back to rest my palms in the dirt as I stared up at him.

Talon laughed and Elu swallowed his smile before Kishil noticed. I grinned up at him as his nostrils flared with his temper. He mumbled something under his breath I couldn't quite catch, but it must have been amusing because the other two laughed. Kishil stomped into the woods, tossing a rude hand gesture over his shoulder.

"Did he just..." My words trailed off with laughter as he crashed into the bushes.

"He did." Elu grinned. "I'm going to join him. We'll make sure our trail is covered, in case the traders come looking." His eyes drifted down from my face to my arms. I had a feeling he could read the markings there, even if he wasn't born of the Sun People.

"I don't know a lot about your people," I began, as Elu made his way away from the fire and toward the trees. "You all know what a matriarch is. Do you have a matriarch, or...?" I bit my bottom lip. I had always been the curious one, and it sometimes came off as rude or insensitive.

"No." Talon smirked from his seat across the fire. "We don't have a matriarch. Kishil's mother was from the Sun People and made sure he knew their ways. The rest of us, well..." His voice grew softer and his eyes flicked to the shadows of the trees around us. "Elu is a healer, by nature. He's closer to what you'd describe as a shaman though, I think. He's very curious and always wants to know everything, matriarch." He leaned forward, his elbows resting on his knees as he stared at me through the flames. I couldn't help but stare. The firelight flickered in the green pools. He had beautiful eyes.

"Why do you keep calling me matriarch, like you don't know my name?" I slid my feet underneath my bottom, resting on my calves.

"It's respectful, isn't it?" His eyebrows drew down into a line above his nose and I smirked. He looked confused. He was built large, with a broad chest and thick, muscular arms that drew my eyes. The war paint I'd noticed earlier was still intact above the tattoos that seemed to twine around every piece of his skin.

"It's not *disrespectful*, if that's what you're asking." I chewed on the tip of my thumb, trying to think. There was something about him that seemed innocent. The tattoos probably weren't a punishment for some huge crime... but I wouldn't know unless I asked. "Why do you have so many tattoos?"

Talon grinned and glanced down at his body as if he'd forgotten he was covered in the black ink. He shrugged and winked at me. "You think I'm a murderer. That's how your people mark their evil, isn't it?"

I nodded hesitantly. I didn't want to offend him. They were being so kind to me, these three scalies. If I upset them, who knew what would happen? Beyond that, I didn't *want* to upset them. They had been through just as much as me today.

"I'm not a murderer, Sage," he murmured. A shiver ran down my spine when he used my name. The fire still separated us, even as it grew lower. The flames had died down significantly since Kishil was no longer here to stoke them. I stood and grabbed the stick he'd been using earlier, stirring the embers until the flames rose again.

"Why is your name so different from the others?" I couldn't help it. I was on a roll and Talon didn't seem to mind my questions.

"You are curious, aren't you? Your name is Sage. It means clever, doesn't it?" He laughed and I ignored the throaty sound. Everything Talon did oozed sex appeal. What made it worse was the fact that he seemed completely unaware of his own charm. I bit my lip, shuffling to the side as I found a seat once again—a little bit closer to him this time. His eyes flicked to the space between us, there was enough room for one person to sit comfortably between us now, but neither of us moved to fill it or shift away.

"It does." I nodded. "Kishil called me 'Clever Girl.' It was cute, but I'm pretty sure he was being an ass." I bit back a laugh as Talon snorted. He nodded and held out a hand. I peered down at his offering warily.

"I'm not going to bite you, come here." His soft, green eyes shone in the low light and I couldn't deny him. He'd had plenty of opportunities to hurt me during the battle at the camp. He'd been in a Bloodlust—or at least that's what it seemed like—and still he hadn't harmed me. I slid my hand into his and let him pull me closer, until I filled the empty space that had rested between us. "Take a closer look if you want, Clever Girl."

I ran my fingertips down his arm, grazing over the raised lines where some of the tattoos had scarred during application. They were beautiful and they told a story of some kind, but I couldn't read all of it. Some of these symbols were universal, but not all of them were. A few were specific to the dino-shifters and I'd never learned to read the scaly runes. I'd never had a need to.

The shaman spoke about the scalies like they were *equal but separate*. A tribe we didn't war with, but a woeful adversary if we ever did. They didn't go out of their way to see us, and we didn't go out of our way to see them. It was a strange arrangement, one I was beginning to question, wondering who made it. It was odd to think there was an entire culture living a breath away from my village whom I knew nothing about.

"What do they mean? Why do you have so many and Kishil none? And Elu has them on his head instead?" I scrunched my nose up when I realized I was rambling. I did that when I was engrossed in a topic. It was hard to back off a subject once I was interested in it. It was part of what made finding a suitable man so hard. Either I bored them to death or they bored me. There seemed to be no in-between.

"Well, I'll let Elu explain his marks to you. These aren't punishments in our culture. They're much like the paint your people wear. I have a tattoo telling each story I've been a part of."

My mouth fell open as I grazed my fingers across the tattoos over his chest. They were beautiful. They were deaths. This man was a decorated warrior among his people, but he seemed so... soft hearted.

"They're lovely," I murmured, tracing one design from his hard chest up to his neck. I began to pull my exploring fingers away, but his hand flew to mine, holding it there. My fingers curled instinctively around his neck and my eyes widened.

"You don't have to stop touching me, matriarch," he whispered.

"Sage." I swallowed, staring up at him. Even sitting down he towered above me. I was tiny compared to all of these men, but Talon might be even taller than Kishil. I blinked, pushing the other man from my mind. Something was happening here, and it wasn't fair to Talon to be thinking of his pack mate. "Are you all related? Brothers, cousins, or just pack mates?"

"We're not blood relatives, no," Talon answered, then coughed out a laugh, shaking his head. "Thank the Creator. I think I'd murder them if we'd been nest mates."

"Nest mates," I repeated the word he'd used, and raised an eyebrow as his hand grazed down my arm to my elbow. Goosebumps erupted across the flesh as he nodded.

"We do family a little differently. Scalies don't believe in marriage, not like humans do." His head cocked to the side and I almost laughed. It reminded me a lot of the Mockingbird. These men were just as much animal as they were human, it was interesting.

"How so? No commitments at all between—" I struggled to remember the word I'd heard the shaman use. "Mates. That's right, isn't it?"

Talon nodded, his dark hair shaking, reflecting the low light around us. My fingers itched to touch it but I refused. I wouldn't be the one to cross a boundary, not when I was so adamant about my own being respected. My bottom lip sucked between my teeth as I pondered the arrangements that might be common in the scaly tribes.

"You're really interested in our culture, aren't you?" His face drew closer to mine and I sucked in a breath, my heart pounding in my ears. How long had it been since a boy—man—had tempted me to want a kiss?

"I'm interested in everything," I whispered. It was true. "I want to know as much as I can about this world before I leave it. I don't know what my calling is. They say I'm supposed to be the next matriarch, but I don't think someone like me is meant for that." The words fell from my lips before I could stop them. It should be embarrassing to admit that I was fully prepared to let my people down, but I didn't see any judgment in Talon's green eyes. Only understanding was reflected back to me.

The corners of his mouth twitched up in a sad, understanding smile. He brought my hand to his lips and kissed my fingertips softly. "I saw you in battle, Sage. You were fierce. You demanded your people be avenged—and they weren't even your people to stand up for. No one could ask for more from a leader than that." His lips brushed across my fingertips again as he finished speaking.

I tried to keep my breathing even, but the soft lips against my skin were going to be my undoing. I looked up at the man who seemed willing to answer all my questions and wondered if there'd ever been a more attractive trait in potential suitor. There hadn't been. It was as simple as that. There was absolutely no way I could ever find anything more sexy than knowledge.

"You have more questions, don't you?" he inquired, chuckling against my hand before he brought it slowly to his side. I nodded, but didn't answer him out loud. I didn't trust my voice just then. Why was I so affected by him? My eyes fell to the tattoos swirling down his chest to his stomach. I wouldn't look lower, not when I was this close to him. My traitorous eyes tried to dip, but I fought the urge and focused on his eyes instead.

Maybe that had been a mistake.

Maybe I should have known better than to meet his gaze when things already seemed to be getting out of hand between us. I'm not sure how a conversation about his peoples' culture was turning me on, but it was. My core clenched and I sucked in a breath when I noticed his nostrils flaring. That's right. *They can smell me.* My cheeks instantly heated and I pulled away from him, moving to return to my place across the fire.

Talon pulled my wrist, spinning me until I landed on his knee. I threw my free arm around him for balance, watching with wide eyes as his lips crashed down on mine. The kiss started off rocky, our teeth met at first and the clink made me smile against his mouth. This wasn't a perfect moment, but that made it more interesting to me.

His lips softened against mine and plucked at my tender flesh like a reed instrument. A sigh escaped my lips and he took the opportunity to trace his tongue ever so gently inside my mouth, teasing my tongue with his own before he pulled back again. His eyes gleamed with need, and my own chest rose and fell faster than I was proud of as his head tilted to the side, listening. He lifted me from his lap and set me down beside him, forcing his eyes shut.

"What are you—"

"They're back. I don't mind if you don't. But I didn't think you'd appreciate the audience." He winked at me and I flushed again. I had to get this blushing under control. I was not a virgin and this was far from my first time kissing a man, yet here I was acting like a hormonal youth. I pulled my braid over my shoulder and began untying it. Eventually, the dark locks fell into my face and I hid in it as the sound of Kishil and Elu grew louder.

Elu hovered at the edge of the fire, glancing between Talon and me, his eyebrow raised, almost imperceptibly, but he said nothing and I was thankful. Kishil bent to adjust the embers in the fire once more, and his eyes met mine as he did.

"Did you have a good chat while we were gone, Clever Girl?" His voice sounded thick, like he was hiding some emotion I couldn't quite catch. Goosebumps blasted down my arms, and I rubbed my hands up and down my flesh to warm myself. I scooted closer to the fire, and by default, closer to Kishil.

"I asked him a lot of questions about scaly culture," I admitted. I wouldn't mention the kiss. I wasn't sure if Talon wanted them to know, I wasn't even sure if *I* wanted them to know. I didn't even understand their mating rituals. For all I knew, I could be signing myself up for monogamy and that wasn't something I'd ever be satisfied with. My mother had found one husband who captured her entire heart but I was too curious, too unsatisfied with the world around me to ever be tied to only one man. I also wasn't sure how I felt about this play on my name. *Clever Girl.* It was cute, but I wasn't sure if they were making fun of me or not. I sighed and shook my head as I curled down on myself and hugged my knees. I needed to get some sleep, as hard as that would be. My heart was still hammering against my chest after that kiss.

I raised my head for a moment, searching for Talon, and found three sets of eyes staring back at me. They glowed strangely in the firelight, like animals. Talon's lips stretched in a gentle smile, while Kishil and Elu exchanged a glance, and then looked to their pack mate. I closed my eyes tight, chasing sleep.

"You fuck," Kishil whispered, as I gave in to the darkness and the warmth of the fire. At least that's what I thought he said. I could always be mistaken.

Chapter 10

Elu

I glanced from Kishil back to Talon and raised my eyebrow. The human was falling asleep, her breathing had slowed significantly. The gentle whistle of her breath was loud in the otherwise quiet moment, but it was comforting for some reason.

"Did you—" Kishil's fists clenched at his side, his words ending on a snarl.

"Shhhh!" I hissed, pointing to an area away from the fire, away from the sleeping woman. The idiot would wake her up.

"Don't order me around, Elu, not right now," he grumbled softly, even as he moved toward the place where I'd been pointing, with me following behind. Kishil was funny that way. He was going to lead our pack one day, and he liked everyone to know he deserved it, but he would still take direction from those he respected. It was an important quality in a leader.

Even if he was an absolute asshole sometimes.

Talon followed us reluctantly, glancing over his shoulder at the matriarch. I crossed my arms over my chest and glared at the two of them. We had never fought over a female before and we definitely weren't going to start now. Not over this human. She was interesting, I'd give her that. There was something sweet about her that the raptor females in our pack were missing. My eyes drifted back to the fire, to the matriarch, and I steeled my spine. Sweet wasn't the right word. She wasn't sweet—she was wholesome. There was an air about her that seemed untouched, and it wasn't her body. She knew what she wanted, even if she was too afraid to ask for it.

I swallowed the slight twinge of jealousy that clawed at my belly. There was nothing to be jealous of. Talon sleeping with that woman made no difference to me, he'd still be mine in the ways that mattered. I looked at him and shook my head.

"What happened?" I asked on a sigh. Kishil was angry—as usual —so this was probably going to get messy.

"Nothing," he whispered. "We only kissed, and barely for a moment. She was asking about my tattoos and things may have gotten a little out of hand for a second." I nodded, refusing to follow his arm down to where his hand was no doubt wrapped around his cock.

"Why are you kissing a *human woman?*" Kishil hissed, his anger swelling between the three of us. "And get your hand off your dick, man. I can't concentrate when you're doing that shit. I need to know the human isn't-isn't—" He stuttered over the final words and then huffed. He couldn't articulate his point when he was upset, as usual.

"Corrupting me? Seriously, Kishil? I'm not a child. You're half human and I know you hate how they treated your mother, but—" Talon began, but Kishil quickly cut of him off.

"Don't talk about her right now," he whispered. His fists balled tight at his sides as he glared at our pack mate. I stepped between them, holding a hand on both of their chests, and took a deep breath.

"Stop, both of you." I shook my head and looked from one man to the other. "You can't let your personal shit pull you into a frenzy like this. What has that woman done to you?" I raised my chin and turned to face Kishil squarely. "Tell me."

He held my gaze, his pupils thinning as his eyes shifted to his raptor's. The blend of brown and blue captivated me. He was angry, and one thing was always certain when he was angry.

Kishil wrapped his hand around the back of my neck and pulled me in close for a kiss, his lips testing mine. I bit his bottom lip, snarling at the distraction he was trying to give me. This is what he always did. Plus, bloodlust had been riding us all pretty hard since the battle at the camp.

Talon's hands roamed over my back and I shuddered as his lips grazed the curve of my neck. These two knew exactly how to distract me. They always had. We'd grown up together and our relationship had progressed from friends to something slightly *more*.

Raptor packs were different. Monogamy wasn't something raptors necessarily participated in. There were family groups, usually large ones, but sexuality was something that was accepted and embraced, and various forms of it blended together. There was love and there were other types of love. None was more important than the other, but other species didn't always see it that way.

I stifled a groan as Kishil pushed my head down, slowly bringing me to my knees. My mouth trailed wet kisses down his chest, his abs, and finally his cock. I flicked my tongue out along the tip and waited to see what would happen. Behind me, Talon's hard length ground against my ass cheeks as he, too, kneeled, though he hadn't made any move to spread them or enter me.

Talon bent down, dragging his teeth over the sensitive flesh across the back of my neck. Goosebumps rose across my skin as Kishil's hands came to my scalp, pushing my face against his dick where it bobbed in front of me. My mouth watered and I opened, slipping my tongue around the head of his cock before it slid in and out of my mouth. Kishil set the pace he wanted, he always did. I twirled my tongue as much as I could while he fucked my mouth, bumping the back of my throat. His fingers dug into my shaved scalp and I loved it.

"What do you want, Elu?" Talon whispered near my ear as his hand came down on my ass. I moaned against the cock in my mouth, and Kishil grunted at the sensation before pausing and pulling back. His abs flexed in front of me, and I licked my lips, arching my back.

"I won't say it. If you want something from me, take it," I dared him. Talon had a wild side. His passion didn't come from anger the way Kishil's did. It was just as hot, even if it was completely different. A snarl ripped from his throat behind me at the challenge.

My eyes nearly rolled back in my head as I felt a wet finger circling my ass, dipping inside slowly to tease me. A whimper crawled its way out of my throat, but was cut short when Kishil slid his cock back into my mouth.

"Fuck," he moaned as I sucked on his length. Every time the head bumped against the back of my throat, I gagged the tiniest bit. Talon's free hand slid to the back of my head, pushing me farther down on the cock until I was gagging. Kishil groaned as he bottomed out in my throat, my nose pressed against his groin.

"That's it," Talon murmured. He rewarded me with a second finger in my ass. His hand suddenly left my head and I almost whimpered at the lost connection. The new sound of him stroking his own dick was music to my ears. The gentle slide of flesh on flesh was mesmerizing. Kishil's hips jerked away, and air rushed into my lungs at the same time Talon's fingers were pulled from me.

"By the Creator, if you tease me—" I gasped as the head of Talon's cock pressed against my ass and slid inside. He felt wet, but I wasn't sure where he'd found anything to use as lubricant. I wasn't worried about it right now. It could be spit for all I cared, I just wanted to be filled. I needed it.

"What was that?" he rasped behind me. His voice shook and it was clear he was trying to stay in control. The bloodlust was harder on him than it was on most of us. I shuddered as he slid farther inside me, stretching me open until I was full.

Kishil mumbled incoherent words as his hips began rocking once again, pushing his cock in and out of my mouth. My tongue curled, massaging the underside of his dick. A series of clicks spilled from him and I shivered, rubbing my hand along his balls, cupping them as I sucked him down.

"Mmm," Kishil murmured, bucking faster against my mouth. My heart hammered against my chest as my need built higher and higher. Talon set a slow, hard pace as he slammed in and out of my ass. I whimpered every time the smack of his thighs meeting my ass sounded through the night.

"Wrap your hand around your cock for me, Elu," Talon ordered behind me. His pace increased, becoming erratic. He wasn't going to last long like this. Kishil's dick swelled in my mouth and I groaned, stretching my mouth wider to accommodate him. My fingers wrapped around my cock now that I had permission, and I stroked it in time with Talon's thrusts.

Every time his cock slid inside me, I glided my palm down my own dick. Kishil's hands moved from my scalp to just behind my ears, where he held my head still and thrust wildly inside my mouth. My jaw burned as I held my mouth open as wide as I could. He groaned as his cock slipped into the back of my throat with every push. My grip tightened on my cock and my speed increased.

"Elu," Talon gasped, his cock swelling. My name on his lips would never get old. I shuddered as his thrusts shortened into quick bursts, warmth filling me as he slowed. Kishil snarled but the sound ended on a chirp, and I stared up into his eyes, my neck craned at an awkward angle as he rammed his cock against the back of my throat. Warm cum shot against my tongue and deep into my throat, his hips stuttering as his orgasm rolled through him.

Talon lay against my back, panting, as I sucked Kishil—he had long orgasms, he always came so much. I nearly jumped when Talon's hand wrapped around my cock from behind. My eyes rolled into the back of my head as he set a hard, fast pace. He worked his palm up and down me as his cock softened inside me. I shuddered, the first wave of the orgasm crashing into me.

"That's it," Kishil murmured, pulling himself from my mouth and rubbing the tip of his cock across my lips. My tongue darted out, even as my body seized through the orgasm. Talon grunted and I sighed, leaning my head forward against Kishil's stomach and breathed in a deep, shaky breath.

Hands slid across my back and my skull, comforting me, assuring me. This was what we did. We took what we needed from one another and then made up for it after. I smiled at the thought. A soft gasp caught my ear and my head snapped to the side, meeting Sage's gaze.

Oh Great Mother... Panic flooded my system until I scented the air. Desire coated everything. My desire mixed with Kishil's and Talon's, but her desire smelled brighter than any of ours. There was something completely different about an aroused female.

Chapter 11

Sage

My head jerked up and I fought through the pull of slumber to consciousness. Sleeping in a seated position tended to make me feel like I was falling. My heart raced and I looked around the fire, searching for the guys—searching for Talon, if I was honest. I blinked, noticing the fire had nearly burned out and letting my eyes adjust to the dark. A strange noise just beyond the dim ring of light drew my gaze. It was hard to see, and what little light there was made it hard to focus on the shadows. I strained my eyes and covered my mouth.

Elu was kneeling, sucking Kishil's cock. My eyebrows shot up to my forehead. I had *not* seen that coming. There were plenty of men and women who preferred the company of their own gender, but these guys hadn't struck me as the sort. I knew I should look away, but I couldn't. Kishil was pumping his hips against Elu's mouth and I felt my core grow slick with need. There was something erotic about watching him please Kishil.

A loud smack made me refocus my eyes and I realized Talon was also there. Behind Elu... *behind* Elu. He was making love to him. My pussy clenched, and I couldn't peel my eyes away from the three of them. The sounds of skin smacking skin rang out in the night and I wished I could see them more clearly. My fingers skimmed the edge of my skirt as I considered what was happening.

It's rude to intrude on their private moment.

But it's so damned hot...

I bit my lip, before sliding my hand between my knees where I sat. My fingers slid to my wet center, stroking lazily over my clit as I took in the display before me. Talon bucked wildly against Elu's ass and someone moaned. A shiver ran down my spine as their voices carried to me.

"Elu," Talon groaned, and I almost moaned myself. His voice was the sexiest thing I'd ever experienced in this life, and if I could fuck his mouth, I would.

My fingers circled my clit faster as I watched Elu wrap his hand around his own cock, pumping his fist up and down. Kishil fucked his mouth with no restraint. My mouth watered as I watched Elu gag and moan—he loved this. *I* loved it. I bit my lip harder, fighting back a moan as sweat beaded on my forehead, and heat rushed through my body as I chased the friction I needed.

Talon groaned and his thrusts slowed. Kishil moaned and adjusted his grip on Elu's head, mastering his mouth. The muscles in his arms and side tensed as he pumped in and out, over and over again. Elu released a pleasure filled cry and my eyes drifted down to find the cause.

Talon lay collapsed against his back, his arm wrapped around Elu so he could slide his hand up and down Elu's cock. My eyes fluttered shut as the noises grew in the darkness. I adjusted my wrist, sliding a finger inside myself as my hand rubbed against my clit more forcefully than before. I moaned as my orgasm crashed into me. My shoulder shuddered and I leaned forward involuntarily, my eyes flying open.

My gaze met the almost glowing yellow stare of Elu, as his face rested against Kishil's stomach. Talon was still buried in his ass, panting. Aftershocks drew goosebumps across my chest and arms. Our eyes stayed like that for what felt like a long while, until Kishil began to move. My eyes widened but I quickly adjusted my skirt and leaned my head down against my knees again.

I focused on remaining calm, and I convinced myself that if I focused hard enough on what I smelled like that I would be able to accomplish that scent. The sound of footsteps drew near and I kicked my leg out, pretending to jump awake.

"Calm down, matriarch," Elu murmured. "It's only us." My gaze rose from his feet and slowly up his legs. I paused at the softening cock dangling freely between his legs, my face heating. I quickly met his eyes with a shy grin.

"Good morning," I whispered. I shuffled nervously to my feet, desperately needing to be at eye level with these men instead of getting a face full of crotch. It was unnerving. My throat went dry as I thought about what I'd seen. It was shocking in the best way.

"Good morning, Clever Girl," Kishil replied with a laugh. He was in a good mood. My eyebrow cocked and my lips pursed against the words threatening to spill out. I'd be in a good mood too if I'd just gotten my dick sucked.

Great Mother, help me keep my mouth shut.

Elu settled by the low-burning fire, his eyes focused on me. His gaze held a promise. I shivered and turned to face Talon, only catching the end of whatever he'd been saying.

"...village. We'll get there before the sun sets if we leave soon. You can rest for a few days and when we're sure the traders aren't following, go finish your—"

"Spirit Walk. She's supposed to be passing some test set out for her by the Spirits." Kishil grinned, kicking some dirt into the fire. I glanced down at his bare feet and noticed him eyeing my boots. "Where did you get shoes like this?" he asked, crouching down low to inspect them.

"I had to take two gator hides to a neighboring village, where they made the soles. They're great for the terrain here." I cleared my throat as his fingers wrapped around my calf, inspecting the sides of the boot. His hands were warm and I desperately wanted to pull my leg away. Everywhere his fingers landed my skin seemed to catch fire. I bit my lip, looking away from him.

"Who helped you kill the gators?" he inquired, finally releasing my calf.

"No one. I killed them." I tipped my chin in the air, watching as he rose to his full height.

"You killed two gators on your own?" Kishil glanced to his side and Talon quickly came into view again.

"Yes. I had to trade them so the villagers would make the soles for my boots." I shrugged a shoulder, fingering the hem of my skirt nervously.

Talon's laughter boomed through the woods and Kishil shook his head. "One hide would have been payment for boots. They *are* nice though," Kishil mumbled as he finished smothering the fire. I huffed a breath. It figured that I'd been ripped off.

"I can't believe they didn't eat you up. You're so tiny," Talon teased as he moved to my side. His hand hovered above my hip, not quite touching me, but close enough that I could feel the heat radiating from it.

"Why are you so warm?" The question popped from my mouth before I could even stop myself.

"Our metabolism is different than humans. When we're in this form, that metabolism produces a lot of heat." His fingers brushed against my bare side, in the gap between my top and skirt. It took everything inside me not to lean into his touch. I shook my head and forced my eyes open, coming face to face with Kishil.

"H-Hi," I stuttered. My heart skipped a bit as his cold gaze met mine.

"What are you doing?" His question seemed direct enough, but I had no idea what he was talking about.

"I'm just standing here?" I looked around, confused as to what he meant.

"What are you doing to them?" His lip snarled up over his teeth, and he shook his head. It was a strange movement. Talon tensed behind me, his fingers curling into my skin as if to hold me in place where I stood. Elu's eyebrow arched and he pointed a stick at his pack mate.

"Calm down, Kishil," he murmured.

"Talon can't stop touching her." A low sound built in his chest, tumbling out behind his words. It was something between a snarl and a growl. I didn't know what to call it, but it was definitely unnerving. I shook my head and stepped to the side, away from Talon and the other scalies.

"I can keep my distance. I don't have any intention of taking your *friends* from you."

"My..." He blinked, a look of confusion passing over his face. "You saw us?"

I twisted my mouth to the side and nodded. I'd planned on keeping that information to myself, but it seemed that Kishil was feeling jealous. He didn't want Talon touching me. Maybe these three were an official item?

Elu coughed and rose from his squatted position. Kishil's face twisted with some emotion I couldn't understand. Anger mixed with some other emotion, but I couldn't tell what. An audible sigh slipped out and his eyes narrowed on me again.

"Kishil—" Talon began.

"No problem," he snarled, and stomped away from our tiny, makeshift camp. "Let's go."

I cringed as I watched him march away from me. Something about that man was infuriating and enticing, but every time I turned around he was snapping at me and I didn't understand why.

"I'm really not trying to cause problems here," I whispered to the two remaining scalies.

"You're not causing problems," Talon sighed. "That," he waved his hand in Kishil's general direction, "is just Kishil. He's an ass."

"I can hear you!" Kishil snapped from several yards away.

Elu caught my eye and tossed me a quick wink. I shook my head as I watched him follow after Kishil. Adjusting my satchel, I turned to follow and ran into Talon. I craned my neck back to look him in the face, and studied the expression I found.

"So, you saw?" he asked on a barely audible whisper.

"I did. I didn't mean to, but something woke me and I caught the ending." I covered my mouth to hide my grin. It had been a very interesting way to wake up.

"And does that..." He screwed his nose up as he searched for the right word. "Bother you?" My head tilted to the side and my eyebrows drew down low.

"No, why would it? Unless you are being unfaithful to someone—"

"No!" he gasped. "I mean—" Talon coughed and turned to follow the other two men. I glanced at their retreating forms and tried to ignore their perfectly curved asses as they walked away. "I have no one to be unfaithful to. None of us are married."

I nodded, soaking that information up for all it was worth. They weren't married—or committed to anyone—so at least there was that. I still wanted to ask Talon more questions, but it didn't seem like the time. I stretched my arms over my head and maneuvered around Talon's wide body to follow the scalies through the swamp.

I wasn't sure where their village was, as I'd never been to a scaly village before, but they made it seem like it wasn't too far away. I found myself picking my way through the overgrown underbrush beside Elu. His arm brushed mine and I nearly jumped.

"Are you alright?" he whispered. I glanced ahead of us to Kishil's back and nodded. The path we were taking was hardly easy to navigate. I, at least, had clothes on, while the guys were completely nude. They'd been in their raptor forms when we left the traders' camp and had nothing to wear. I couldn't imagine marching through the wilderness naked.

I smacked a hand on my arm and growled at the red and black splat that was left on my palm. Mosquitos were terrible this time of year, and even worse in the swampier parts of the land. I sighed and glanced again at Elu. I bit the inside of my cheek, trying to resist asking the question.

"Go ahead, Clever Girl." Talon's voice rang out behind us and I screwed my mouth up against the smile trying to spread across my face. "I can smell the curiosity on you. What is it?"

"Oh, this'll be great," Kishil snorted up ahead.

"Well," I started, trying to find the right words. "I keep thinking it has to be uncomfortable walking through the woods naked. The mosquitos alone are enough to drive me insane and my most important bits are covered." I focused on moving the brush in front of me, minimizing the scratching against my legs. Silence hung between the four of us for a long moment. I was just starting to wonder if it was too strange of a question when laughter finally echoed around us.

"Did you just ask if we get mosquito bites on our dicks?" Kishil stopped and turned to face me, his chest heaving as he tried to control his laughter.

"I mean, wouldn't that be more sensitive?" My voice got higher the longer he stared at me, and I blushed under his stare. "Forget it, I'm sorry."

"No," Elu laughed as he came to a stop beside me. I hadn't noticed his momentary lag behind while Kishil stared me down with such intense amusement. "We actually don't get bitten by mosquitos."

"What! Why?" My eyebrows flew up my forehead and my hands landed firmly on my hips. I may have been a little bit jealous that they didn't have to deal with the infamous pests.

"I guess we taste different to them. I've been bitten a handful of times my entire life." Elu's eyes trailed down my arms, no doubt taking in the multiple bites littering my skin.

"That's not fair," I grumbled, resisting the urge to scratch my arms.

"Well, you could have always been a scaly," Talon teased, dropping his arm around my shoulder. I tensed under the gesture and looked from Kishil to Elu for any sign of jealousy. Kishil had been really mad earlier.

"It's not like I had a choice in the matter," I argued. "I was born human. I don't think I can magically become a scaly." My eyebrows cinched together and I considered it.

"No, Clever Girl," Kishil replied, as he turned around, still laughing, and begin walking again. "You can't become a scaly. It's not catching."

Elu turned to continue moving and ran his hand along my arm ever so carefully before he did. My heartbeat raced and his nostrils flared. I met his dark gaze and my mouth went dry at the heat I found there.

Why does everything these three do turn me on? And they can smell it... Oh Great Mother.

Elu blinked and looked over my shoulder, a quiet click sounded from him before he turned and left. I sighed, trying to convince my pussy to stop growing wetter by the second. It wasn't the time or place, and these weren't the right men for the job, obviously. Kishil probably wouldn't let me enjoy the other two even if I wanted to—which I absolutely didn't.

"Something wrong, Clever Girl?" Talon whispered dangerously close to my ear. I swallowed, before shivering as he moved past me with a wicked grin on his face.

"Of course not," I quipped, walking fast to catch up to the rest of the group. These scalies were going to be the death of me.

Chapter 12

Kishil

I stomped noisily through the undergrowth, trying to ignore the scent of desire that clung to the matriarch as thick as her sweat. I didn't trust her. She was from the Sun People and we were scalies, that was all there was to it. I wanted her to make it home safely, and thought her staying at our village to rest while we waited for the traders to pass through the country was the best idea in that regard, but I did *not* want her.

I didn't *want* to want her anyway. I glanced down at the growing erection that swung out as we marched toward the village. At least Sage was in the back, between Talon and Elu. If she saw how turned on I was, it would probably be the end of this argument I was having with myself.

She was willing. I think she wanted all of us, actually, if her scent after she witnessed our tryst in the woods was any indication. That in and of itself was one of the reasons I was having a hard time concentrating. The scent of her desire could drive a man wild. Her aroma— wildflowers and honey—mixed with the familiar scent of my pack mates was hell on my resolve.

The sound of rushing water met my ears and a weight lifted from my chest. We were almost to the river, almost home. We hadn't lived in this strange land long, but wherever my people were was home for me. I thought about the tyrannosaurus we'd fought in the woods, the one who'd been killed by the traders. I couldn't imagine being rogue, it would kill me to be separated from my pack indefinitely. Maybe other scalies were different. Tyrannosauruses didn't live in large communities like raptors. Usually they had small family units, consisting of mates and their offspring. I ran my hand through my hair as we came to the edge of the river. The ground didn't slowly give way to the water here. Instead, it came to an abrupt halt, ending in a steep embankment.

"Wow," Sage whispered as she came to a stop at my side. I angled my head to see her reaction. She focused on the wide river and the land beyond. The forest we'd just tramped through was crowded with trees and undergrowth, but across the water the land was flatter. The pack had claimed the northernmost part of the area that other tribes referred to as the peninsula.

"What?" I busied myself by gauging the depth of the water. The river was low right now and wouldn't be very deep. I knew from experience the middle was the deepest part of this crossing. Where the water sat now, it shouldn't be more than six feet deep. We could make it across fine, even in our human forms, but I worried about the woman.

"It's gorgeous. I've never been here before," she murmured. Before I could reply, she was scaling down the side of the embankment, holding on to roots and rocks.

"What are you doing?" I called down to her.

"Getting ready to cross the river, of course." She smiled up at me, her light brown eyes twinkling with mischief.

"We're going to change to cross, you should get on one of our backs," I replied as I climbed down after her.

"Awe, Kishil is worried for her," Elu snickered quietly from above. I glared up at the ledge before focusing on lowering myself down the embankment.

"No," Talon gasped in mock shock. "He hates humans. He

wouldn't dare be worried about our clever girl." My teeth ground to the tune of his amused words and I shook my head. Below me, Sage had reached the end of the embankment and clung to the dirt wall as she surveyed the water.

"Aren't you worried about gators?" she inquired, peering into the dark water.

"I'm not, but you should be." I bit my lip against a smile when she cursed under her breath. "You'll be on one of our backs. Predators tend not to attack predators that are bigger than them."

"I've seen a gator attack a panther," she countered.

"They're not the same breed of predator. Scales. Scalies. Think of gators like our wild, distant cousins. We should be fine, matriarch," Elu answered as he came down beside me.

"We will jump in and change, then you come in after. Okay?" Talon directed. He didn't wait for an answer before he let loose from his place above me and fell into the water below. A small gasp from the matriarch pinged my ears at his fearless action, and I shook my head as loose dirt rained down into my hair.

"Dammit, Talon!" I shrieked, a series of clicks bubbling up my throat. I jumped down toward the water, intent on throttling him. The cool river rushed against my stomach as my feet sank into the muddy bottom. We'd been in a drought for a while, but the rains would start coming more frequently soon, and hopefully that would help. Prey animals were harder to find during the dry season, especially when there was a drought. They moved where the resources were plenty.

The snap of bones to my right let me know that Talon was already changing. I splashed some water in his general direction and called my own raptor forward. My eyes drifted to the embankment where Sage clung to a root as my face elongated and my vision changed. I blinked, focusing on her face. The white paint that swirled along her arms and legs looked more crisp, and her light brown eyes held even more depth than normal. The markings on her forehead seemed to glow in the light, the more I focused on them. A bird sang a tune somewhere in the trees above and Sage gasped. Her eyes shot upward, searching for the source of the sound, and my head canted to the side as I studied her. Why was she so concerned with a bird?

Elu dropped into the water, shifting from man to raptor almost seamlessly as soon as his feet hit the mucky bottom. I stretched my neck out, nipping at his tail as it twitched back and forth just above the water, only inches from my face. Sage's eyes crinkled and she dropped down into the water in front of us. By the Creator, she was tiny. The water had only come up to my belly button in human form, but rose to about the middle of her breasts. She slipped in the mud and my heart raced, and several shrieks came from both of my pack mates as we rushed toward her.

"Calm down, guys. Great Mother, you're worse than old nannies," she muttered, as she fought her way through the murky water toward Elu. I swallowed the jealous snarl fighting its way up my throat and shook my head. There was no reason to be jealous, she wasn't trying to take Elu from Talon or me.

But what if Talon or Elu chooses to be with the female... a voice whispered in the back of my mind. I shook my head and snorted, waiting for her to climb on to Elu's back. He bent down, easily holding his head above water as she looped an arm around his neck and swung her body over his shoulders. He rose back to his full height and Sage squealed, sliding backward onto his back. Elu chuffed and she nodded.

"Oh right, sorry, I forgot." Sage adjusted her grip from his neck down to his shoulders, her fingers digging into the scales there. Beside me, Talon bumped into my side, his tail swinging over mine as he watched the matriarch climb on to our pack mate. He chirped happily, drawing my eye. I turned so I could see him out of one eye, and Sage and Elu out of the other. It shouldn't take us long to cross the water once Sage got her balance. I chuffed and began a slow pace toward the middle of the river. On either side of me was a pack mate. To my right, Sage sat on Elu's back, and to my left was Talon.

"You're slippery when you're wet," she murmured. Clicks

rippled from my snout before I could stop myself, and similar sounds came from the other two raptors. "Are you laughing at me?" Sage accused, her voice turning sharp. I focused my right eye on her, noticing how the sun glinted through her long black hair, highlighting parts of it brown and red. Her braid must have come loose at some point during the walk. Her eyes narrowed on me as her grip tightened around Elu. The current was stronger here in the middle of the river. I glanced behind us and then across at the land we were moving toward. I'd feel better about the traders once we put the river between them and us.

Even though there hadn't been any sign of them on any of my patrols, I was still nervous that they were following us. Now that they knew what we were, I was worried they'd try harder to find the village. The pack. A snarl built in my chest and I surged forward in the water, my talons digging into the bottom of the river as we pressed through the current. It was slow going. This was the worst place to cross, but it was also the closest crossing to where we'd evaded the traders, so it would have to do.

"Are you okay?" Sage's soft, lilting voice called out over the sound of the water.

I couldn't answer her in this form, but I nodded and pushed on. Something was pricking my senses, making me jumpy. The sound of a bird sang out, and it changed its tune midstream. *It must be a mockingbird,* I thought.

"Are you following me, now?" Sage grumbled, as she looked skyward. Was she talking to the bird? She shook her head and adjusted her grip on Elu's shoulders, leaning forward to rest her forehead against the back of his skull. The soft clicks that came from him stirred something inside me. I kept an eye on the matriarch as we came to the edge of the next embankment. My claws slipped in the mud and I clung to the slippery substance with everything I had, jumping onto the muddy ground. I closed my eyes, envisioning my human form, and tucked away my raptor.

Soon Sage was standing beside me as the pop of bones rang out, before Talon and Elu moved up next to us. I turned to face the opposite side of the river, back the way we'd come. "Talon, climb up. Then the matriarch will follow so you can pull her up if she needs help." I didn't turn to watch him scramble up the embankment, but the gentle slide of feet on ground let me know he was obeying. I narrowed my eyes, peering into the woods on the other side of the river. I felt watched. The hair on the back of my neck bristled and I turned to Elu. "Boost her up, now, move!" I hissed.

"What is it?" Sage asked, her voice panicked as she dug her fingers into the dirt wall, searching for a root to hang on to. Elu grabbed her by the hips and flung her upwards, pulling a squeal from her throat. I turned in time to see Talon grasp her hand and pull her over the ledge.

"Go, Elu," I ordered, turning to climb alongside him. We leapt up, almost in unison, digging our hands into the wall before we began to fall again. I shoved my foot into the dirt, making a hole where there was none, and climbed the last few feet to the top. Rolling onto my belly, I peered through the weeds toward the riverbank and waited. Someone was coming.

"Is it them?" Sage whispered, raising on her elbows to look with me. A click from Talon told me to look to my left. My eyes followed the tree line to the left until a figure came into focus. The copper-skinned man wasn't a trader. His long black hair was pulled into a ponytail at the nape of his neck, his bow slung over his shoulder.

"Rain?" Sage sounded shocked.

"You know that man?" I side-eyed her, gauging her reaction. "Is he one of your people?"

She nodded, leaning up to stand. Talon pulled her back into the dirt and she crashed down between us, her ass landing right on my side.

"Why would he be here? None of your people come near this land." Talon was right. It was odd. We hadn't dealt with any Sun People since we claimed this area. Even the closest tribes knew to stay out of our territory, so there weren't any misunderstandings.

"I don't know why he's here. Maybe he's followed me?" Her eyes hardened and I could see the thought crumbling in on itself even as she spoke it. "If he was following me this whole time, why didn't he help me out of the trader camp?"

"Clever girl," I nodded and pressed my finger to my lips. I scooted on my belly backward, then barely rose onto my feet and scurried into some nearby bushes. As I waited for the others to join me, I plucked a purple berry from the bush and chewed on it. The sweet juice filled my mouth and I pulled a handful more before they came dashing to my side.

"What do we do?" Elu asked.

"We will go back to the village," I mumbled around a mouthful of deliciousness.

"There is something odd going on with him following the matriarch," Elu noted, plucking a berry from my hand. I bared my teeth at him and scooped the rest of the berries in my mouth.

"Get your own, there's a whole damned bush right there." I waved toward said bush and shook my head before pushing to my feet. "Regardless of why he's tracking her, the safest place for the woman is at the village."

"You do realize I can hear you, right?" Sage snapped, her hands flying to her hips. I glanced to her for the first time since they'd joined me at the blackberry bush and swallowed. Her clothes were wet, clinging to her body. Pebbled nipples peeked through the fabric of her top and her skirt hung on to her hips for dear life. My gaze slid slowly back up to her eyes and I offered her a sheepish smile.

"I'm aware."

"Ooookay then," she sighed. "It's been nice knowing you guys, but I'm not going to be bossed around by men I hardly know. Goodbye." She turned to leave and Talon caught her arm. My eyebrow cocked as I watched his face morph from shocked to angry.

"I did no such thing." His eyes narrowed on the small woman, his large hand holding her still.

"He did." She pointed with her free hand toward me. "And you apparently listen to the oaf, so I'm leaving. I won't tolerate it." Sage glanced down at where Talon's hand dug into her skin and he immediately released her, as if he realized what he'd done. She rubbed her arm and nodded, as Talon's gaze fell to the ground. He probably thought he hurt her.

"Don't manipulate him," I snapped. "If he hurt you, say so. But don't play hurt and cause him shame."

"Excuse me? I am not manipulating him. I'm not hurt. He grabbed me and it stung a bit. Excuse me for having *weak human flesh*." Sage rounded on me, her finger flying toward my face, stabbing the air to punctuate each and every word.

My eyes narrowed and I swatted her hand away, shoving my face toward hers. "Watch your tone, matriarch."

"Don't say that word like a curse, or I'll slap the taste from your mouth, scaly." Her eyes flared with anger and something inside me honed in on the lack of fear in her scent. She wasn't scared of me at all. She was pissed. Her copper skin flushed a darker tone beneath the white markings drawn across her body, and whether it was the sun or the anger causing her to turn red, I wasn't sure.

"Is she going to hit him?" Talon asked Elu quietly on the side.

"I hope not," he murmured in response. "I've never had to stop him from eating a woman before."

Talon snorted and shook his head, crossing his arms over his chest. "I think our clever girl can take him, if he doesn't shift." My eyes flew to the two of them, my lips curling over my teeth in a snarl.

"Can you two shut up, please?" I begged, pinching the bridge of my nose. Sage huffed, crossing her arms over her chest, perfectly mirroring Talon. That fact didn't escape me.

"I'm going to go home. I'll deal with Rain. I don't need to be coddled. Not by him, and not by you," she spat.

My hand fell from my face and I studied her expression. It wasn't just anger, it was betrayal. She didn't know why this man was out in unfamiliar woods, apparently following her. She also didn't seem comfortable with the idea that he was tracking her... for her protection.

"Is he some boyfriend of yours?" I gaped, wondering if she was spoken for. "Are you promised, matriarch?" Sage snorted, Talon snarled, and Elu just stared openly at her.

"Why do you care?" She smirked up at me, her wet hair dripping more water onto her top. Barely resisting the urge to track the water droplets that ran down the curve of her neck to her breasts, I bit my cheek.

"If he's just some man who is trying to protect you, then we have nothing to worry about. Is that the case?"

"Maybe," she mumbled. "He doesn't belong to me though. I've avoided him for a long time on that subject." Sage's face softened and I scented the air. She didn't smell or look defensive, but she did look a little uncomfortable. I licked my lips and nodded, dismissing the subject.

"So we will go to the village. You're welcome to come with us." I paused, making sure she knew the decision was hers. "Or you can go on your own now. I think it's smart to wait the traders out."

"We do have some experience avoiding them," Elu interjected. Sage turned to scowl at him and he only shrugged in response.

"When you're not getting captured by them," she pointed out with a smirk.

"When we're not getting captured by them," I conceded with a sigh.

"I didn't get captured by anyone," Talon grumbled. "Kishil ran off into the woods in a rage when the arrows started. That was on you, brother." His smile widened when a snarl began rumbling my chest.

"Let's go," I snapped, plucking another fistful of berries off the bush and passing them to the matriarch. "Here, eat these. It should hold you over until we get to the village. Then you'll have plenty of food until you leave." She gave me a sweet smile and took the gift, immediately popping a berry in her mouth.

"She'll have plenty with her when she leaves, as well, if the women have anything to say about it," Talon muttered, shaking his head.

"The women? I thought you were all unmarried. Who are *the women?*" Her words were jumbled around the berries she chewed as she fell in step beside us. I shrugged and bumped into Elu on my left out of habit.

"Raptor packs are a little different than what you're used to." My spine steeled with every step we took closer to the village. "I think maybe we should change and run in. I still feel a little wary," I murmured to my pack mates.

Talon nodded, already crouching to shift. I bent and let my raptor take my body once again, the sound of bones crunching in my ear as my form changed. Sage gasped, looking from me to Elu, the last one of us in human form.

"They're alright," he whispered.

"It looks like it hurts!" Sage whispered. "I don't think I could ever do that."

"Well, the good news is that you don't have to. Like we said, it's not contagious." With that, Elu picked her up and placed her on my back. I chuffed as her weight settled on top of me. "Hang on, Clever Girl. Kishil is the fastest runner I know, and this land is a little more his style."

"Oh, I'm sure, he almost took my head off in that for—ahhh!" she squealed when I broke into a run. The sound of Elu's laughter followed after us as Talon fell in at my side. There was a long stretch of almost flat land ahead. My legs pushed harder, pulling ahead of Talon with ease as I left him behind us. I felt Sage twist around on my back—she must have been looking back at my pack mates—and she laughed.

"THIS IS AMAZING!" HER WORDS WERE PUNCTUATED WITH giggles as her fingers dug into my shoulders. The warmth of her against my back was comforting, somehow. My feet flew over the grassy field, my talons digging into the dirt beneath the grass as I pushed harder. Talon and Elu weren't far behind, but they wouldn't catch me unless I wanted them to. Not on a flat run like this.

"Slow down," Sage hissed, clinging tighter to my shoulders. Clicks rolled from my snout and I pushed harder, running faster just to see what she would do. Her thighs and legs clenched against my flanks, and a small squeal escaped her before she buried her face against the back of my neck. I came to a slow stop when we reached the edge of the field, the flat, empty ground giving way to bushes and small trees.

I twisted my head around and caught a glimpse of the matriarch on my back as she sat back up. Her fingers combed through her wind-blown hair, braiding it as she went. The ride had dried it at least. I bent down, chuffing at her.

"You want me to get off?"

I snorted, shimmying ever so slightly until she slid off my back and down my side. Sage placed her hands on my flank, steadying herself. I called my human form back, and my bones popped and creaked as my scales receded into my skin. I shuddered as the last of my human skin reappeared and realized that a hand still rested on my side, right along my ribs. I glanced down at the fingers covered in white paint. My gaze rose until I met her eyes and I sucked in a breath.

"What's wrong? Did I—"

I slid my hand around the back of her neck, my chest rising and falling from the run. That had been amazing. I cupped her cheek with my left hand, stroking it with my thumb, it was a question, a chance for her to say no.

Instead, she said nothing, her eyes flickering with something unreadable. I bent down, pressing my lips to hers. I kissed her over and over, a series of soft, fast kisses that left me wanting more. Her lips were so smooth and soft against mine. A few chirps I couldn't control filled my chest and spilled out as I plucked at her bottom lip with my own.

I slid my tongue against the seam of her mouth until she opened for me and I delved inside. I caressed her, pulled her into me until she was panting against my lips. Finally, I pulled back. The sound of Elu and Talon approaching grew closer by the second and I didn't want them to see. Call it pride, but I didn't want them to know how much this human affected me.

Sage's fingers flew to her lips, her eyes wide and bright as she stared up at me. "What was *that?*" she murmured.

"Well, I won the race. Call it a victory kiss," I whispered, smoothing the top of her hair back before I stepped away from her.

"A victory—"

"You have to stop outrunning us, Kishil," Talon panted as he jogged up to us in human form. My eyes dipped to his cock as it bounced around between his legs. A quick glance to the side confirmed that Sage was also eyeing it. Talon's nostrils flared and he came to a stop beside us, glancing first at Sage and then me. "What did I miss?"

I shook my head, my hair falling around my face with the movement, and turned toward the trees. "Nothing. Hurry up, Elu! We're almost home," I mumbled. Once my back was to them, my fingers flew to my own lips, tracing the path of the kiss we'd just shared.

I wanted the matriarch, at least for a night. Inside me, I could feel my raptor clawing to get back to her, to touch her again. He was fond of this human as well. I ran my hand down my face, trying to clear my head, and pushed deeper into the trees. This was going to be an interesting couple of days.

Chapter 13

Sage

I trudged along beside Talon, trying to ignore the way his arm brushed against mine every few minutes. It was unintentional, I was sure, but the small touch was driving me wild inside. I traced my fingertips across my lips for the hundredth time since kissing Kishil. That man confused me. Talon and Elu seemed straightforward enough. They were both interested in me, from what I could tell, and had no problem with that. Elu was a little more shy about it, but I knw I hadn't imagined the lust in his eyes when he'd caught me cumming over their show in the woods.

Kishil seemed to dislike me sometimes and flirted with me other times. Then that kiss had happened... I hadn't been expecting that at all. He'd been so tender with me, completely different than what I'd expect from such an angry man. Maybe there was more to him than I'd thought. I licked my lips and dug through my satchel for a rune bone. I pulled out one painted blue, and glanced to Kishil's back. His eyes were brown and blue. That was probably a coincidence.

"Something bothering that mind of yours, Clever Girl?" Talon rumbled by my ear. Shivers rushed down my spine and I rounded on him, my eyes narrowed.

"Stop doing that," I snapped.

"Stop doing what?" he enquired, in an all too innocent tone.

"You know exactly what!" I slipped the rune back into my satchel and chewed my lip. This was frustrating and he had to know that. "You're—" I paused, searching my mind for the proper word. "Bothering me."

"Oh, the matriarch is bothered," Elu teased from up ahead. He and Kishil were quickly pulling ahead of us. I rubbed my thighs together, glaring at Talon who only laughed.

"You smell very *bothered*," he growled. His eyes roamed across my body and I shuddered. I tried not to notice the way the tattoos on his chest seemed to come alive with each breath, drawing my gaze lower and lower. I pressed my eyes closed before I got farther than his belly button.

"I'm going to turn around and follow your friends toward the scaly village. Hopefully, I won't get eaten when we get there." I spun around on my heel, but a soft touch grazed my bottom and a slight moan spilled from my lips.

"You may very well get eaten, matriarch. But I don't think you'd mind," he whispered, almost too low for me to hear. I bit my lip against another sigh and marched forward, stomping after Kishil and Elu. Laughter rang out behind me as I ran to Elu's side, slipping my arm in his.

"Save me," I whimpered. He chuckled and patted my arm.

"I don't know that you're any safer with me," he teased. "But I'll try to behave if that's what you want." His eyes twinkled with mischief and I groaned, only making him laugh harder.

"That's the problem," I mumbled.

"What was that?" Elu asked, his tone growing more serious. Kishil glanced over his shoulder, a smile tugging the corner of his lips.

"Nothing," I replied. I decided to focus on the landscape. This was a part of the peninsula, I was sure of it, but I'd never been here. The trees were larger, older, and the underbrush was littered with honeysuckles. The air smelled sweet, thanks to the flowers, and I pulled one off a bush as we passed it, plucking the stem from the flower and licking the sweet nectar I found.

I could feel eyes on me, and I glanced around at the three men who were staring at me intently. My tongue darted out to take the last drip of nectar from the honeysuckle before I tossed it to the ground. Two groans echoed around me and I scrunched my mouth to the side, trying to hide my smile.

This was fun, even if nothing could come of it.

"We're almost to the village," Kishil grumbled as he turned back around, pushing through the bramble ahead of us. The ground beneath us was firm here, not swampy like it was near my village.

"Yay," I mumbled. I was nervous about being in a village full of scalies. Raptor scalies no less. Not only were they predators, but they were organized predators.

The rest of the walk was quiet. Every now and then one of them would touch me, using our surroundings as an excuse. My hips were held, and fingers brushed against my back, or across my arms. Talon even ran a finger across the line of my neck, moving my hair away from my skin when I complained about being sweaty.

It was maddening. My core clenched every time one of them touched me, and I was about two seconds away from letting them fuck me on the forest floor when Kishil cleared his throat.

"We're here," he murmured.

"I don't see anything." I glanced around, raising my eyebrow as I tried to spot a clearing or some kind of village. We were still in the thick of the woods, and there was no clearing in sight.

"Just wait," Elu promised. My hand rested on my hip, my fingers tapping—patience had never been my virtue.

"Elu?" an unfamiliar voice called out from the bushes ahead of us.

"Yeah, it's us!" Kishil snarled, clearly as impatient as I was. The bushes shook and then spread apart. I rubbed my eyes even as my jaw dropped, trying to understand what I was seeing. How were the bushes moving?

"Welcome home, brothers. Everyone has been worried." The young man who was speaking couldn't be as old as me, he still need to fill out quite a bit, but he was tall, with eyes as black as night. He'd be a handsome warrior when he grew up. His eyes drifted from the three scalies to me, and his eyebrows cinched together. "Who is this?"

"This is a matriarch from a Sun Tribe." Talon's voice was calm, even. His fingers closed around my shoulder, and they were warm and calming against my skin.

"A matriarch?" The boy's eyes bounced from me to the three men accompanying me. "Is she a prisoner? Did the Sun People take Kishil? When you returned home before, you made it sound like traders had attacked your party." His questions rattled off so fast I could barely keep up.

"No!" I shook my head. "I did not take Kishil. I was imprisoned with him," I whisper-screamed. The last thing we needed was a conflict between my people and theirs over a misunderstanding.

The young man nodded, casting me one more wary glance before he waved an arm through the path in the bushes.

I made my way between them, glancing around at the foliage to see how they'd managed it. My jaw dropped again. I'd stepped into a massive clearing full of small homes. They weren't raised off the ground like our chickees were, instead resting directly on the hard surface. I shuddered as I imagined all the bugs and critters that must end up inside them, but I pushed that imagery away. Maybe there weren't as many crawling things in this part of the land. The land was different enough that I could believe it to be true.

Eyes lingered on me as I followed the three of them through the center of the small village. A group of tiny raptors—children, I guessed—ran past us, nipping at one another as they went. My lips curled into a smile while I watched them chase after each other. One tumbled over onto its side and bayed out. It was a chilling sound, coming from such a small creature.

"When you're born, are you in your human skin or your raptor form?" I bit my lip after the question, since it was probably incredibly rude, but I was curious. Were these small raptors human children who could shift into raptors, or were they raptors who would one day shift into humans?

"We're born just like you, naked and human-looking," Talon answered with a chuckle.

Kishil muttered something under his breath I couldn't quite catch, and I narrowed my eyes on his back for the hundredth time.

"We don't change until we're older. Every child is different, but it happens before they're five. If they don't change by the time they're five, they never do." Elu ran a hand over his bald, tattooed head and shrugged. Someone laughed and I peered to the side where a group of women stood near a house.

"Who is this you've brought home, Kishil?" The woman speaking was beautiful. Her skin was darker than mine, and her amber eyes seemed to glow in the afternoon light.

I raised an eyebrow, wondering what the hostile tone was all about. Though the woman had addressed Kishil, it was Elu who answered her.

"A matriarch, she—" Elu paused, glancing at me with some pained expression written across his face. "She needs our protection for the time being."

"I absolutely do not," I scoffed. "You *told* me that I should come here and avoid the traders."

The group of women went still and the one who'd been speaking turned her attention from Elu back to Kishil.

"I know, Storm. This woman isn't an enemy. We only want to keep her safe until we are sure the traders have left, and then she will go on her way." His hand slid to my arm, just above my elbow. It seemed almost aggressive, like he was trying to assert his control over me.

My eyebrow raised and my eyes drifted down to where his fingers clasped my arm. I shrugged out of his hold, turning away from the spat brewing between Kishil and this woman, Storm. I wasn't sure why Elu was intervening, actually. It was obvious to me that Kishil was the leader among them . . . but if he wanted Elu fighting his battles with his lovers, then so be it. That was certainly *none* of my business.

The young boy was moving the foliage back into place. It was woven into pieces of wood, making a fence that surrounded the village, and anyone walking by would only see green forestry. It was a brilliant idea. My eyes circled the clearing, noting that the strange fence encircled the entire village.

"Your village is very... remote." I turned to find Talon mere inches from me. I almost face-planted his chest. I craned my neck, looking way, way up at him. "Excuse me," I mumbled.

"The elders are coming, just do as we do, please." Talon's green eyes tightened at the corners and I swallowed, turning around to face this new threat with my head held high.

"I'm the next matriarch of my people, I won't cower for anyone," I murmured, tilting my chin a little higher in an air of defiance. Talon's mouth clacked shut. Kishil and Elu moved to stand beside us. Kishil stood to my left, our shoulders almost brushing as we watched the group of grey and silver-haired elders approach. With each step the elders took toward us, the guys seemed to close in around me. They had been so adamant that I come here and now they seemed worried about the reaction their people would have. Typical men, never thinking clearly.

The elders drew closer, their faces coming in to focus. A woman with long silver hair stood at the front, her face scarred on one side by what looked like claw marks. She inclined her head to me and I repeated the gesture.

"Matriarch," she whispered.

"Elder." My voice rang out much clearer and stronger than I felt at the moment. A small smile quirked her lips and she looked from her left to right at the two men accompanying her. Apparently, their pack only had three elders, which seemed strange to me for some reason.

"That's alpha, dear one. To what do we owe this unexpected pleasure?" Her voice was smooth, alluring. It was a trap. I'd grown up living with a matriarch. I knew full well how deceiving the matri-archs of other tribes could be when they had to meet and discuss things.

"You should ask your men that question. They decided it would be safer if I waited here until the threat has passed." I schooled my face into a bored look, before rubbing some dirt off of my arms that had marred the bright white markings.

"I see. I'm sure Kishil knows best," she replied, and with that she turned to Kishil. "I'm glad to see you're well. We were all concerned."

"So concerned you sent only two men as a rescue party?" Kishil's fists clenched at his side. I did my best to ignore the tension between them, since I had no idea how scaly politics worked. Their society was hierarchical like ours, but different.

"Obviously it was plenty," the alpha huffed out, waving to the other two men. "I'm surprised you don't have more faith in your brothers."

"That's not what I said," Kishil snapped.

The old woman smiled, revealing a mouth full of sharp teeth. Kishil stilled beside me, growing quiet.

"Remember your place, child. You're not in charge here *yet*. Maybe the humans have it right," she lamented. "Maybe women are just better suited for leadership." The old woman inclined her head, her silver hair flowing back and forth. She turned and left without another word.

My teeth dug into my lip to hold back a smile. The tension and tone between them had been easy enough to decipher. Kishil and this woman were related somehow, I was sure of it. Maybe she was his grandmother?

"One day I'm going to—"

"And the matriarch is welcome to stay within the pack for as long as she wishes. I like her spunk. Watch your tone, Grandson," the woman called over her shoulder. I outright laughed then, I couldn't help it. She was a sassy old lady and she reminded me of Nova.

Kishil glowered at me as I tried to control my laughter. I couldn't help it. My hand clasped over my mouth, and my shoulders shook with pent-up amusement.

"I'm glad you're amused," he grumbled, kicking a patch of grass in my direction. The motion brought my attention to what was swinging between his legs. I swallowed hard, my eyes quickly darting back up his body to his face.

"Don't you want to put some clothes on?" My cheeks heated under his attention. I glanced away, only to find Elu and Talon equally amused.

"We do have clothes, yes," Elu began, while Kishil erupted into his own fit of laughter. "Our people aren't upset by nudity though. Clothes often get ripped during changes, and when we're coming back from a long time out as a raptor, we will be nude. Look around, half the village is nude now."

I did peer around at the people again. Several wore animal skin clothing, slightly thicker than what I was used to seeing, and some were completely nude. One young girl quickly shifted into her raptor form when she felt my eyes land on her. Her raptor was beautiful, light grey with blue speckles on her back.

"You shouldn't watch them change," Elu whispered beside my ear. A shiver ran down my spine, but I didn't turn to face him. The heat of his breath on my ear felt amazing.

"Why not?" I lowered my voice to match his, though I knew they could probably hear us speaking anyway.

"It's considered rude to watch a scaly shift. It's when we are our most vulnerable." His hand trailed down my neck to my shoulder, holding me as he pointed to a group of raptors running through the clearing.

I'd known they were vulnerable during their shifts, that was true for all scalies, but I didn't know it was considered rude to watch them change because of that. It made sense when I thought about it. That meant I'd offended all of them at some point already.

"Should I apologize to you all?"

"No," he said, laughing and spinning me around, before cupping my face in his hands. "You didn't know."

I stared up into his brown eyes, which were blissfully human at the moment. This could almost be a moment between any woman and any man. My tongue darted out to wet my lips, and Elu's gaze traveled down, following the path of my tongue across my mouth like the predator he was. Heat pooled into my core, and I knew the moment he smelled it. His nostrils flared and his eyes closed tightly like he was trying to concentrate.

"Do you want to see where we live?" he asked, opening his eyes to reveal slitted pupils.

I nodded, trying to keep my mouth shut. Somewhere in the back of my head, I knew this was a bad idea. Being enclosed somewhere with him—or any of them—was going to lead to some serious awkwardness. Or sex. My core clenched at the thought of it. When was the last time I'd taken a man? Maybe the man from the Tree Tribe? He'd been fun.

I walked beside Elu, our shoulders barely touching, as we made our way to a house settled away from the others. Images of the painted warrior from the Tree Tribe flashed through my mind. They had started a huge fire in the middle of their village, and I'd been so confused as to where the homes were until I'd looked up. The Tree People lived in a forest full of thick, tall trees farther north. They built their homes in the limbs of the trees. An entire village was nestled in branches of that forest, and you could walk under and never notice if you didn't know it was there. The warrior had pulled me into the trees with him, after he'd also asked if I wanted to see where he lived. I'd said yes then, just like I had now.

Maybe men were cowardly that way. They didn't want to face rejection, so instead they asked a different question that might get the same results. I pondered that as I briefly paused outside the door to the small house. Elu waved an arm toward the door and I pushed it open, sticking my head inside first to see what was in there. No monsters or beasts lay waiting for me, only Kishil sprawled out on a large bed of furs. I wondered for a moment how he'd beaten us here, but pushed the thought aside.

The house was one large bedroom, with no individual rooms divided by walls or hanging tapestries. There was only one bed. I swallowed hard as images of the three of them tangled up together flashed through my mind. Kishil had been so rough with poor Elu, but he'd seemed to like it. My eyes drifted back to Elu, he had a soft smile on his face.

"You can sit down if you want, Kishil doesn't bite." Elu made his way toward a cabinet of some kind and began pulling things out. "I want to put some medicine on those cuts on your legs, if you don't mind."

I glanced down at the gashes on my thighs. I'd almost forgotten about them, but at the mention of them, they sprang back to life, burning once more. I padded toward the large bed, which was higher than the beds I was used to. Instead of being a few layers on the floor, this bed was piled high. The furs reached my hip. I situated myself on the edge and crawled into the middle, beside Kishil.

"He lied, I definitely bite." Kishil winked, and then took a bite of the food I hadn't noticed he was holding.

"I bite back." My chin jutted out in the air and I stared him down. I refused to be cowed by a man. It wasn't going to happen. Not ever.

"Clever girl," he murmured, reaching out to brush a strand of hair from my face.

"What are you—" I was interrupted by the door swinging open. Talon stepped into the room, his hair soaking wet and dripping droplets of water down his broad chest. I swallowed again, even harder this time, briefly wondering how in the world he'd managed to get soaking wet in the short time we'd been separated. Thankfully, everyone seemed to be wearing clothes now. Even Elu had covered himself in some breeches.

Thank you, Great Mother. You're not making it easy to stay on task, you know that?

Outside, a bird sang and my eyes searched for an opening in the wood, a window of some kind so I could see where the noise came from. A tiny window on the west side of the home was all I found. I peered through it, searching for the bird. A mockingbird, with black tips on its feathers as black as night, flew by.

Don't pretend to know what the Great Mother wants from you, young matriarch.

Elu dropped the bowl of medicine he'd prepared, looking around the room. Talon moved toward his friend, laying a hand on his shoulder. He didn't speak, only stood there looking concerned. I shoved a hand into my hair, pulling it through the dark tresses in frustration. The Mockingbird was going to drive me insane, if he was even real.

I'm very much real, young matriarch. I think you may have bigger problems at the moment . . .

"Who's there?" Elu called out, spinning around.

"What do you mean?" Talon asked, worry coating his voice. "Did you hear someone outside?" Kishil bounded from the bed, heading for the door.

"No, no. Someone is speaking to Sage." Elu pointed to me and my eyebrows shot up my forehead. He could hear it too?

"What? You can hear him?" I sputtered, leaning forward.

"Who is he?" Elu demanded, obviously perturbed.

"Um..." I glanced from one man to the other and bit my lip. I wasn't surprised when three sets of eyes dropped to my mouth. I gulped, steeling my spine for whatever came next. They may call me crazy, since I wasn't sure what their beliefs were. "The Mockingbird."

Elu's eyes went round and he sat on the edge of the bed, rubbing a hand across his bald head. "The Mockingbird. As in the one who the Great Mother nursed back to health? Restored? Her messenger?"

I nodded, my shoulders going limp with each addition to his question.

"Why is he speaking to you?" Talon inquired, looking between Elu and me. He was tense, I could tell he wanted to help, he just didn't know how.

"She's on a Spirit Walk, Talon. He must be her guide." Kishil dove back into the middle of the bed, sighing. I scooted away from him, his head was dangerously close to my thigh.

"Just like that, you believe me? And why can't they hear him?" I slid my hand into Elu's and squeezed, offering some support.

"I've always been able to hear them, the Spirits. I've never met the Mockingbird though. Only more minor spirits have ever come around here." His eyes flicked to Kishil and my eyebrows cinched together.

Kishil seemed to bristle under the attention and flipped his friend off.

"Why?"

"The Spirits are drawn to leaders, Sage." Talon seemed to have relaxed once he realized me and my Spirit friends weren't a threat. He sank down onto the bed directly in front of me. His head plopped down in my lap like it belonged there.

I glowered down at him, but he only grinned in response. "You're a child," I muttered.

"You think I'm childish?" His eyebrows cinched together as if he was puzzling over what that meant.

"Well, at least she sees you for what you really are," Kishil quipped. "Unlike Storm."

"Storm prefers *you*," Talon accused, rubbing his hands down his face. "She only tolerates me because she knows we're a package deal."

"A package deal?" I repeated, genuinely curious. "And is this where I'm sleeping? Do you have a bedroll?" My fingers ran through Talon's drying hair absentmindedly as they bantered and I waited for my answers.

"Well..." Elu began as he dabbed some medicine onto my thigh. I hissed under my breath and he offered me an apologetic smile. "Sorry. What you saw in the woods, that's... we're..." He paused, struggling to find the correct words.

"You're together," I finished for him.

"Sort of. It's more complicated than that. I have no problem with either of them going out and finding a female for fun. But when it comes to mating—that's our version of your marriage—it would be best if we had mates that understood our relationship. Actually, it would be best if we mated with the same woman."

I winced again, resisting the urge to yelp as the medicine stung my thigh. My teeth dragged back and forth across my bottom lip while I worked out what he meant. So, the raptors accepted multiple marriages like my people did, that was an interesting tidbit.

"You can sleep in the bed if you'd like. No one will touch you unless you ask them to." Kishil caught my eye as he spoke and I swallowed. Since we met, he hadn't often been sincere with me unless he was angry—that particular emotion he expressed very well. He was being genuine right now though, and his strange brown and blue eyes seemed to soften in the dim light of the house.

My fingers stilled in Talon's hair and a few clicks tumbled from his throat. *Awe, the big bad warrior likes being petted.* I focused on Kishil, he seemed like a different person within these walls. I couldn't put my finger on the change, but he just seemed more relaxed, more comfortable. He was being... considerate. I nodded to him, and resumed twining my fingers in and out of Talon's hair.

"I can sleep here. It's a very nice bed. I've never seen one so thick before."

Elu, who'd been in the process of sliding onto the bed, burst into a fit of laughter. I looked from him to Kishil, who was also barely containing himself. I narrowed my eyes on Talon, tugging at his curly locks.

"What's so funny?"

"You said you've never seen such a thick one before," Talon bit out between chuckles. My cheeks heated instantly and I snatched my hand away from his hair.

"Oh Great Mother," I hissed. "You're children, all of you!" I clamped my mouth shut, scared I'd give them more fodder. Eventually, the fits of giggles gave way to more conversation about the traders and the woman named Storm.

"So your people have history with the traders. Why don't you just organize and fight them? Surely a bunch of scalies can take out some humans." I shrugged. Elu offered me a piece of dried meat and I took it gratefully, tearing off a bite.

"Their weapons are metal. They're stronger than what you're used to fighting against, Sage. We won't see our people captured and held for entertainment by some ignorant humans."

I cleared my throat and leaned forward—over Talon—to face Kishil. My finger prodded his chest repeatedly as I spoke. "Some ignorant humans respect scalies, I'll remind you."

"Yes, yes, you're very respectful, Clever Girl. You didn't tell the traders what I was and I'm grateful. Your kind still tends to demonize mine." His eyes looked sad and I wished I could understand his distrust for my people. I'd never heard scalies be *demonized*. Sure, there was a lot about them that we didn't understand, but they were a very secretive people, that didn't mean we hated them.

"Why do you hate humans?" I leaned back, lifting Talon's head up so I could crisscross my legs. He grumbled but readjusted fairly quickly. Elu began rebraiding my hair, his fingers combing against my scalp was mesmerizing. My eyes couldn't leave Kishil's. The look on his face was hard to read and I was fascinated.

"I don't *hate* them," he eventually replied. "I just don't trust them. Your people have a tendency to fear what they don't understand, and shifters aren't something that they understand." He shrugged and stole a piece of meat from Talon's chest.

I wrinkled my nose up at the sight. That couldn't be healthy. Then again . . . I'd seen them do less sanitary things to one another.

My cheeks flushed. The sound of someone inhaling deeply brought me out of the memory that had begun flashing through my mind.

They can smell you, remember. I groaned inwardly at the thought.

"Some of them do, Kishil. Not all humans are like the tribe your mother grew up in," Elu all but whispered behind me. Kishil went still, his gaze hardening.

"Your mom is from the Sun People! I forgot that, Talon mentioned it but I just—"

"Has everyone been discussing my private business behind my back?" he snarled, looking between the other two men.

My shoulders sagged. I wanted an answer, but I was going to have to drop it. Forcing a man like Kishil to speak wouldn't do anything but lead to an argument or a brawl. Except, some wild part of me thought fighting him would be fun.

"Why don't you get some sleep, matriarch." Elu fastened my braid as he finished speaking and tugged on it, pulling me backward. The slight pain in my scalp caught my attention and my neck whipped around to face him, my lip snarling back. "I think you might be a little feral, Clever Girl. You've snarled at me more times than Kishil has snarled at you."

"That can't be true," I huffed, my eyes darting back to the man in question. "All he does is snarl."

Talon burst out laughing, earning a kick from Kishil. The big, tattooed man crawled up and dumped himself onto the bed beside me. I opened my mouth to ask what he was doing, but before I could speak, an arm snaked around my waist, pulling my back flush against Talon's chest. I gulped. I could feel every inch of his body against mine. Every cut muscle pressed against my back in a titillating dance each time he breathed.

I bit my lip, resisting the urge to move against him in any way. They'd promised to let me sleep unmolested and I was going to take that offer for what it was worth. The past few days had been exhausting. Elu leaned back, bracing his head on his elbow. His hand slid down my cheek and I instinctively turned into his caress, sighing as my eyes closed.

"Get some sleep," he murmured again, quieter this time.

I didn't respond, only settled into the darkness behind my lids. I felt more than heard Kishil move around on the bed. I wasn't sure where he was laying but he wasn't touching me, which was the only thing that mattered at the moment. Apparently, my kind was good enough to flirt with, but not good enough to trust.

Fucking scalies . . .

Chapter 14

Sage

My eyes blinked open one at a time, my vision blurry from sleep. I wasn't sure what had woken me. I lay still, listening, and trying to focus on the dark world around me. It was still dark, so I couldn't have been asleep for terribly long. My right arm snagged as I tried to move it. Talon had somehow managed to get his head on top of my arm in our sleep. I pulled my hand back slowly, letting his head fall against the bed. Rolling back onto my left side, I blinked until my surroundings came into focus. Two slitted pupils stared back at me. Amber swirled with gold and blue in the most gorgeous pattern I'd ever seen. I didn't jump, I wasn't afraid for some reason.

"Why are you awake?" I whispered.

"I don't sleep well," Kishil replied in a soft voice. He inclined his head behind him, and I rose up enough to peek over his shoulder. Elu lay sprawled across half of the bed, while Kishil was pressed to the center, not far from me at all. I covered my mouth to contain a laugh.

"He sleeps like a child."

"He does." Kishil smirked. He seemed relaxed, even though his raptor eyes would suggest differently. From what I could tell, their animal traits surfaced when they were stressed or experiencing some heightened emotional response.

My hand snaked out toward his cheek, but was stopped short by his hand clamping down on my wrist. A small gasp slipped past my lips.

"What are you doing?" he asked, a snarl in his throat.

"I just..." The words wouldn't come. Kishil's grip tightened on my wrist and he pulled me toward him, my back arched awkwardly as my chest pressed against his.

"Just what?" His voice was rough, his gaze heated. I swallowed and tilted my face so my lips brushed against his. It was soft, barely even a kiss. Kishil went completely still under my touch, his grip loosening on my wrist. I turned my head with my newfound freedom and plucked at his lips gently with my own. His lips didn't move, but neither did he try to pull away. Confused, I pulled back, staring at him.

"I thought, after—"

His lips sealed against mine in an instant, his hands slipping into my hair as his mouth devoured mine. Kishil swallowed whatever words I was speaking without any further hesitation. My hand slid up his arm to his neck, winding around underneath his hair. Kishil's tongue swiped along my own, delving into my mouth like he owned it. A tiny moan rose in the back of my throat when his leg slipped between mine and he rocked his thigh against my core.

Clicks echoed from his chest, and I gasped when he rolled me on top of him as he pushed up into a sitting position.

I sat straddling him, with one leg on either side of his, and my arms wrapped around his neck. Our chests pressed together and my forehead leaned against his as my breasts rose and fell with each breath.

"I..." Kishil shook his head, closing his eyes as he tried to find the words he was looking for. "Now's the time to say no, Clever Girl. If you're as smart as I give you credit for, you will."

I reared back, my eyes going wide as I stared at the man in front of me. Did he just insult me? His hips rocked beneath me, his hard length grinding against my core, but his pants were in the way. Why was he wearing pants? They'd all been nude in the woods, but of course Kishil *would* have pants on right now just to spite me. I bit my lip, grinding down against him.

"Sage," Kishil warned, a snarl building in his chest. I slipped my hand between us, tugging at the laces to his pants.

"Yes. Just for tonight," I whispered.

That was all Kishil needed to hear. His hand rushed to join mine, pulling the laces apart, and his hips lifted as he pushed the material down his thighs just enough for his cock to spring free between us. My hand wrapped around it—just barely—stroking as I watched him. His nostrils flared and he slipped his fingers to my wet center, brushing across my clit in a lazy pattern. My lips parted on a moan and Kishil's free hand went to my mouth, clamping down on my lips.

"Shhh," he murmured.

My grip tightened on his cock, working my hand up and down slowly. The angle was awkward, but Great Mother this was heaven. Kishil dipped a finger inside me and I almost came undone. I stared at him with hooded eyes, rolling my hips down against his hand.

Kishil tore his hand away from my mouth, his lips descending on mine. His hand went to the back of my hair, sliding against my scalp and beneath my braid, angling my head for his kiss. I whimpered against his mouth when he pulled his hand away and slid it between our bodies, before quickly closing it over my own, and moving his cock toward my entrance. The head brushed against my slick center and I pressed my hips down against him.

I pulled my hand away, wrapping my arms around his neck once again. Kishil slid inside me slowly. He was wide, and even as wet as I was, it would take a moment for my body to adjust. I bit back a moan when he finally bottomed out. I'd never felt so full before.

"Fuck," he moaned quietly, his hips grinding against me as his hands fell to my legs. Kishil pulled on my calves until my legs wrapped around his back. I crossed my ankles, whimpering at the new pressure.

Kishil's eyes met mine, his fingers digging into my legs as he set a pace beneath me. I rolled my hips down against him, unable to break the eye contact. Every time I writhed, he pulled back the slightest bit, then bumped into my cervix all over again. He was as deep as he could possibly get. My teeth grazed my bottom lip as I tried hard to be quiet. I didn't want to wake our bedfellows.

As if summoned by the thought, a noise to our side drew my attention. Kishil's hand darted up, gripping my throat while his forefinger rested along my cheek. He shook his head, gritting his teeth as his gyrations sped up. I couldn't resist him even if I wanted to right now. He filled me so completely, and his hands... a breathy moan slipped out when his thumb circled my clit. I rolled my hips, trying desperately to get something more, when another hand pushed my top down, revealing my breasts. Fingers twisted and pulled my nipples, then a wet mouth replaced one of the hands, latching on to the budded flesh and sucked hard. I cried out, my hand going to their head—Talon, it was Talon's curly hair I found—as an orgasm rocketed through my body.

Kishil muttered under his breath, a snarl building in his chest. His grip on my throat tightened, and even though I'd come I couldn't stop moving, my pussy was chasing the friction he gave me. Beautiful. Wonderful. Perfect friction.

"Cum for me, Clever Girl," he demanded. One of his hands lifted my ass off his thighs, creating enough distance between us for him to slam deep inside me. I screamed when his cock filled me. Wild sounds filled the air as he pummeled me from below. Talon abandoned one nipple for the other, biting down on my breast hard as he palmed my stomach. My senses were overloaded. So much touch at once...

"I can't!" I cried out, my body shaking as Kishil pounded against my g-spot over and over.

"*Now*," he ordered.

My eyes flew open. Elu sat leaned back on one elbow with his hand wrapped around his cock, watching the display unfolding around him. I met his gaze as his lover slammed deep inside my pussy. Kishil swelled inside me, and my skin erupted in hot goosebumps as a shiver wound its way around my spine. I could feel the edge of my orgasm, but it was just out of reach.

A tongue slid between my cheeks where Kishil's hands spread them. I glanced down, wondering how Talon had moved from my front to my back without me noticing. Talon's tongue dove into my rear, stretching it open for the first time. His hot mouth pushed me over the edge.

I shattered around Kishil for the second time, pulling him into oblivion with me. Hot jets of cum sprayed inside me, coating my inner walls over and over. Clicks and chuffs rang out around me, but I had no idea what sound came from who. I couldn't see straight anymore.

I'd never come so hard in my life.

I leaned forward, away from the mouth teasing my rear, and arms encircled me, laying me gently on my back. My eyes blinked, trying to focus on the world around me once more.

"I think we broke her," Talon whispered.

Elu laughed somewhere nearby, and Kishil brushed a sweaty strand of hair from my face.

"She's fine," Kishil whispered. He turned my face to the side by my chin, as if he were examining me. "By the Creator," he groaned.

My eyes fluttered shut. He could turn my face whatever way he wanted as long as I could close my eyes. Everything was still a little fuzzy, and some of it was spinning a little. The bed dipped as someone moved around, followed by a loud smack.

"You *know better*," Talon snarled.

"It's not like I meant—"

"Don't finish that sentence." Talon's voice was rough. He sounded angry, but I knew he was also turned on.

"Have you forgotten who the alpha is here?" Kishil snarled.

"No, she's asleep across the village unless your mate woke her up. Have *you* forgotten?"

Kishil mumbled something I couldn't quite catch. A set of lips brushed against my temple before the bed shifted again. I turned my head to the side, squeezing my eyes shut tighter. I wanted to sleep. That's what I wanted. An annoying, burning pain zipped through my neck when I turned again and I hissed in a breath.

"Shh, I know it stings. It won't for long. Open your eyes, Sage," Elu murmured. Something cold met my neck and I opened my eyes.

Elu dabbed medicine along my neck and throat. It stung for a moment before it turned cool. Goosebumps erupted along my skin once again as I watched him move above me. His hard cock swung freely between his legs. I looked behind him to find Talon, lazily palming his dick. My core clenched at the thought of him filling me. He looked even bigger than Kishil.

"Elu," Talon ground out as his eyes fell on me. I whimpered under his gaze, daring to brush my fingertips along Elu's legs where he straddled me.

"Tsk. Talon first, love, if you're willing."

"She smells willing enough," Talon murmured, crawling up between my legs, behind Elu.

"She has to say it, you barbarian," Elu scolded, winking at me.

I opened my mouth to speak but no words came out. I'd initiated this tryst with Kishil, and now it was spiraling into some kind of orgy. My core tightened again. I had just had Kishil and was about to take at least one—probably two—more men tonight. That's exactly what was going to happen, because I wasn't going to tell him no, as long as it wasn't a problem.

"Did Kishil leave because I want you as well?" I glanced between the two of them and waited for the answer.

"No, Clever Girl. He left because he needed to deal with some-thing. It's nothing you need to worry about right now, I promise." Talon's green eyes were liquid heat.

I swallowed hard and nodded, staring at the two men above me on the bed. My skin was peppered with sweat from the encounter with Kishil. And Talon, he had definitely been involved there at the end.

Elu smiled at me and leaned down, pressing his lips against mine in a chaste kiss. Everything was still so sensitive, and it felt a thousand times more involved than I thought it should. His soft lips moved against mine like water, taking my bottom lip between his and pulling until it let loose a soft *pop*.

"My turn," Talon whispered.

Elu slid to the side, out of the way, and ran his fingers down my arm. He traced my markings carefully, reverently, while Talon lowered himself above me.

"All you have to say is no," Talon murmured against my cheek as he kissed across my jawbone to my ear. My head turned to the left of its own accord, giving him better access and bringing Elu into sight.

"I don't want to say no." The words tumbled from my lips and Elu smiled at the same time Talon snarled. My eyes were ripped back to the tattooed man above me. He'd leaned away from my ear, his dark curls falling like a curtain around us. My fingers twined through them as his hand slid from my breast, down my ribs, and then to my stomach.

"Are you protected?" Talon's hand cradled my belly and I blinked, trying to process his question. Everywhere his fingers touched lit a fire inside me. My eyes fluttered shut as Elu's mouth kissed down my shoulder to my arm.

"I take the thistle water, if you know what that is." I had been drinking thistle water daily—with a few exceptions—since I came of age. The shaman taught all young women how to make it, so that they never fell pregnant without their own consent. It was a blessing to have a child, but it should always be up to the woman whether or not a sexual encounter led to one.

"Thistle water is similar to the milk our women drink, Talon. She'll be fine." Elu breathed the words against my elbow, and I had never realized that part of my body was so sensitive until now.

135

"Sorry," Talon murmured, cupping my cheek as his lips pressed against my own. "I wanted to be sure. I wouldn't want to—"

I silenced his words with my lips, kissing his worries away. He was so sweet, so different than what I'd imagined he would be like. This tattooed behemoth was gentle and caring, and he didn't want me to do anything I'd regret. That only spurred me on more. I hooked my legs around his waist, deepening our kiss and pulling his body closer to mine. My tongue slid along Talon's as a hand massaged my breast, tweaking my nipples until they were as hard as tiny rocks.

"So beautiful," Talon gasped between kisses. His hand slipped between our bodies and soon I could feel the head of his cock pressed against my entrance. He teased me, sliding the head inside and then back out.

My fingers scored his shoulders, silently begging for more. I arched my back, pressing my hips closer to his.

Finally, he filled me, but Talon did so at his own pace. His cock slid in inch by inch, stretching me wider than I'd ever been stretched before as he sank his teeth into my lip. The bite wasn't hard enough to break the skin, but it was close.

"Oh!" I gasped as my eyes flew open. Talon's eyes bore into mine, the slitted pupils of his raptor staring back at me. His jaw clenched as he pulled back and sank inside me once again. Every time he moved, his cock brushed my clit and a moan slipped from my lips.

"Shh," Elu murmured, moving his hips beside my head. His hand circled his cock, pulling slow strokes that seemed to match Talon's thrusts.

I turned my head toward him, flicking my tongue out against the tip of his cock. Elu gasped, his hand flying to my hair. He frantically looked from me to Talon. I kept my eyes on his and opened my mouth, letting him know it was okay.

"I..."

"Do it, Elu," Talon groaned as he slammed deep inside me.

I cried out, my face bumping into Elu's dick. I slid a hand around the base of it, steadying myself, before I covered the tip of his cock with my mouth. My tongue swirled around the edges of the head and probed against the sensitive slit at the top.

"Oh Great Mother," Elu murmured, fisting my hair. I didn't mind the sting in my scalp, it actually egged me on. I worked my mouth down as far as I could and began twisting my hand up and down to meet my lips as I set my pace.

"She is a clever girl, isn't she?" Talon moaned, as he slammed deep inside me once again.

"Fuck! Yes, yes she is." Elu's voice was strained already. It hit me that he probably never got this treatment from his lovers—at least the two I knew—as they were more dominant than him. That didn't seem fair to me, but made sense in an animalistic sort of way. I was determined to make the experience one he'd never forget.

Carefully, I pulled my other hand from between Talon's shoulder and cradled Elu's balls. I massaged them in time to the rhythmic sucking pattern I'd began. My hands made up for anything my mouth couldn't take, I was sure of it.

Elu's hard stomach rose and fell in pants while I sucked him. A finger brushed against my clit, then pinched it, and I groaned against the cock in my mouth. My hips rolled up against Talon, begging for more.

"She's perfect," Talon groaned, his pace quickening. He pounded in and out of my pussy, slamming my mouth farther down on Elu's cock.

"S-Sage!" Elu cried out, his grip in my hair tightening. His cock swelled against the entrance of my throat and I pressed farther down, forcing my throat to open for him. The head of Elu's cock popped into my throat with a slight burn, and his hips jerked as he spasmed against me. Warm cum coated my throat, easing the burn the friction had created.

"Look at me," Talon demanded.

I sucked as I slowly released Elu's cock from my mouth, turning my attention fully on Talon as Elu panted beside us. The middle of his eyes were so green, my fingers brushed under his eyes, wishing I could touch them somehow. Talon's face softened at the gesture, his thrusts slowing as he wrapped his arms around me, pulling me as close to him as possible.

My back arched, my hips rocking against his, pulling him as deep inside me as I could. Each pass between my legs added more pressure to the explosion that was brewing. My flesh burned, my core clenched, and I was so close. So. Close.

"I want to fill you over and over," Talon murmured in his deep, sexy voice. My skin broke out in goosebumps. Who said things like that out loud? "And when I'm done, I want to watch Elu clean you until you cum on his tongue." With that, he slammed his cock deep inside me until he bottomed out.

I screamed out in pleasure, nonsensical words that even I didn't understand. My eyes tried to flutter shut, but Talon's strong hand on my neck and his thumb on my cheek kept my eyes glued to his. I came hard. It felt like my pussy seized around his cock forever.

"Good girl," he groaned as his own release came. Talon was true to his word. He filled me with large jets of cum until I could feel the fluid rolling down my thighs. Finally, his hips jerked to a stop. Talon leaned his forehead against mine, his lips brushing against my nose.

A strange feeling spread through my chest, like warm butterflies flitting beneath my skin. My eyes slid shut and I smiled, my legs tangled up with Talons and Elu gripping my hand for dear life.

"Well," Elu chuckled and a grin split my face.

"That was definitely something, boys," I whispered.

"Indeed, it was," Talon murmured, sliding off me and to the side. His arm draped over my waist, his chin pressed to my head. He was so warm beside me, but I didn't mind it. Not even in this heat. It was a cozy warmth that made me want to shut my eyes and go to sleep.

"Nu-uh." Elu clicked his tongue against his teeth, pulling my gaze to him. "You owe me something, matriarch." His mock formal tone got my attention as I tried to figure out what I could possibly owe him.

"Mmm, that's right. I did promise you a meal, didn't I?" Talon pulled me over on top of him. My back lay against his chest, my cheek pressed against his. His cock sprang to attention between my thighs and my eyes widened. There was no way he was hard again already... but his cock slid inside me and he swirled his hips from below. "That should work for lubrication," he murmured, lifting me up and depositing me on the bed beside him once more.

"Lubrication?" I blinked, trying to understand what was happening.

Elu quickly crawled between my legs, spreading them wide as he braced his forearms on my thighs. My mouth went dry. *He's not going to... not after I just...*

His mouth closed over my pussy, his tongue darting between my slick folds as he searched for my clit. I gasped when he found it, causing a shudder to rush through my body. I was incredibly sensitive after the earth-shattering orgasms I'd just enjoyed. My hips ground against his face as he licked and sucked at my sensitive flesh. I bit my lips, trying to contain the moans that desperately wanted to escape.

"Arch that back for me," Talon's voice called from somewhere nearby. His words confused me. I was beneath Elu, how could I—

"Yes, love," Elu purred into my pussy. I whimpered and he slid his tongue farther down, dipping into my core.

"Oh Great Mother!" I called out. His tongue was doing wicked things to my body. He fucked my pussy with his tongue like it was a cock, delving deep inside and curling into my inner walls. I'd never felt anything like it. The bed shifted as Talon arranged himself behind Elu. I stared into his eyes as he ran his cock between the other man's ass cheeks. He was going to fuck Elu while Elu pleasured me. My heart hammered against my chest as that realization dawned. Talon smirked at me, taking a few leisurely strokes of his cock, before he aligned himself with Elu's entrance.

"You enjoyed watching us out in the woods. Didn't you, Clever Girl?" Talon's voice sent shivers down my spine. That velvet tone was something I wanted to bottle up and keep for myself, and never share with another soul. I quickly nodded, my teeth marking my bottom lip.

Elu's tongue swirled inside me then ran up to my clit once again. He moaned against my sensitive nub when Talon slid inside him.

Talon took no time to let Elu adjust. His thrusts were wild and punishing from the start. Every time he pounded into Elu, Elu's face rocked against my pussy. The difference in friction was going to drive me insane. Soft, wet tongue. Rough contact from his face being pushed against me. Soft, wet tongue. Rough face. Over and over and over... the pattern repeated until I was a writhing mess, digging my fingers into the fur pelts the bed was made of. I grabbed a fistful and let out a long, throaty moan.

"Yes," Elu groaned against my pussy, his tongue darting in and out of my entrance, teasing me. His tongue was longer than what I'd grown used to. The tip of it prodded my g-spot, spurring me toward another orgasm.

"Beg," Talon demanded.

"Please," Elu and I moaned out at the same time. I wasn't sure who he'd been speaking to, and it didn't matter. His hips slammed hard against Elu, once, twice, and then he pulled out completely.

"Wh-what?" Elu whimpered, arching his back for Talon.

"Move up. I want you to be inside her while I'm inside you," Talon snarled.

Elu shuddered, his eyes flicking to mine. I quickly nodded, slipping my hand over his bald head and pulling him to me by the back of his neck. His lips descended on mine slowly. He was shaking. His hand found his cock and he slid it along my entrance, but never pressed inside.

"I consent, sweet man. Please," I whimpered. My swollen clit begged for attention, and my aching pussy wanted him inside me as badly as Talon did apparently.

Elu bit his lip and slid inside me slowly. He wasn't as thick as Talon, but he made up for it in length. Within moments, he was rolling his hips between my legs, sliding in and out of me at a slow, agonizing pace. His steady movements were going to make me lose my mind.

"Here we are," Talon grunted.

Elu moaned, slamming deep inside me, and the wind rushed out of my lungs. He'd been going slowly so Talon could line himself up. I swallowed hard as the sound of skin smacking skin filled the room, and every time Elu moaned his cock slammed deep inside my pussy.

Talon was fucking him, forcing Elu to fuck me harder with each thrust. My core clenched and Elu cried out, clicks bubbling from his throat.

A snarl ripped from Talon's chest. His hand came around Elu's throat from behind, his mouth by his ear. "You love it, don't you, Elu?"

"Yes!" Elu whimpered. His hips had ceased moving on their own. Talon drove into him harder and harder, pushing Elu's cock deep inside me.

I moaned, drawing Talon's gaze. He leaned farther forward, brushing his lips against mine. Elu turned his head, his tongue darting between our lips, inserting himself in the kiss. It was an odd feeling, two tongues swirling against mine.

"Ohhhh," I moaned when Elu's cock grazed my G-spot with *just* the right amount of pressure. We were so smooshed together that he rubbed my clit with every movement. It was too much. I clamped my eyes shut against the soft dawn light that seemed to be crowding the room and growing brighter by the second. My skin felt like it was going to burst into flames. The orgasm shook me, my pussy spasming around Elu's cock until I pulled him into oblivion with me.

"Please, please, please," Elu chanted over and over, his cock jerking inside me as he came.

Behind him, Talon roared his release, slamming into Elu's ass with a loud smack. His hand dug into the flesh he'd just spanked as his thrusts slowed during his orgasm.

We stayed like that for a moment, everyone panting in a tangle of limbs. Elu was the first to raise his head. He brushed his fingers through my hair, my braid long since unraveled, and smiled.

"You are amazing, sweet matriarch." Elu grinned at me with his honey-brown eyes and my heart warmed.

"You are pretty great yourself. You all are," I whispered.

Talon rolled off to the side and then Elu followed in the opposite direction. They cradled me between them, my back pressed against Elu, and my head laying on Talon's chest. Fingers ran across my arms and back. I wasn't sure whose were whose, but the soft caresses slowly lured me back to sleep.

Chapter 15

Talon

I pressed my nose to her scalp, inhaling her scent for the hundredth time since she'd fallen asleep. Sage and Elu were both snoring quietly—completely exhausted by the lovemaking we'd done. I shook my head, shoving my hand into my curls to push them back.

Not lovemaking, fucking. We fucked. She will go back to her village soon.

I choked on the thought of her leaving. My hand curled into a fist and I fought the urge to snarl, just barely able to control it. I slid out from behind Sage and swung my legs over the bed onto the wooden floor of our home. Despite all of Kishil's moaning, this *was* our home now. We'd come to this place to start a new life for our pack and to get away from the traders.

Apparently, the traders were making their way to this part of the land as well, but there wasn't much to be done about that until our alpha gave us permission to attack and end this. It wouldn't be an easy war to win, there would be lots of casualties, but if it stopped the strange traders from trespassing onto our lands in the future, it would be worth it.

I pulled my pants up my hips and secured them as I moved

toward the door. The scent of smoke hit me before I made it outside. Someone bayed somewhere in the village and I looked over my shoulder at the two motionless bodies in my bed. They'd napped for an hour or two, I could wake them. Well, I had to wake them anyway. I didn't know what was going on outside, and if there was a threat, they needed to be alert.

I padded back to the bed on silent feet. I woke Elu first, my finger going to my mouth so he wouldn't speak when he opened his eyes. He nodded groggily and swung himself out of the bed.

Sage rolled over in her sleep, snuggling down into the furs. I hated to wake her, but the sounds outside our home were growing louder and I smelled humans. I shook her shoulder gently and waited. She didn't immediately wake and I stared at her for a moment, puzzled. I shook her again, harder this time, and she jumped up, swinging wildly.

My hands circled her wrists, holding her blows back from my face. "Sage!" I snapped, trying to maintain a hushed tone. "Be at peace, woman. It's me, Talon!"

"I'm sorry, you startled me," she whispered with wide eyes. She looked me over, then her eyes slid to Elu who stood by the door. "What's wrong?"

"I think the traders have found us." I kept my voice low, I didn't want to be heard by anyone walking around outside. "I can't be sure until I go out there and see, but Kishil still hasn't come back and I smell humans. I need you two awake and ready to fight or run. You understand, Sage?"

Sage snorted and jumped off the side of the bed and began rummaging through the house. She moved several piles of clothes over before I finally interrupted her search.

"What are you looking for?"

"I don't have my blade, those *traders* took it. I'm going to borrow one of yours. If it's them, I'm going to get my knife back, and I can't wait." Her eyes seemed to shine with an inner fire. My hand lifted, seemingly of its own accord, and I pointed to a wooden box we kept in the corner. There were boots thrown on top of it at the moment.

"There should be a few blades in there, maybe a bow and quiver if you know how to use one." I clacked my mouth shut with a smirk when she stopped moving to meet my gaze. Her nostrils flared and I inclined my head in a mock bow. "I'm sorry. Of course, the matriarch knows how to use a bow. What was I thinking?"

"You're a fool," Elu muttered, peeking out the door. "And you were right, it's the traders. Two just ran through toward the other homes. Are we ready?"

Sage cussed under her breath and ran for the box, knocking the boots over and quickly rummaging inside for the weapons she wanted. I watched as she pulled a bow, some arrows, and a knife before she skidded back to the bed. I handed Sage her clothes, my eyebrow raised.

"Oh," she muttered, her cheeks flushing that cute color they always turned when she was embarrassed. She snatched the clothes from my hands, stepping into her skirt in a rush. She tied the top around her side, adjusting her breasts until it fit the way she wanted. Next, she slung the bow over her chest and slipped the knife into the belt of her skirt. I grabbed the arrows and slid them carefully into her boots—I'd seen Kishil do that before. He wore his arrows like shin guards until he used them. It was a smart move, even if I hated complimenting him.

"Alright, ready?" I glanced between Sage and Elu. She nodded and moved to the door, standing beside Elu who also nodded gravely. I brushed my fingertips along both of their backs as I stepped through the door.

Everything smelled like smoke, it was much stronger out here than it had been in the house. A scream tore through the air and I sprinted toward the sound, giving my body over to my raptor midstride. Behind me, the sound of bones popping let me know that Elu had also shifted. I glanced over my shoulder to see him stalking alongside our girl, keeping her safe.

A bay caught my attention from another direction. That sounded like Kishil... I shook my snout, running toward the scream. It had been human and female. It could be one of our women in trouble and that wasn't something I could live with on my conscience. Kishil would have to wait.

I glanced over my shoulder one last time to see Sage and Elu turning in that direction. Sage looked confused, but Elu was pushing her, urging her to stay with him while he checked it out. Clicks rippled out of me at the sight of him taking care of her.

I skidded to a stop at the second home I came to. The house beside it was the source of the smoke, it was in flames. I hoped no one had been inside when the fire was lit. A group of men stood around the home the scream came from, pointing toward another group of men fighting two raptors. I recognized Storm and our alpha fighting side by side. My instincts warred with each other. I needed to find out what was happening in this house, but our alpha was in trouble. I snorted, shaking my head to clear the confusion.

One thing at a time.

My talons dug into the earth and I launched myself into the group of men. They hadn't heard my approach. My claws slashed into one while I bit into the neck of another. A crisp jolt of pain in my side drew my gaze and I snapped at the man holding the long knife. These weapons were much sharper than the ones we'd fought against before.

SCALIES HAVE THICK HIDES, IT WAS A TESTAMENT TO THE blade's deadliness with how easily it sliced into me. A snarl ripped from my throat as I turned, lashing out at one of the men. I jumped and landed on two more, digging into their abdomens with my claws as I gnashed at more with my snout.

"Someone kill the beast!" That voice was familiar. I focused on my right side, watching the man with long, yellow hair approach.

His hand fisted in the long, dark hair of a man I didn't recognize. I scented the air, stepping over the fallen bodies around me. The captive was a human man. Focusing on his face, I came to realize I *did* know this man. He was the one from the river, the one Sage knew. I was sure of it. Pain seared my side and I snapped at to my right, trying to reach it. One of the humans had landed a good blow. I took another step forward, scanning the area. Storm was injured but still defended the alpha. Our alpha snapped a head clean off a man's shoulders and bayed out, calling for more of her raptors. I snarled as I drew closer to the yellow-haired man. A group of humans to my left slipped between a home and fled the village, trampling our fencing in the process.

"Stop. I'll slit his throat if you come any closer, dragon."

Clicks bubbled out of my chest as I watched the trader draw a dagger against the man's neck, a small line of blood welled along his skin. I bared my teeth, preparing to lunge at the trader, when a voice caught my ear.

"Talon! Stop! Please!"

I turned to see Sage running toward me, bow drawn. She loosed an arrow, piercing a man in the chest. Elu and Kishil trotted along beside her. Kishil bayed and a weight lifted from my chest. He was okay.

Our alpha bayed again and I snarled, unable to resist her call anymore. Kishil and Elu could handle this. I needed to help the females. I turned my head back to the trader, and then darted toward the fight circling the alpha and Storm.

Chapter 16

Kishil

My heart thundered against my ribcage when I saw the prisoner the trader was holding. It was the man from the river, the one Sage knew from her village. I chuffed, shaking my head. Sage's gaze shifted as she took in the scene around us. I could tell the moment she realized who it was.

Her rushed walk became an outright run. Another arrow flew from her bow, disarming a man with his weapon raised high.

"Talon! Stop! Please!" she yelled, pointing toward the man with the knife against his neck. Blood dripped from the shallow wound and a high-pitched shriek poured from my snout. This man was important to my mate.

I pushed the absurd thought from my mind, even as my eyes scanned her neck for the claw marks that meant I now belonged to her. *What in the fuck had I been thinking?* My eyes snapped to the alpha when she bayed—she was injured. Storm limped beside her, lashing out at human after human as they assaulted them with long knives and pikes. I pressed my flank closer to Sage, using the newfound pull I felt toward her to ground me, and stop me from lashing out at the rage bubbling inside me. Tonali was a strong alpha, she could handle herself.

Talon surged toward the fight around the females. They would definitely be fine now. Beside me, Sage came to a slow stop, nocking an arrow, and aiming the bow at the trader holding her friend hostage. Gunner, their leader.

"Let him go, Gunner," she demanded. She pulled on the bowstring, lining up her shot, and I chuffed. On her other side, Elu snarled. He wanted to rush the man too. But that wouldn't help. These traders had heavy weaponry that we weren't used to. A few of them had found me near the village, where I was roaming to clear my head after I'd realized what I'd done in bed with Sage. I'd fought them, but their knives pierced my scales so easily. I was on the edge of succumbing to their nets and spears when Sage and Elu had shown up. Sage had shot one man through the throat with her bow, while Talon tore another to shreds. I'd finished off the one who'd stabbed me with a sick satisfaction.

"I can't do that, woman. These dragons are *men*. Did you know?" His wild eyes searched the area, as if looking for more proof that we could shift between dinosaur and man.

"There is no such thing as dragons!" Sage screamed. "Your people idolized *dinosaurs*. Whether they knew that scalies could shift between two forms, I don't know. Things get lost in lore over time, Gunner. It's happened to my own tribe. Leave these people alone." Her eyes dropped down to the man with the knife against his throat. "And let Rain go. He has nothing to do with this."

"Ah, so you do know him then," Gunner purred. He kicked the man in the back, holding his hair as he fell to his knees.

"Don't give him anything, Sage." Rain's dark eyes searched for something, roaming over the matriarch, then Elu, and finally me. "Our people need you, not me. Just go! Run!"

Gunner tightened his grip on the man's hair, pushing the knife against his throat again until he couldn't speak without slicing his own skin.

"Well, that's interesting. You seem to inspire loyalty, woman. I found this one when I was tracking you. Apparently he was tracking you as well. A lover, perhaps?"

A snarl flew from me as I took a step toward Gunner. I was going to rip his smug face to shreds and enjoy doing it. Screams rose throughout the camp, human screams. I shook my head, weighing my options. Quickly—before I could talk myself out of it—I called my human form. My skin and bones stretched, shrank, and reshaped themselves until I once again looked like a man.

"Let him go and leave, Gunner. Go find the rest of your party and call this a loss. You tried to ambush a *raptor* pack, you fool. You caught me alone," I murmured, taking another step toward him. "Raptors hunt in packs. We're stronger together, more organized than you could imagine." Several bays went up in the distance and I smiled.

"Those were victory shouts." I wiped a hand down my face in agitation. "Leave while you can. This is a generous offer, believe me."

"Let him go!" Sage seethed behind me. "He's a *healer*! Do your barbaric people threaten healers where you're from?"

"I don't care about him." Gunner pointed the knife first at me, then at Elu. "I only want one of them, alive. I need to show my people what sort of magic is in this land. It's the last thing I need—" Gunner cut off midsentence and shook his head. "Give me one of your dragons and I'll give you back your healer. A fair trade."

I went still, my pulse pounding in my ears as I listened to Sage inhale sharply.

Chapter 17

Sage

I hissed in a breath at the offer. I was becoming a leader for my people, so I had to consider all the options. Elu and Kishil's eyes bore into me so hard my skin prickled under the attention, but I refused to look at them. I had to consider it. Even if it was something I would say no to. Even if it was something I couldn't physically pull off.

I shook my head, tipping my chin in the air.

"I won't trade a life for a life, neither of them are yours to take. You're a trespasser here, in this village, in this land. You have no right to my people, or to the scalies, even if they remind you of your dragons."

"You'll regret that, woman," Gunner ground out between his gritted teeth. The man who'd held me captive, threatened me, and tried to bend me into something *he* saw fit, offered me a sick and twisted smile as he drew the knife closer to Rain's throat.

"Stop!" I shouted. My fingers trembled on the bow. I was a decent shot, but I wasn't a warrior. It wasn't my calling. How I wished I could change that now. If I shot Gunner, he could still kill Rain. If I did nothing, he was probably going to kill him regardless. He was a cruel man. That was one thing I was certain of.

Memories flashed through my mind as I stared at the boy I'd grown up avoiding. The man who'd given me my first kiss. The one who'd waited on me, time and time again, while I ran off and found myself—even when that search found me in another man's bed. He'd tried to romance me over and over, and while he wasn't the man of my dreams or the man I'd settle for... Rain was a piece of my life. He was someone I was attached to in a strange sort of way.

"Please, stop," I whispered. I wasn't proud of the tremble in my lips.

"It's okay," Rain whispered. His back straight, his eyes on me. "You've found your loves, matriarch. Be well until we meet again, Sa—"

He never finished his goodbye. Gunner drew the blade across his throat and I loosed my arrow with a scream. A hole burned in the center of my chest as I watched my childhood friend fall to his side, his hands clasping his throat. The arrow went astray, hitting Gunner in the side instead of the chest. I let loose a war cry. All the emotions bubbling beneath the surface, all the memories that had just been stolen from me, and everything that was wrong in my world went into that scream as I charged Gunner. He lumbered backward.

"Loose yer arrows!" he screamed. "Now!" I paused, searching for who he was speaking to. Most of the traders had fled already. Behind me, Elu and Kishil snarled, prowling closer by the second. I didn't want them harmed, not for me. I didn't want anyone else to get hurt because of me.

Kishil gripped my arm, a snarl on his lips. "There's more in the woods. *Run!*"

He pulled me to him, turning and sprinting in the other direction. A loud whistle sounded behind us and I glanced up at the sky, only to find what looked like hundreds of arrows flying toward us.

"Faster," he hissed, pulling me behind him.

"I'm trying! Where's Talon?" I began to turn for him, but Elu's snout crashed into my chest, blocking my view. He snarled at me, pushing me in the direction Kishil was pulling me. "Talon!" I cried out.

"He was with the alpha. He will have heard everything. Just run, Clever Girl. Please." Kishil's eyes brimmed with moisture for the first time since I'd met him. He must have been more worried for Talon than he was letting on. I swallowed and nodded, following him until we were safe behind a house. Elu changed back in an instant, running his hands down my face and arms, then spun me around to inspect my back.

"Are you okay?" His voice was a ragged whisper. Elu was a healer at heart, a caregiver.

I glanced at Kishil and nodded. His hand wrapped around his upper arm, with blood seeping between his fingers. I pointed to him.

"He's hurt," I murmured to Elu.

He quickly pushed past me, examining Kishil. Kishil, for his part, grumbled through it. It seemed to be a flesh wound, something that his healing would make quick work of. I took advantage of their distraction and glanced around the corner of the home, surveying the damage.

Rain's body lay on the ground, riddled with arrows. Not far from him was a raptor. A dead raptor. I covered my mouth as my stomach turned. The green raptor seemed to have been running toward the traders instead of away from them.

Talon was green.

My heart raced as I strained my eyes to see if the raptor was tattooed. I couldn't tell from here. My hand searched behind me, coming into contact with a warm body. I didn't care who it was. I—they—needed to know if Talon was dead. My stomach wrenched as a head popped over my shoulder.

Kishil sucked in a breath and shook his head.

"Great Mother," he murmured.

"Is it him?"

"No. Sage, you have to go." Kishil turned me toward him, his eyes wide with fear. I'd never seen him look scared before. Pissed, annoyed, worried maybe, but never scared. I steeled my spine against his gentle shakes.

"Why? If it's not Talon, what's going on?"

"By the Creator," Elu whispered as he peeked around the edge as well. "He's right, Sage. You have to go. Now." He turned to Kishil. "One of us needs to go with her."

"I'll go," he murmured. "My mate, my responsibility."

I cocked my eyebrow at his words. I wasn't his—my hand flew to my neck and realization sank in. He had marked me... accidentally, but he had marked me, nonetheless. From what little I knew about scalies, that was the same as a marriage dance. Unbreakable.

We could worry about the implications of my wound later. There had to be a way around it. I would find a way to let him out of his obligation. Right now, I needed to know what was going on. The traders seemed to be gone. There were bodies everywhere. Mostly human, or human looking. I only saw one raptor dead, but there was the rest of the village to consider.

"Tonali. My grandmother," Kishil explained as a tear leaked from his eye. "The green raptor is Tonali, the alpha. We have to move. There's going to be a bloodlust. The alpha is dead and humans were responsible. When the pack realizes she's gone, things are going to get crazy. *Run*."

My throat went dry as I took in what he was saying, and my feet seemed to fly on their own without my permission. There was an entire village—or what was left of it—of angry scalies who may be about to turn on me.

"I had nothing to do with this!" I whisper-screamed as we ran toward the woods.

"It doesn't matter. When bloodlust hits a warrior, it's strong. Add animal instincts to that, Clever Girl. It can be damn near uncontrollable. Our leader was just murdered by humans, and despite being a decent human being..." Kishil chuckled as he jogged at my side. My full-out run was a leisurely pace for him and it was infuriating. "You still smell human. You have our scents on you from the mating this morning, but you still smell human, even to me. They may not be able to tell the difference and I'm not willing to take the chance."

We reached a piece of the fence that was still intact after the assault from the traders. Kishil pulled it to the side and ushered me through. When he followed, he pulled the piece back in place and pointed in the opposite direction.

"We have to get as far away from here as possible, as fast as possible. They are going to want vengeance. I know I sound like I'm repeating myself, but I need you to understand. We are just as imperfect as humans..." His face looked pained at his own words. I nodded, waiting for him to finish. "We're stronger than your kind, Sage. Even though we are equally imperfect, we outmatch you in a massive way when it comes to combat."

I knew all of this already. My expression must have seemed bored because Kishil shook his head, grabbed my upper arm, and started walking at a brisk pace into the woods.

"If they killed you and your people found out, there would be a war. Your people would lose that war. I'm trying to prevent it."

My stomach lurched at the thought of what a pack of angry raptors could do to my village. Bloody visions passed across my lids and I nearly retched. I quickened my stride. Kishil was right. We needed to put as much distance between us and that village as we could, as fast as possible.

"Thank you," I whispered.

"What for?" His chin tipped in my direction and I dropped my eyes, careful not to trip on any roots or underbrush.

"For saving me. You are a good leader, Kishil."

His cheeks flushed and he shook his head, focusing on the path in front of us. In the distance, a raptor bayed. A shudder rippled through my body and I focused on the path we were cutting in the forest.

My legs ached. All the sex and then the tension of the day, the running, the walking, it was exhausting me. I was a few seconds away from breaking down and asking Kishil to shift and let me ride on his back when a noise caught my attention.

I ran into Kishil's back and he threw an arm out, blocking me from whatever was in front of him.

"Give me the human," a voice rasped out.

I peeked around Kishil's shoulder to see an elderly man, naked with his fists curled at his sides. He had been one of the men at The Alpha's side when she'd welcomed me into the village.

"Let us pass, Edutsi. The matriarch had nothing to do with what happened. Tonali wouldn't—"

"Don't speak about her!" the man fumed. He took a step toward Kishil, but stopped short when a loud shriek ripped from Kishil's chest.

"She was my family too! I'll be the next alpha when the village comes back to their senses. Listen to me *now* and stop this. Harming this woman will not settle your need for vengeance." Kishil's voice was strained.

My chest ached for them. They'd lost someone very special, it was the equivalent of losing a matriarch, and the entire village would grieve if something happened to my mother. I understood.

"I mean you no harm," I murmured from behind Kishil.

"Sage, don't," he warned.

"Let your pet human speak, Grandson. I can smell you and your friends on her from here." He sounded disgusted.

I straightened my shoulders and pushed my way around Kishil to face the man who might be the end of me.

"I came to this village because I was invited. Your alpha welcomed me. She knew the traders had been in the area, I'm assuming—since your people have experience with them, from what I hear—she knew the risks. I would never punish someone my people protected, just because they were harmed during that time." My voice shook a little and Kishil wrapped a hand around my wrist, pulling my back to his chest.

"You sound just like her," the old man whispered.

"That's because Tonali was a leader, just like this woman is—or will be, if you let us pass and let her leave unharmed." Some of the tension seemed to be leaving Kishil's body. I didn't know this man like he did, but he seemed to think we were making progress.

"She's gone..." His words barely carried to me. The ache in my chest grew stronger and I held my hand out, an offering of peace.

"She waits for you. You know that as well as I do. I lost someone today too." My eyes filled with tears at the thought of Rain. His final words haunted me. *You've found your loves, matriarch.* Even as he faced death, he was looking out for me, letting me know that he didn't harbor any ill will for my new bedmates or me. Were they bedmates or mates? Kishil was the only one who had marked me, but they had said they were a package deal.

The old man stared at my hand, tears flowing down his face. He reached his hand out, clasping my forearm and nodded. His eyes drifted to Kishil behind me and then went wide.

"Get her out of here, Grandson."

"What is it now?" My shoulders sagged. I wasn't proud of it, but how many times was I expected to face utter doom in one day without feeling a bit inconvenienced?

"Storm..." Kishil's voice was low, deadly. I stepped forward, behind the older man. Storm was the woman who'd eyed Kishil like a piece of meat when we first arrived in the village. The one the other guys weren't fond of. The one who wanted to be Kishil's mate.

Not only had her Alpha died—and I had a feeling those two were very close, based on how she was defending her during the battle— but the only human in the vicinity for her to inflict her rage on was the same human who was now somehow *mated* to the man she wanted.

I did *not* want to be involved in any sort of fight with Storm. She was a strong warrior, that much was obvious. I swallowed and took another step backward.

"I can smell her fear, Kishil. Give her to me."

157

"No." His voice left no room for argument. "Turn around and go back to the village. That's an order."

"Oh, an order from my *alpha*?" she sneered. Storm sidestepped Kishil, drawing closer. Her eyes locked with mine and a wicked grin curved her lips. She was covered in blood—some of it was her own, proof of the many closing wounds on her body, but most of it belonged to others.

"Yes," Kishil growled, quickly backstepping to put himself between us. "You will not touch her."

"Why are you defending her?" she screeched, her hands flying around as she spoke. "Why would you abandon your people when they need you most, for a human?" Her lip curled back in distaste, revealing the razor sharp teeth I'd come to recognize as a raptor's.

"If you touch my mate, I'll end you. Don't do this, Storm. We're all hurting—"

"Your *what*?" Her eyes flashed a brilliant green, her pupils slanting as her face twisted with rage.

My heart fell into my stomach. *You idiot...*

"Go home."

"You've claimed her? A human? I knew you were fucking her, but you really chose this woman as your mate for *life*, Kishil?" The skin at Storm's elbows and knees broke out in scales then receded into flawless, human skin. I watched in wonder as her skin switched back and forth, over and over. The change was fluid, like a gentle wave rolling along the shore. I couldn't help but stare, even as I backed away from the confrontation.

"Tonali wasn't prejudiced against humans, Storm. Why should you be?" the old man asked.

Storm seethed with anger, her chest rising and falling rapidly as she glared between Kishil and his... grandfather? I was having trouble keeping up with all the relationships in this pack of scalies. A twig creaked under my foot and Storm's eyes snapped to me again as she shouldered her way past Kishil.

He snarled, gripping the woman by the back of her neck, and

brought her back to face him. His lip curled up, revealing teeth that looked sharper than normal, even from here.

"You will not—" His words cut off on a loud shriek. His hand dropped from her neck and fell to his stomach, blood seeping between his fingers as he staggered back a step.

"You'll heal, and when you've come to your senses, you'll thank me for this," Storm spat, as she turned around and stepped toward me once again.

"Storm," the old man murmured, holding his hands out.

My eyes flicked back to Kishil. He sat on his knees, his hand covering his stomach, as blood poured from the wound. He coughed, his hand slipping during the jarring motion, and I finally saw what she'd done. Storm had gutted him. Three long, deep wounds carved into Kishil's stomach. Anger burned my chest and I pulled the knife from my belt, narrowing my eyes on the woman. I had no doubt she was going to make it to me before Kishil could recover.

I also knew she would willingly assault her own elder to do so.

Her eyes glowed with rage as she stalked to the side, trying to find a way around the elder without having to harm him.

"Get out of my way!" Her shrill voice hurt my ears. I dipped into a crouched position, preparing for her attack. I wouldn't try to run from her when she was already this close, it was pointless, since I couldn't outrun her—the guys had already made that clear when I was forced to run with them. I swallowed, turning the knife in my hand until it felt comfortable.

"You want to fight me, little human?"

"No, I don't. But I'm not going to stand here and be sacrificed to your bloodlust either." My brow cocked as I took her in. Maybe Storm could be reasoned with. Kishil was finally beginning to move again, even though the gashes to his stomach would have been a killing blow for a human. My nostrils flared with my anger as I circled away from the elder. I wouldn't let someone get hurt on my behalf. It wouldn't be right and my conscience wouldn't allow it—

even if it would be really nice to be defended in this particular situation.

"You killed my alpha!" Storm roared, lunging toward me.

I sidestepped, bending through her attack and narrowly missing the talons sprouting from her fingertips. *That's awfully convenient,* I thought to myself as I spun, slicing through the air with the blade.

Where I lunged, Storm twirled away. When she leapt, I stepped to the side. Her talons scraped along my skin, peeling the flesh with it. A grunt parted my lips as I searched for an advantage. She was toying with me, Storm was a warrior, and she could have ended this already. I turned my blade in my hand, examining the handle. Before I could overthink it, I flung the knife at her, and it flew through the air. Storm tried to dodge the blow, but it landed in her shoulder.

I smirked as she roared, her hand gripping the handle. I rushed to Kishil, ignoring the elder who was playing spectator.

"Are you okay?" I murmured, brushing his hair away from his face.

"It'll heal. You need to go, quick, while she's injured." Kishil's hand went to my arm. Warm blood smeared along my skin but I ignored it, my stomach twisting at the thought of leaving him.

"I can't leave you." I held up a finger to stop him from interrupting, before his lips even moved. "And even if I did run, she would catch me. I'm not as fast as your kind."

"No, you aren't," a feminine voice whispered by my ear.

My eyes went wide as I was wrenched to my feet and dragged toward the village by my hair.

"Stop!" Kishil snarled from his place on the ground.

"You're not healed enough to fight me yet. Stay down, *alpha*. I'm starting to wonder if you even deserve the title." Storm's tone exemplified her disgust. I twisted my neck, clawing at her hand with my fingernails. Anything I could do to break free, I tried. Despite my efforts, I couldn't overpower the warrior. That didn't mean I had to make it easy on her though.

I dug my feet into the ground, trying desperately to slow our progress into the woods. Kishil struggled to his feet, taking a step toward Storm and me. My fingers reached out for him. If I could just touch him, he'd be able to help me. It was a childish thought, but one I was holding on to for the moment.

"I challenge you," a male voice declared, clear as day as it approached us. I whipped my head in the direction of the familiar voice and fresh tears fell down my cheeks. Talon was bloody, his tattoos were smeared with crimson, and some of the beautiful patterns were interrupted by open flesh. Part of me mourned the loss of those tattoos, they looked like they belonged on his skin and someone had taken them away.

"For what? Challenge your new alpha, he's unworthy." Storm laughed, throwing me to the ground as she turned to face the new threat.

My head hit the soil with a thud, and I blinked away tiny stars until my vision cleared. The voices around me sounded like they were under water. The only clear sound was lilting song of a mockingbird. I squinted my eyes, staring up at the trees for the bird that was singing.

"No. I challenge you, Storm, for the position of beta." I could tell Talon was losing his patience.

"I accept," Storm hissed. The sound of flesh crashing into flesh tore through the forest. I scrambled up onto my elbows, watching the two of them battle for a position within the pack. Storm's hands were fully scaled, her talons long and dripping blood—my blood—as she circled Talon.

Talon grinned a split second before his raptor exploded from him. Even Storm seemed surprised by how fast he'd been able to change. He was on top of her in an instant, and I couldn't see what was happening. The snarls didn't sound promising however.

"I yield," she ground out between gritted teeth. "I yield!" she yelled, louder this time.

I made my way to my feet, staring down at the pinned woman. Talon had his mouth around her neck, his teeth slowly piercing the flesh of her throat. She couldn't change, or she'd slice her own throat. Even scaly healing wasn't *that* good—she'd die.

"Talon," I whispered, approaching the raptor slowly. Storm's eyes were wide with fear, searching my face for something. I should let him kill her. I wasn't even sure if I could stop him, but there was no mistaking that was his intention if I didn't intervene.

Kishil stumbled in our direction. His waist was covered in blood, and his legs were also coated in the wet, sticky liquid. He held his hands out, his eyes on Talon.

"Be still, brother. She submitted, you have to let her go."

Talon's grip on Storm's throat tightened, as several clicks and a snarl rolled from his chest. Kishil's head snapped to Storm, a scream bubbling from her lips.

"You know what he wants, give it to him!" Kishil shouted, pointing at the woman fighting to breathe around the teeth constricting her throat.

"I'm—" Storm rasped in a breath. "Sorry. I'm sorry. Won't touch your mate." Talon snarled, released her, and backed away. The green raptor with the swirling tattoos came to lay beside me as Kishil walked toward Storm.

He offered her his hand and dragged her to her feet, wincing. He wasn't completely healed yet.

"You could have killed me or her." His finger pointed toward me and I slid my hand down Talon's back, focusing on the roughness of his scales.

"She's a matriarch. We just lost our alpha, you want her people to feel that same pain?" Kishil's eyes were wild. The wounds on his stomach were closing slowly, they were deep and there was a lot of tissue for his system to repair.

"I'm sorry, *alpha*," Storm spat. Her hands flew to her neck, covering the wounds Talon had left. "He would have killed me, even though I yielded..."

"Yes. You should have known better than to accept a challenge from Talon. We all know what happened with his father—"

Talon snarled at my side, taking a single step closer to the two speaking in front of us.

"Settle yourself," the elder murmured, as he stepped back into the fray. "It is done. The challenge was accepted and settled. Storm has accepted her place in the pack. Since she is no longer a threat, Talon, you need to stand down."

"He's right, change back," Kishil snapped. His voice was harsh, even to my ears, but there seemed to be a purpose behind it. Beside him, Storm winced at the tone. My attention turned to Talon, his scales shuddering beneath my fingertips as they receded into skin. In seconds, a man kneeled where a raptor had stood.

Talon rose to his feet, his hands sliding along my cheeks to cup my face. Before I could stop him, his mouth descended on mine and I gasped against his lips. His tongue slid across mine, desperate for something. I gave myself to the kiss, as embarrassing as it was to be watched by my *mate*, an enemy, and someone who had wanted my head on a pike only to decide he simply didn't care what happened to me.

"You're okay," he whispered.

"Me? You're alive! I thought you were the green raptor, the alpha," I choked out. I wasn't sure where all this emotion was coming from. I hardly knew these men, but I didn't want anything bad to happen to any of them. Hopefully, Elu would soon join us.

"Of course I am. I don't die easily, ask anyone." Talon winked, pulling me in for a gentle hug.

I rested my face against his pec, soaking up his warmth, even through the grime that coated his skin.

"I'm going to hold you to that. It seems like death has been chasing us," I whispered. Kishil ambled over, throwing an arm around my shoulder. As I turned to face him, a sharp pain burned across my shoulder. My head whipped around to figure out what had happened.

Talon stood there, with blood dripping down his fingertips, a guilty smile across his face. I glanced at my skin, my eyes going wide. He'd just clawed me!

"What in the Great Mother's name?" I groaned, pressing my hand to the wound to staunch the bleeding.

"Now I'll have to live up to my oath, because we're bound. I won't leave you alone, Clever Girl, don't worry." Talon tucked his hair behind his ear—a self-conscious habit—and waited for whatever was to come. He looked like he expected me to yell.

I'd be lying if I said I didn't think about it. I swiped my hand against my shoulder, cringing at the stinging pain left behind. Kishil marking me in a fit of passion—accidentally—made sense. This was bizarre. I stared at Talon, my mouth slack as I tried to figure out what to say.

"I guess that makes sense." I clicked my mouth shut and pressed my fingers to my temples.

"Excuse me?" Kishil laughed.

"You three are a package deal. When you accidentally claimed me, you signed me up to be claimed by them as well, didn't you?" It made sense in an archaic way that I didn't quite like, but I felt something for these men, and there was no sense in arguing with myself about it anymore. There was something between us. Kishil and I shared a passion hot enough to rival the sun, while Talon, my protector, was a mystery I loved unraveling, and Elu... sweet Elu. He was the glue to this tiny pack.

That's how I thought of them, as their own pack within the raptor pack. Yes, there was definitely something between us. I wasn't sure how comfortable I was with being bound to them permanently... but that was a problem for another time.

"That's right, Clever Girl," Talon purred by my ear.

A shiver darted up my spine and a snort pulled my attention back to Storm and the elder. She shook her head, a look of disgust on her face. I opened my mouth to say something but thought better of it.

Storm and the elder began to make their way back toward the village. The old man looked completely dejected. He'd lost his love. I couldn't imagine a pain like that. With each step he took toward the home of the raptor pack, his shoulders slumped further.

Kishil turned to me and brushed a hand through my mess of hair. "Thank you for being okay."

I twisted my lips up and shook my head, ignoring his strange statement. These men were odd.

"Kishil," Storm called out over her shoulder.

"Yes?" he replied, his body tense.

"Do not stay gone too long, or you may find the position of alpha filled."

Beside me, Kishil bristled, and his chest swelled with whatever words he was going to yell. I laid a hand on his cheek, staring at him and willing him to calm. His skin was always so hot. I knew they'd explained it to me, but it still caught me off guard whenever I touched one of them.

"Peace," I whispered, low enough that I hoped no one else heard.

Kishil nodded, leaning his head down against mine as Talon wrapped his arms around me from behind. We stood like that in the woods for what seemed like forever. Finally, enough time had passed that we decided to move on, toward my village, without Elu.

"He'll find us later," Talon promised. "He is a fixer, it's his nature. He is probably helping settle everything in the village."

I nodded, following them through the woods once more. I hoped Elu showed up soon.

Chapter 18

Sage

Once I recognized where we were after we'd crossed the river again—in a different spot than the last time—I began to lead the way back to my village. A mockingbird flitted through the trees nearby, singing whatever tune it felt like at that moment. It had been following us since we left the raptor village.

"Do you think that's the Mockingbird?" Talon whispered.

I craned my neck to look up at him and grinned. The behemoth was afraid of the Spirits, it would seem.

"At this point? Probably. He's... challenging."

"Did you just call one of the Spirits annoying?" Kishil scoffed.

I blinked my eyes innocently at him, tracing the symbol painted on my forehead as I turned to continue walking.

"Would I do something like that?"

"Yes," three voices answered.

I wheeled around at the same time as the two men behind me. A few feet away from Talon stood the man from my dream—the Mockingbird. His eyes were black as night, dotted with stars that shone brilliantly. I swallowed hard, staring into those dark orbs.

"Who are you?" Talon snapped, putting himself between the Mockingbird, and me and Kishil.

Behind me, bushes rustled and I spun around, my hand going to the knife in my belt.

"It's Elu," Kishil whispered.

"That's not Elu," Talon pointed out.

"No, you idiot. Elu is coming... to help us deal with," Kishil waved his hands in the direction of the Mockingbird and shrugged, "whoever that is."

"Young matriarch," the Mockingbird purred. I winced at the formal title. Was this when the Spirits would finally tell me that I'd failed? That I didn't deserve to be a matriarch and there had been some kind of grave mistake?

My heart clenched. I'd changed my mind somewhere during this little journey. I'd come to think of *myself* as a matriarch. Maybe it was because everyone kept using it as if it was my name, I wasn't sure, but I had begun to think of myself as a matriarch. I didn't know if I'd be able to handle having that new identity stripped from me now.

The identity that the three men surrounding me—I smiled to Elu as he stepped from the bushes and came immediately to my side—seemed to like.

"Be calm, young matriarch. I'm not here for that." The Mockingbird canted his head in a very bird-like way.

"What is he tal—" Talon sputtered.

"Sage, who is this?" Kishil interrupted, turning to face me directly.

I swallowed, opening my mouth to speak. The Mockingbird was here. He wasn't just speaking in my mind, flitting around as a bird to torment me. He was here. It was indisputable proof that the dream I'd had wasn't just a dream.

"This is the Mockingbird," I whispered.

Kishil's eyes tightened. He didn't seem to like that answer. Elu's eyes widened and Talon simply stared.

"You came looking for me once, asking about your task," the Mockingbird began.

"Yes, and you told me you couldn't tell me what it was." I crossed my arms over my chest, waiting for him to give us whatever news he'd come to deliver.

"You've grown even sassier since you began your journey, young matriarch. It's endearing," he commented with a chuckle.

"Excuse me?" Kishil snarled.

"Be calm, faithful one." The Mockingbird's eyes glinted with something, joy maybe. He did seem to enjoy confusing everyone.

"He can hear your thoughts," I whispered. "So try very hard not to blaspheme."

The Mockingbird's laughter boomed out around us as each man's eyes widened.

"Literally, every single one of them took the Creator or the Great Mother's name in vain the moment you finished your warning. Humans are hilarious." He wiped at his eyes.

I peered closer at the moisture rimming his eyes during his laughing fit. Stardust twinkled in the tears spilling from the corners of his eyes. It was bizarre. The Mockingbird was mocking us—as ironic as that sounded—and he was crying stardust. I shook my head, dispelling the strange thoughts.

"If you're not here to tell me I've failed my test..."

"Your test isn't over yet, young matriarch."

My throat went dry. Each of the guys moved closer to me, touching me in one way or another. It was strange to think that two of them had claimed me as their own in the short space of time we'd actually known each other. Elu hadn't participated in that particularly reckless decision yet. I viewed them as a packaged deal, so I was sure it was coming at some point.

"What do you mean?" My fingers dug into a hand, I wasn't even sure whose it was.

"I can't tell you anything else, only—" The Mockingbird looked pained, his face twisted up as he spoke. "Be wary. When you think it's finally over, be wary. I wish I could say more." With that, the Mockingbird folded in on himself with a flash of light and flew away, singing out as he glided through the trees around us.

I spun around to face the three of them. Talon's expression worried me. He looked cagey, like he might lash out at any moment. Kishil's anger seemed to be bleeding into a different emotion, finally. Elu was the only one who didn't seem shocked at all. He looked... awestruck.

"Are you okay?" I asked him, holding my hand out in invitation.

Elu grasped my fingers in his, pulling me into a hug. "I'm so glad you're okay," he whispered against my hair. His fingers slipped over the fresh marks on my shoulder and he pushed me away from his chest a little to examine me. "What's this?"

"Well—"

"I claimed her," Talon piped up. He didn't sound apologetic at all. I wasn't sure if I wanted him to, but this entire situation as odd. Elu's face was an unreadable mask as he glanced down at the marks on both my neck and my shoulder. His fingers traced each one, and it stung but I let him continue, it seemed important to him.

"I see," he finally murmured, brushing my hair away from my neck and smoothing it back. It had become a tangled, unbridled mess in the drama of the morning. I yawned, leaning my head against his hand. "What do you think he means, that it isn't over?"

"I don't really know," Kishil muttered. "Unless the traders are planning something else, I'm not sure. She survived them twice and managed to avoid being killed by two different scaly warriors."

"Who?" Elu snarled.

"Edutsi, at first, but Sage managed to talk him out of it. Storm wasn't so easily swayed. She almost gutted Kishil trying to prove a point. Our clever girl was brave. Then I challenged Storm for beta." Talon shrugged, reaching down to pick up a stick he could play with.

"You sound very calm about that," Elu remarked.

Talon grinned, shrugging again as he broke the stick apart into tiny pieces. I cringed as I watched him break it until there was nothing left but minute slivers of wood at his feet. It was such a destructive thing to do and served no purpose. I sighed, holding up my hand.

"The traders are probably the problem. Elu, you stayed behind. Were any of your people taken?" All eyes went to him as we waited for his answer. That was exactly what they didn't want to happen. They didn't want to be caged entertainment for these humans who didn't understand what they were.

"No. A few losses, but none were taken," he whispered.

"Who was lost?" Kishil inquired, his voice rough.

"Tonali, Jitsu, and Bright." Elu's eyes fell to the ground as he spoke the names.

"Until we meet again," I whispered. My hand fell on Elu's shoulder. He was a healer, or shaman of some kind, so this would hit him harder since he was spiritual.

"Damn. Bright was a good warrior, do you know what happened?" Talon asked.

"Decapitated," Elu whispered, his face twisting with his own rage as he said it. "In raptor form. The human who did it tried to make off with the head, but was stopped and killed."

Kishil nodded, rubbing his fingers over his eyebrows. It was a nervous tic for him, I'd noticed.

"What do we do now?" Talon questioned, glancing around the woods. The sun was high in the sky, the heat beating down on us while we discussed things and weighed our options.

"I think we stick to the plan. I need to get back to my village. Whatever final test the Mockingbird was trying to tell us about will happen on the way there, I'm sure."

"How do we prepare for that? This test?" Talon asked, his eyes searching the area for a threat.

"We can't. If he hadn't told us, we wouldn't have known it was coming. I think we should go on as if we don't know anything. I'm not sure if that makes sen—"

"It does," Kishil interjected, nodding. "If we change our course of action, it will cause the enemy to change theirs. Acting as if nothing has changed and being wary is the best course of action we have. Good thinking, Clever Girl."

I swallowed a smile, trying not to soak up his praise too much. He was fickle, that one. I took the first few steps in the direction of my village and looked over my shoulder. "Are you coming?"

The guys all muttered something under their breath to one another, something I couldn't quite catch. My lips quirked up in a smile as I pushed through the brush ahead. The ground was already giving way to more soggy soil. We would be in the swamplands soon. Once we reached them, my village wouldn't be far away at all.

I PICKED MY WAY THROUGH THE SWAMPY EARTH, GLANCING around for snakes. I preferred to use canoes when I had to go through the swamps, since the gators and snakes could be vicious here.

"You okay?" Talon murmured by my ear.

I jumped, swatting him on the arm as I did. I lost my footing and nearly fell, only to be saved from tumbling into the murky waters on our left by one of Talon's strong arms.

"Don't. Do. That!" I shrieked.

"Save you? Oh okay," he snickered, letting go of my hand.

I popped him on the arm again, narrowing my eyes. He knew exactly what I meant. He just wanted to be annoying. He was awfully playful for someone who looked so intimidating. My eyes scanned the tattoos weaving around his body and I tried to keep my eyes above his waist.

"Stop gawking at him and come on," Elu teased.

My cheeks heated and I marched past the two of them, catching up with Kishil. I looped my arm in his, tossing a look over my shoulder at the other two.

"I wasn't gawking."

"You're always gawking at him, I think he might be your favorite," Kishil quipped.

"I don't have a favorite," I huffed.

"Uh-huh, sure. If you had to choose one of us, I know it wouldn't be me." His tone was filled with humor, but a quick peek at his face let me know he believed some part of what he was saying. I slipped my hand up his arm to his neck, pulling him down to me.

"I don't have a favorite," I whispered again, staring into his brown and blue eyes. The colors swirled in such a delicious way that it was hard to look away from them.

Kishil offered me a weak smile, turning his head to kiss my wrist, before he started walking again.

"It's okay if you do, you know. I know this isn't how your culture works."

"What do you mean?" I picked my way around the puddles we were maneuvering through while I stayed beside him.

"Your people don't choose mates the same way we do. For scalies, we mainly let our animal choose. My raptor never took notice of any females before you, as much as I hate to admit that."

My eyes stayed glued to the ground in front of me. I was scared of what I might see if I looked at Kishil just then. I wasn't used to him being sincere, or sweet for that matter.

"All I'm saying is that I know your people do things differently. These marks," his hand brushed against the wound on my neck and then the one on my shoulder, "may not mean as much to you. When we get to your village, you might denounce us completely, or denounce only one of us," he whispered.

"I wouldn't do that to you," I replied. I was frustrated. He was right, this wasn't how my people did things. I should have been consulted before either of them claimed me and been given a choice of some kind. "I wouldn't separate you three, not for the world. It's easy to see how much you love one another."

I raised my eyes to glance at his face and smiled. His mouth was twisted to the side and he shook his head, waving me off.

"I don't love those idiots."

"We can hear you," Elu chided.

"I love all of you," Talon boomed out, his words laced with laughter.

I shook my own my head, my shoulders shaking with mirth as I listened to the three of them banter back and forth. They did love each other, it was easy to see once you were looking for the signs—they loved each other like brothers when they weren't in bed, and as lovers should when they were. It was a perfect relationship—one I had encroached upon. I didn't want to take anyone's place. Elu hadn't really spoken about the claiming marks, and I thought it might be because he was a little threatened by my presence.

From what I could tell, he was the least dominant, most sensitive one out of the three of them. I could be a threat to his position and I didn't want that. In the deepest parts of my heart, I hoped he knew I wasn't trying to take anyone from him.

If I didn't renounce their claim on me—and Kishil was right, I probably could since it wasn't my culture and they didn't ask for my consent—I'd be with all three of them, I understood that. Multiple marriages were common in my village. Nova had three husbands. Rain's mother had several husbands. My heart stuttered at the thought of him.

"What's wrong? She smells sad," Elu whispered, jogging up to my side. Before I could answer, he pulled me into a hug and I let myself get lost in his scent. He smelled like smoke and oils, a testament to his trade as a healer.

"I'm sorry, I'll try to control my emotions better." I sniffed, swallowing the tears that were clawing their way up my throat. There wasn't time to cry over Rain. I needed to get home and tell his mother what happened to him. His fathers should know how brave he was, how much honor he brought to his family.

"You don't have to control your emotions—if you even can—it's not a problem. We are used to knowing what other members of the pack are feeling, Sage. We're just worried about you. What's wrong?" Talon's voice was calm, soothing, as his chest pressed against my back and he wrapped his arms around both Elu and me.

Kishil remained to the side, just watching.

"I was thinking about how Rain's mother and fathers should

know how brave he was at the end. He brought a lot of honor to his family. He died gracefully, even though he was murdered. It's a big deal for my people." My voice shook and I buried my face in Elu's chest once again, soaking up all the good and happy energy he seemed to possess all the time.

"Shh," Elu whispered against the top of my head. "It's okay. It's a feat for our people as well."

"Yes," Talon murmured. "Our warriors value good deaths. Dying in battle or as an elder in your bed is the only acceptable way to go. Gunner tried to take that from your Rain, but he didn't succeed. Rain accepted his fate so that you could be the best matriarch you can for your people. He was very brave."

"Thank you." The sniffles were embarrassing. I pulled away from Elu, wiping at my nose and drying my cheeks. Despite my best efforts, some tears had spilled over. At least I wasn't on the ground sobbing like I wanted to.

Kishil pulled me into a hug, holding me tight against his chest. His heartbeat thudded loud enough for me to hear, even with my weak human ears.

"I'm sorry that things have been taken from you, Clever Girl. I'll do what I can to right the wrongs that have been done to you, like a good mate."

"Thank you." I shook my head, unable to hold back the tears now. Kishil's random spurts of sweetness were going to push me over the age. "You'll be good mates, all of you. I mean, both of you. Elu hasn't—"

Elu huffed and a nick of pain made me cry out. I glanced down to my other shoulder, surprised to see three marks that mirrored Talon's. My eyes went wide as I glanced at him.

"I was going to wait and claim you the way it's meant to be done. These two have no respect for tradition," he muttered. "But I can't have you thinking you're unwanted. The four of us are stuck together now, matriarch."

I swallowed, letting that sink in. He was right. The four of us were bound together now. I glanced at the wounds on my shoulders and my hand flew to the cuts on my neck. They were deep enough to scar, which was the point apparently. I took a deep breath, watching their faces as I nodded.

"The four of us, I think I like that," I finally whispered. "How is it supposed to be done?" I asked Elu, as I began walking again. We were making good time and we'd be at my village before nightfall at this pace. It was strange to think that the raptor village had been so close this whole time and I'd had no idea. I didn't think my mother did either, but I'd have to ask her to be sure.

"You're supposed to mark your mates in front of the village—yours or theirs, it doesn't matter—and say your promises to one another." Elu bumped his shoulder against mine playfully as we walked side by side.

The back of my skirt flew up and I swatted at the hand—probably Talon's—that was responsible.

"Stop that! So you owe me promises, hm?" I looked over my shoulder, glaring at Talon. He punched Kishil in the arm and I laughed. Maybe I'd been wrong about who was assaulting my rear end.

"I made you promises already," Kishil reminded me with a wicked grin.

"That you did," I hummed the words, tapping my chin.

"I promised to never leave you." Talon's smile was beautiful, his curls falling in his face and making him look shy, even when I knew better.

"I guess I'm the only one who owes you promises," Elu grumbled, sliding his hand into mine.

"I suppose you're right. So what do you promise me, Elu?" His eyes met mine for a moment, his pupils elongating as he chewed his lip.

"I promise to be the glue in your life that holds everything together. When things are wrong, I'll fix them. If I'm what's wrong, I'll fix myself. If our other mates are the problem, I'll knock their heads together until they stop acting like the fools they are. I'll be the best mate I can, and I won't leave you unless you ask."

My heart skipped a beat and my feet came to a stop as I listened to his words. It was the sweetest thing anyone had ever said to me. Elu halted his steps, smiling at me as he backtracked until he was face to face with me once again. I tilted my chin up, offering my lips for a kiss

"Do you accept my promise, mate?" His voice was husky.

I nodded, leaning up on my tiptoes to brush my lips across his. I'd never been patient. Elu kissed me sweetly, softly pecking my lips until I opened for him, letting his tongue slowly massage my own. A soft moan escaped me when his teeth grazed my tongue. Elu's hands changed, sliding from my sides down to my ass, gripping it roughly beneath my skirt.

"By the Creator," Kishil muttered, glancing down at his hardening cock.

"Me too." Talon audibly swallowed, his eyes shifting to his raptor's as he watched Elu play my body like an instrument.

"I want to have you, here, in the middle of these woods," Elu breathed against my mouth.

My pussy clenched at the thought of them taking me on the ground. It was wild, but so were they. It was fitting. My heart fluttered when a new set of fingertips grazed my sides, pulling me back against a hard chest and an equally hard cock. I took a deep breath, rolling my hips against whoever was behind me. A tattooed arm came into view as a hand loosely collared my throat. Talon.

"I second that idea," he growled against my ear. His voice was pure sex dripping against my skin. I could listen to him talk forever. And the things he said during sex...

A warm mouth pressed against the back of my knee and I almost fell over. It tickled and felt amazing all at once. Kishil chuckled, steading my legs with his hands as his mouth move up the back of my thigh, nipping at the skin as he went.

"You're all trying to kill me," I murmured, my heart racing. Three sets of laughter rang out in the quiet woods.

Elu tossed me a wicked grin as he slipped his hand beneath my skirt, testing the wetness between my thighs. He groaned, slipping his fingers between the slick folds he found there, circling my clit. I shivered, leaning my head back against Talon.

He took the opportunity to kiss down the column of my neck, closing his mouth over the bend near my throat. He sucked, hard, and I hissed in a breath as so many sensations filled me at once. Pain. Pleasure. Mouths. Fingers. I was starting to wonder how women handled multiple lovers on a daily basis—this was sensation overload.

"We won't kill you," Kishil murmured against the back of my leg, just below my ass. He kept finding the most sensitive, strangest places on my body to kiss. I wiggled when his breath tickled the area again and he bit down, punishment for moving.

"Eeep!" I squealed, instinctively leaning forward against Elu.

Talon took his chance to push my skirt up my hips, his fingers digging into the soft flesh and pulling me back against his hard cock. He didn't enter me, just slid against my wet seam, bumping into my clit and Elu's hand. It was pure torture.

"What do you want, love?" Elu whispered, pulling his hand away and slipping it into his mouth. I watched as his tongue curled around his fingers, sucking away every bit of me.

It was hypnotizing. I opened my mouth to speak, but a tongue on my clit cut me short. My fingers flew down to Kishil's hair, holding him where he sat on the ground between my legs, his tongue slipping between my wet folds and tantalizing my clit.

Talon rocked his hips back and forth, slipping along my entrance, and then rubbing across my clit where Kishil's mouth lay. My eyebrows shot up my forehead as I peered down between my legs. Kishil's eyes were on me, his tongue flicking along my clit and the head of Talon's cock, daring me to answer Elu's question.

Something about seeing Kishil, the alpha, kneeling between my legs with a cock brushing over his tongue, pushed me over the ledge. I slid my hand up Elu's neck to his tattooed scalp, and pulled him toward me, biting down on his lip.

He snarled in response.

Talon's hand came down on my ass hard and I moaned.

"Please," I whimpered.

"Please what?" Talon growled behind me. "Tell me what you want—exactly what you want—and you'll get it, Clever Girl."

"I want—" My body shuddered again when Elu pushed my top down, my tits falling free. He plucked at my nipples, twisting and teasing them, while I tried to answer Talon. I bit my tongue, trying to focus. "I want you to take me from behind while Kishil licks me—and you—and I want Elu to take my mouth," I answered, panting the words as Kishil's mouth did wicked things between my legs. I was soaking wet and needy.

"Mmm, we'll need to resituate for that," Talon purred, pulling on my hips until I lost my connection with Kishil.

I felt the loss immediately. Kishil lay on his back and beckoned me closer. I kneeled above his face, before leaning forward on my hands and knees over his body, my spine arched for Talon. I looked over my shoulder to see he and Elu kissing. Their tongues darted slowly in and out of the other's mouth, taking what they needed. Elu's hand wrapped around Talon's cock, pumping up and down.

It was so damn hot. I adored how they loved one another. It was the perfect arrangement.

Kishil's hands pulled on my hips, bringing my pussy closer to his face and he began licking me from my entrance to my clit. I moaned a low, throaty sound that caught the attention of both Talon and Elu.

Talon kept his eyes on me while pushing Elu down to his knees. I saw Elu's mouth close on his cock and I nearly lost it. I turned forward, lowering my own mouth down onto Kishil's cock. I wrapped my lips around him, sliding my tongue around the head and down his full length. I'd always loved this. It wasn't something many women in my village did, or so they said. I sucked hard on Kishil's cock and groaned when his hips jerked beneath me.

This was the most power a woman could hold over any man. Kishil was vulnerable, completely at my mercy, and I loved it. My hand cupped his balls as I bobbed and twisted my mouth up and down his length, taking him into my throat. The pop when the head of his cock met the back of my throat was intoxicating.

Kishil's tongue twined around my clit then delved at a different angle, slipping inside me. He fucked me with his mouth for what seemed like a forever, and then suddenly stopped, his mouth moving back to my clit. I moaned against his cock, sliding it out from my throat so I could catch my breath.

Something large pressed against my pussy and I looked over my shoulder, staring up at Talon. He ran his cock along my seam, once again teasing me. Every time the head bumped into Kishil's mouth near my clit, Kishil would slide his tongue over both of us simultaneously. It was maddening. I kept my eyes on Talon's as he wrapped his hand around his dick, lining himself up at my entrance.

"Yes," I panted, arching backward.

Kishil wrapped his arms around my thighs, holding me in place above his face as Talon slowly entered me. I moaned, relishing the stretch between my thighs. He felt amazing.

"By the Creator, you're fucking heaven," Talon muttered under his breath, slowly rocking his hips against my backside until he found his pace.

I turned my head back around, with my body rocking forward with every thrust from Talon. My eyes fluttered shut, focusing on the sensations between my thighs. Kishil sucked on my clit, flicking his tongue against it in a steady, aching rhythm.

Talon filled me, over and over, stretching me as wide each time he slid inside my core. He bottomed out against my cervix, pushing my head forward, and I felt something warm against my face.

My eyes flew open to find Elu kneeling in front of me, his hand wrapped around his cock as he watched our little show, straddling Kishil's thighs. His eyes flashed with need and I licked my lips, watching the tiny drop of precum that beaded on his cock. I flicked my tongue out to taste him, relishing the salty flavor.

Talon pounded harder inside me and I whimpered when I felt Kishil's tongue leave my clit. He shimmied around beneath me until he was kneeling beside me, bent over my back. I blew across the tip of Elu's cock, trying not to focus on what Kishil was doing when his tongue pressed against my back side. I came, hard, with my hand wrapped around Elu's dick. I jerked him in time to my orgasm and when the worst of the tremors stopped, I wrapped my mouth around him. I slipped my mouth lower, pressing as far down as I could and continued massaging the rest with my hand.

"I think she likes that," Kishil chuckled, removing his tongue and slipping a finger deep into my ass.

I groaned against Elu and his hands twined in my hair as he cursed under his breath. I stared up into his eyes, opening my mouth in invitation for him to take control. Kishil maneuvered himself back underneath me, his hot tongue sliding against my clit.

He didn't need to be asked twice. Elu pulled on my hair, a gentle sort of pain, and began thrusting in and out of my mouth. His cock slipped into my throat, it was hard to breath around it, but I could manage. The snarl building in his chest as he fucked my mouth was worth it.

I moaned out against his cock when Talon clicked behind me, his hips slapping against my ass over and over while he pounded into me.

Every time Talon's cock hit my cervix, a zip of pain arced across my nerves, with just enough pain to make me tremble with need. Kishil moaned happily against my pussy, circling my clit in an agonizingly slow pace. I arched my back as much as I could—Kishil's arms still held me in place above his face—and pulled my mouth back from Elu's cock, swirling my tongue around the edges of the head as I caught my breath.

"That's right, Clever Girl," Talon praised behind me. His thrusts never slowed. Sweat beaded on my forehead—body heat from four people could rival the sun, I'd decided.

"Mmm," I mumbled around the cock in my mouth, grinding my clit against Kishil's mouth while Talon thrust into me. I slid a hand over Kishil's cock, working a tight fist up and down in a slow motion. I twisted my hand in sync with my mouth, whimpering when Talon bit down on the back of my neck.

"Oh!" I cried out, my skin prickling with goosebumps as pleasure coursed through my body. I writhed against them, trying to focus on working Kishil's cock as I swallowed Elu's in my throat.

"Oh Great Mother," Elu moaned, his cock swelling against the back of my throat. He pulled out of my mouth at the last moment, jerking his dick in front of me. Warm jets of cum landed on my tits and Kishil's cock below me. I bent down, closing my mouth on Kishil once again, sucking him clean as Talon's cock seemed to get bigger inside me. I rolled my hips back against him, a silent plea for more.

"Stay. Still," Talon ordered between powerful thrusts, digging his fingers into my hips as he slammed mercilessly inside me.

I moaned against Kishil's cock, twirling my tongue along his shaft. He groaned against my pussy as his dick swelled, he was so close. I dragged my teeth gently across his cock and he cried out, shooting cum into my mouth, over and over. I swallowed, trying to catch all of it, but pulled back to breathe, finding more jets headed toward my tits. I watched in wonder as the hot liquid pooled on my flesh.

Talon snarled, pulling my hips back against him as he slammed into me. It hurt but it felt *so good*. I looked over my shoulder at him, noticing his eyes were wild. He slipped his hand around my neck, gripping my throat loosely, but holding my gaze to his.

"Look at me. I want to see you cum on my cock, Sage," he snarled.

I lost it. I could listen to him talk all day long, but when he said things like that, it made my toes curl. Kishil flicked his tongue against my clit at the same time Talon slid a finger into my ass. I nearly screamed, writhing against the two of them. Talon smirked for a moment, my pussy spasming around his cock, milking him, and pulling him deeper inside me.

"Ohh," he moaned as he expanded, coating my insides with hot jets of cum.

I panted through the aftershocks of my own orgasm, resting my hand on his at my neck. His grip loosened and I sighed, my eyes fluttering shut.

"Trying. To. Kill me," I panted between shivers.

Someone pulled me into their lap—I wasn't even sure who—and I curled up against their chest, letting darkness pool behind my lids.

"Nap now, sweet matriarch," someone murmured.

"I love you," another voice whispered.

I opened my mouth to tell them I loved them too. I did. All three of them. Somehow, in the midst of this journey, I'd found three pieces of my heart I hadn't known were missing. But all that came out was a yawn.

Chapter 19

Elu

I stared at the wounds on her shoulders and neck. A satisfied chirp filled my chest as I cradled Sage against my chest.

"You do love her, don't you?" Kishil asked in a quiet voice.

I glanced to where he and Talon were squatting not too far away. I held Sage close, kissing the top of her hair. We'd worn her out, and she'd need a little bit of rest before she could finish the walk to her village. I planned on changing and letting her ride on my back the rest of the way. She was going to be sore after what Talon had given her. I'd been on the receiving end of those thrusts before, and they felt amazing when they were happening, but made it hard to walk for the next couple of days.

"You don't? And don't lie, Kishil. I've seen the way you look at her, even before you marked her. Your raptor wanted her from the beginning, didn't he?"

Kishil swished his mouth to the side, his shoulders sagging. He knew I was right. Talon clapped him on the back and grinned.

"I don't know why you two are so emotional about it. I love her. I'd die for her. I'd have killed Storm for her without question. There's no argument in my mind. That clever little matriarch is ours, she belongs to all three of us." Talon nodded when he was done speaking, as if that was the end of it.

"Do you think she'll keep us?" Kishil whispered.

I sucked in a breath, staring down at the woman covered in white markings. She was the future of her people. Kishil was the future of ours. The villages were close enough that we could travel back and forth, if she was willing to make this work. I scanned the markings on her tawny skin. Some of the white paint had been marred with blood and now showed red against her copper flesh.

"I do," I breathed, running my fingers through the hair hanging loose on her back. "I think we call to something wild inside of her."

Kishil grunted and Talon grinned. I sat there quietly, waiting for our girl to finish her nap after the exhaustion we'd put her through. It probably wasn't the best strategic idea we'd ever had—fucking in the middle of the woods when we knew an enemy was coming for us—but sometimes fucking just happens.

I jerked awake at the sound of a twig snapping. Talon snarled, maneuvering to his feet. Kishil's skin was already stretching, ready to shift into his raptor and shred anyone stupid enough to sneak up on us while we had our—where was she?

"Relax, you foolish men," Sage called out from the bushes as she stepped through, adjusting her skirt to cover her ass again. "I had to pee. I didn't think it would be polite to do it in Elu's lap so—"

"Oh by the Creator," Kishil huffed, trying to rein in the shift he'd started.

Talon snorted and I cocked an eyebrow. "I enjoy lots of things... urine has never been one of them."

"How do you know if you've never tried it?" Sage asked, her voice innocent. I sputtered, looking around to my other two mates for help. She couldn't possibly be serious! Urine! She tossed me a wink and launched herself at Talon, who caught her as if she was light as a feather.

"Someone got her energy back," he snickered.

"Shhh," she whimpered. "I'm convinced you three are trying to kill me with orgasms. It's not a bad way to die, I suppose. But I'd prefer not to die right this moment."

"What she means is, we're the best she's ever had," Kishil sang from his place beside me.

"I never said that!" Sage's face was burning red as her eyes widened and she glared at Kishil.

"Oh, so all of your lovers have made you pass out from cumming too hard?" His eyebrows arched, waiting for her denial.

"Well..."

"Like I said, the best!" He raised his arms in some kind of victory. A boot came flying through the air, smacking him in the side of the head.

Sage scrambled farther up Talon's chest, hiding in his arms.

"Did you just throw a boot at me, woman?" Kishil hissed.

"No. Nope. Talon did it!" she squealed, even as Talon's fingers tickled her side.

"Oh, did I?" he snarled playfully by her neck.

"Eeeep! No! No! Sorry! Can I have my boot back please? Great Mother, you three are the worst," she grumbled. The sparkle in her eyes told me she was enjoying herself though.

Kishil grabbed the boot and stomped toward her, shoving it onto her foot.

"Let's go," he said, pinching the bridge of his nose.

"I'm not the worst," I whispered, batting my eyelashes at Sage. She grinned from ear to ear and shook her head.

"No, no you're not."

I shifted into my raptor, groaning as my body stretched and scales pierced my skin. I shook my head when the transformation was over. Everyone always commented on how fast I changed compared to others, but to me it felt like it took an eternity. Several clicks rang out from my snout, a chirp following them.

Talon moved toward me, placing Sage on my back with care. He was a savage lover but a tender man. It was one of the things I loved about him.

Sage leaned forward, wrapping her arms loosely around the base of my neck. Her thighs clenched tightly against my flanks. The heat of her pressed against my back was titillating, but we had things to do. We needed to get her home, to her people.

Kishil and Talon changed next, and soon we were walking in the direction of her village. Sage gave us directions, telling us when to veer a certain way, what landmarks to follow or avoid.

"There's a gulley not too far from here. The terrain there is treacherous, I wouldn't take a horse through it, so I think we should avoid it. Go left at the split tree," she called out. I don't think she realized just how sensitive our hearing truly was. We could hear her fine without her raising her voice.

I padded along at an even pace, clicking out to Talon and Kishil every few feet. The forest had grown quiet and I didn't trust that. Sage seemed to be on alert as well, as she hadn't spoken for several minutes, which was unlike her.

She was usually full of life and questions, or making observations of everything that seemed interesting to her. I came to a slow stop when we reached a large tree split down the middle. It looked like it must have been hit by lightning years ago, but it hadn't died. Past the scarred bark, new branches grew on each side, filled with tiny blue flowers I'd never seen before. My head canted to the side and a chirpy click rang out as I studied it.

"The shamans say this was a holy place once. The Great Mother gave birth to life here, beneath the Ezeltree. When her creations began murdering one another she stopped bringing new life—new creatures—into the world, and left the Ezeltree as a reminder to us that we should respect life." Sage's voice was reverent. She hadn't struck me as someone who was overly spiritual, but I suppose meeting a Spirit could change that for a person.

I turned left, picking up my pace. We were close. I could smell humans already. Talon snarled at my side and I reached out, nipping his shoulder playfully. I clicked to him in warning, he needed to calm down. We didn't want an incident when we met our mate's people for the first time. They were going to think we were strange anyway. It didn't sound like Sage's people had much experience with scalies. If I could groan in this body, I would. I hoped they weren't prejudiced against our kind, or at least that they were willing to put their prejudices behind them for the sake of their matriarch...

SAGE

THE SMELL OF COOKING MEAT REACHED MY NOSE. WE WEREN'T far from my people at all. I tapped on Elu's side, gaining his attention.

"Let me down," I whispered. "I should be on Kishil when we meet them, since he's the alpha. Small gestures matter in politics, Elu." I pressed my lips softly to the back of his head as he came to a stop, chuffing. Sliding down his side, I turned to Kishil.

He stared back at me with blazing blue and amber eyes. Elu pushed me toward him with his snout and I huffed.

"Impatient," I accused, as I made my way to Kishil. I wrapped my arm around his neck and he bent down far enough for me to throw my leg over. My fingers dug into his shoulders as he rose to his full height, moving to the front of the pack.

Kishil set a slow but steady pace, looking straight ahead the rest of the way to the village.

"Sage!"

I rose up off my bottom to look for the source of the familiar voice. Chayton came running toward us and then slowed, his eyes dropping to my mount and the two other raptors flanking me.

"It's okay," I murmured with a smile. I'd missed him. He came up beside me just as a crowd from the village began to tumble into the edge of the woods behind him. A murmur swept through the crowd as they welcomed me home. I could only pick out bits and pieces of their comments, but I was sure my guys were getting the brunt of it.

"...scalies..."

"...where has she been?"

My chin tilted into the air and I leveled them with the most regal stare I could muster. The crowd split and my mother came running toward me. Either she wasn't afraid of scalies at all, or she was so excited to see me she didn't notice them, because she unceremoniously pulled me from Kishil's back, wrapping me in a hug.

"My curious child," she murmured against my hair. "I kept asking the Great Mother to bring you home. You were gone for so long, I'd begun to worry. But here you are! In one piece, and with... friends? Suitors?" Her eyes twinkled with mischief and I let myself laugh in her arms.

The sound of bones popping rang out behind us and the majority of my people took a quick step back, away from the scalies as they changed. I pulled away from my mother and addressed them.

"It's rude to watch a scaly shift. I didn't know this either, since there is a lot we don't know about their culture. I expect that will probably change soon." I bit the inside of my cheek, searching for the right words.

"Of course." Mom nodded and pressed her palms to her cheeks, looking at me. "You must come tell me and the elders everything about your journey. What was your test?"

I swallowed, trying to think of how to tell her that my test wasn't over yet. An arm came around my waist and I glanced down—it was Kishil. I leaned back against him, thankful for the support.

"Mom, the Matriarch Ayasha, please meet Kishil, the alpha of the raptor pack who live not far from here."

"Well," she sputtered, her eyebrows inching up for her forehead in surprise. "Well met, Kishil, of course. I had no idea there was a scaly village near us." Mom reached out for a handshake.

"Well met, matriarch. We haven't lived here long, we came from the plains." Kishil clasped his hand around her forearm and I moved away, allowing them their introduction.

"And who are your friends?"

"These are my fr—mates—Talon and Elu." Kishil seemed to stumble over the words. It was the first time I'd heard him refer to the guys as his mates.

"Oh, do you share a female mate, then? Or is it just you three?" Mom's smile was transparent.

I could hear the hope in my mother's voice. I almost snorted. She had made no secret about hoping I'd fall in love one day, sooner rather than later.

"I'm Elu, matriarch, it's an honor. We do share a female mate. If you'll excuse Kishil's fumbled words, this is a new development. We weren't all mated until very recently," he whispered. Elu's eyes searched out mine and my cheeks heated. "In our culture, men are not mates until they find the woman that binds them."

"I see," Mom sang, turning to me. Her hands grabbed my shoulders and she pulled me in for a hug, whispering near my ear. "Congratulations, daughter, they look like fine men."

"You aren't upset that they're scalies?" I was glad she supported my decision, but I'd expected some kind of pushback, some sort of emotional response. Instead, I received unwavering support. She was amazing that way.

"No, why would I be? They're here with you and that's all that matters. If The Spirits lead you to them, it was for a reason." Her eyes shone with warmth and nothing but love and understanding. I swallowed the emotion threatening to spill out of me and nodded, hugging her tight.

"I'm Talon," he mumbled, side-eyeing all the people surrounding us. "Our clever girl is the best thing that's happened to our pack in a long time. But I think we need to get your people back into the confines of your village, the woods may not be safe right now."

Mom's eyes snapped to him, her back straightening instantly. She raised a hand and five warriors ran to her side, their spears and knives drawn as they circled our little party, waiting for orders.

"What has happened, Sage?"

"Let's get in the village, like Talon said. I'll tell you everything once we're settled, I promise." I tilted my chin up, looking her in the eye. My mother was the Matriarch Ayasha. She was a legend among my people. She'd calmed a raging scaly with nothing but her wit and kindness, and saved our village the day she was confirmed. I could only hope to be half the matriarch she was.

"You'll be the best matriarch of them all," my father called out from the crowd, and my face split into a grin. I ran to him, letting him wrap me up in a hug. He kissed my hair, laughing as he ushered everyone toward the village.

"I see you've been busy," he whispered quietly as our people moved around us.

"Very."

"Well, well. You'll tell us all about it with the elders momentarily. For now, take your men to our chickee and get them some clothes. Nova might try to steal them from you if they remain naked for to much longer."

I turned, glancing over my shoulder, and sure enough Nova was following behind Kishil, Talon, and Elu. Her bright, mischievous eyes kept falling lower and lower down their backs, with an appreciative grin quirking her lips.

"Ah, you might be right," I muttered.

My father boomed out a laugh, clapping me on my shoulder. "Don't worry, I think they prefer you."

Talon looked over his own shoulder, scowling at the old woman as he batted her hand away from his backside. Kishil's eyes found mine and I laughed at the hopelessness I found there. They most definitely preferred me.

I TOSSED THE PANTS AT THE GUYS AGAIN, PRAYING TO THE Great Mother that they'd listen to me this time.

"You have to wear clothing in the village," I snapped.

"Your men wear strange pants," Kishil whined, stepping into the clothing. As long as he was putting them on, he could whine as much as he wanted to.

Elu and Talon pulled their pants on from their seats on the floor, not making any further comments about the clothing they were being offered.

"Those are my father's pants, Kishil. Stop being a terror," I huffed.

"There are beads on them. Only our women wear beads."

I threw my hands in the air and stormed from the chickee, heading toward the center of the village. The elders would be waiting for me there. I had no doubts that my three guys would be able to find me with their heightened senses whenever they were done pouting over their attire.

I swung up onto the raised platform and strolled to the middle of the room, heading straight for my mother.

"Sage!" She turned and smiled, brushing her hands over my freshly washed face. I had looked rough when we first arrived, and had decided to remedy that before I explained our situation to the elders.

"Where are your men?" Nova asked from her seat at the low table.

"Off being insufferable, as men do," I groaned.

"Ah, young love," she teased. "If they give you any trouble, send them to me. I can train them up right for you, young one." Nova's eyes twinkled with mischief and I couldn't help the smile tugging at my lips.

After the way Kishil had been acting about the damned pants, I was tempted. A night or two with Nova might make him see how reasonable I was. On the floor, beside the table for the elders, my father's shoulders shook with silent laughter.

One day he was going to tell me how he knew the things he knew. It had been a mystery my entire life. I was convinced my mother knew the secret, and I wanted to know as well.

"Ah, there they are. Fine specimens," Nova drawled, elbowing one of the other elders beside her.

I snorted and turned to see the three men clambering into the chickee. Talon towered over the other two, remaining in the back. A series of whispers swept through the elders as my men approached. Talon's eyes found mine and remained there as they crossed the room to me. I held out a hand to Kishil and stood with my back to Elu. Talon remained behind us, guarding our backs if I wasn't mistaken, while we turned our attention to the elders.

"Tell us what happened, daughter," Mom urged.

I recounted everything that happened from the moment I woke up surrounded by the elders that night to my arrival back at our village. I told them how I was taken, how I came to befriend the scalies—skipping over the more personal details, of course—and of the warning from the Mockingbird.

I sucked in a breath when it was over, scanning the room for their reactions. My mother stood with her hands clasped at her waist, her face unreadable. The elders' faces were in varying stages of shock. A woman outside the chickee cried openly—Rain's mother—as her husbands wrapped their arms around her, trying to comfort a wound that would never heal. The loss of a child wasn't something a parent was meant to endure.

"The Mockingbird spoke to you directly?" an old warrior asked me.

I nodded, my spine straight as I waited for the next round of questions.

"Who are these traders? Are they coming to the village?" Nova asked, her eyes hard. Several grunts of agreement came from the outskirts of the room. Only The elders and the matriarchs were allowed to speak during this, but anyone could watch.

I chewed my bottom lip, nodding.

"I don't have all the answers about the traders. The time I spent with them was limited to threats and their weak abuse. If it's okay, I'm sure that my mates can explain them to you. They have been dealing with these traders for years, where they're from."

"Did they follow them here?" I wasn't sure which elder had spoken. My shoulders sagged at her words. It was a possibility that the traders finding this part of the land was in part the fault of the raptors, but I couldn't reconcile blaming them for it. The scalies had migrated, that's all.

"We haven't seen the traders since we moved to the area, and we've been here for a couple of years now," Kishil began. He clasped his hands behind his back, standing tall as he addressed the elders directly. I knew this had to be hard for him, being questioned by humans. Knowing that a Sun Tribe had banished his mother for loving his father broke my heart. My people were not cruel by nature and it made me question the leadership of the other Sun Tribes.

"They aren't traders at all, though that's how they introduce themselves. They're raiders. They come to our land on ships—large canoes with wings—that they load up with our goods, in exchange for very little. That's the best-case scenario. The worst-case scenario, as Sage witnessed, is they burn down a village and enslave its people. Their weapons are superior to ours, harder, deadlier. They use metal in them. We aren't sure where they come from, but they showed up every summer on the plains. When entire tribes began to go missing, we moved our people out of their reach, or so we thought." Kishil's eyes fell to the floor.

"They're dangerous," he continued. "They do not respect our ways, though at least one of them can speak the Language of the Sun."

"What? What do you mean?" My mother demanded, her eyes growing fiercer by the second.

"The village that he's speaking of," I started, my voice catching on the emotion the memories brought back. "They razed it. The Matriarch there was murdered in front of her people and any survivors—mostly women—were chained together. It was unlike anything I've ever seen."

"And you believe these men are coming here?" Mom's voice was hard, her eyes searching out the edges of the chickee for her favored warriors.

"Yes. The Mockingbird said to be wary, this is me trying to heed his warning. These men will stop at nothing until they get what they want."

"What do they want?" Nova's bright eyes bore into me. I had a feeling she already knew the answer.

"The scalies. They call them dragons, and when they found out they were partly human as well as dinosaur, they made it clear they wanted to capture them and take them to their homeland, wherever that is."

Nova rose to her feet, moving to the middle of the room to stand by Mom. The rest of the elders followed her, and one by one they touched their hands to the mark on my forehead that named me as the next matriarch.

"We will stand with you. Invaders have come to these lands before and they will come again. We'll prepare the warriors for whatever is going to come, young one. You've been given a gift by the Great Mother with this warning—don't take it for granted."

I nodded to Nova then turned to my guys. "Let's get the village prepared for a raid."

Their eyebrows shot up their foreheads before they followed me out of the chickee. It seemed not even Kishil knew what I meant. Maybe his mother had been better at keeping our people's secrets than I thought.

Chapter 20

Kishil

I screwed my nose up as Sage pulled thin lines of twine through the trees near the village. My eyes dropped to the random objects in the basket I held. Turtle shells, bones tied together, a few pieces of broken pottery, all things that would make a lot of noise when rattled. It was a good alarm system, I was proud of her.

She glanced over her shoulder at me and winked. I was staring again. It was strange, being in a human village. These were some of the same people who had exiled my mother for nothing other than falling in love with my father. They didn't approve of what he was, and they had thought he would be a danger to her and any children they had. She'd died from the breathing sickness when I was young, and I remember my father crying, wishing he could share his shifter-healing with her. He'd loved her more than anything in the world.

He died in the next battle our people fought in. To this day, I think he may have just given up. I shrugged away the morbid thoughts. Elu was in the village, speaking with their shaman and healers. He was too curious about such things to be denied the chance to learn new methods.

Talon prowled nearby in raptor form, scenting and listening for any signs of danger.

"What will we do when this is over?" The question flew from my lips before I could stop it.

"What do you mean?" Sage turned to me, taking the clinking objects and tying them to her perimeter wire.

"Once the danger has passed, I'll have to return to my people. We just lost an alpha, it will be hard for a while."

"I've been thinking about that," Sage admitted.

I prepared myself for her response. She was going to tell me that the distance would be too hard, that not seeing each other every day would be torture. If she asked me to leave my people behind, what would I d—

"I think since you three are mates, as well as being mated to me, you could share the responsibility of your people. That way, only one or two of you ever needs to be there at once, except for special occasions of course. And if you're not taking me, you can travel much faster between my village and yours."

I blinked, my mouth flopping open like a fish out of water as she spoke. She'd gone and fixed the thing that had been worrying me since I marked her. I wrapped my hand in her hair and pulled her in for a kiss. I sipped at her lips, savoring the taste of her.

"What was that for?" Sage laughed against my mouth, brushing her lips across mine between words.

"You're amazing, Clever Girl," I murmured, staring down into her light brown eyes. She really was too. It wasn't just something that I needed to say to get her in my bed. She was amazing. A weight was lifted from my chest. "I think Talon and Elu will agree to that. My people shouldn't have any qualms about it either, since they know how close we are."

"Good," she sighed, pecking my cheek before going back to her task.

I made myself busy tying the loud trinkets along the line as we made our way closer to the village. Children brought basket after basket of the items to us as we made our way around the perimeter. When the work was done, Sage examined her new alarm system.

"What will you do about the river?"

"Someone will have to watch it. I could cross and tie a line through the trees on the other side, but I'm not sure we'd hear it. I don't think they'll approach from that direction anyway. If Gunner is following us, he will have to come the same way we did." Her fingers smoothed the braid hanging over her shoulder. Sweat beaded on her brow, proof of the work she'd just done for her people.

"Daughter! Come!"

My head snapped in the direction of the village. Talon shot past us, a blur of green, as I took Sage's hand in my own.

"What do you hear?" she asked, her voice beginning to tremble.

"Your mother. Let's go." I pulled her along behind me, running for the village. The children who had been bringing us the trinkets for the fence huddled between the legs of a woman who must be their mother.

"Get them into the forest. Don't come back until me or the Matriarch Ayasha find you. Take any children you find, run!" Sage ordered. Her voice was frantic but quiet as we began running again, turning into the center of the village.

In the middle of the settlement, where the grass had long been trampled into bare dirt from so many feet walking on it, Gunner stood with a bow pointed at a young boy.

The young boy who had greeted us first, before anyone else.

A snarl rippled through my throat as Sage struggled to catch her breath beside me.

"Chayton," she whispered.

Chapter 21

Sage

"Chayton," I breathed, searching the area to figure out what the situation was. My mother stood with warriors in front of her and the elders. My father's bow was aimed at Gunner, his finger on the arrow, waiting for the perfect moment.

"There you are, woman," the yellow-haired idiot sang. "I've been looking for you and your friends."

"Well, you've found us," I answered, taking a step closer to my brother.

"Ah, ah, not a step closer. Not until you've agreed to hand over one of your friends there." Gunner tilted his chin to the left and then to the right. Talon prowled on the outer edges of the circle in raptor form and Elu mirrored him in human form.

"That's not going to happen, you know that already." I glanced toward the river, and around the familiar faces in the village. I didn't see any pale faces looking back at me except for Gunner. My eyebrow raised as I took another step.

Kishil made a noise behind me but I waved him off, holding my hands up in the air.

"Where are your men?" I called out.

Anger flashed in Gunner's eyes a second before he schooled his features into something more passive. He drew the bowstring back, aiming his arrow directly at Chayton.

"Nearby," he lied.

"In the woods again? With their bows?" I glanced over my shoulder to Kishil, whose eyebrows were cinched together as he began working the pieces of the puzzle.

"Yes!" Gunner kicked a bag at his feet in my direction. It skidded toward me and I lowered myself into a crouching position to examine its contents. Chains. The bag was full of chains. I tossed it to the side, disgusted.

"You're a liar," I purred. "A coward and a liar. I just came from those woods. If your men were behind us, we'd have heard them. You came from the river... where are your men, Gunner?"

He muttered under his breath, adjusting his aim. Chayton was stock-still but he didn't look afraid, which is all I could ask for. Men like Gunner fed on fear, they relished it, so giving him even a taste of what he wanted would only spur him on.

"We were attacked by water dragons," he hissed. "When we made it to the shore, what was left of my men were convinced that the dragons weren't worth the trouble and left. Is that what you want to hear, woman?"

Talon took a step toward him, a snarl ripping from his throat.

"Control your dragon or I'll kill the boy, I swear it!"

Talon stopped, raised himself high, and bayed out.

"What is it doing?" Gunner asked, his eyes widening in fear.

"Calling for help," I lied. The raptor village wasn't close enough to hear his call, but Gunner didn't know that there weren't more scalies with us. I took another step toward my brother. He was only a few feet away now.

A shrill bay came from the woods and I paused. A beautiful raptor flew toward us on two feet. Storm. I steeled myself for whatever chaos she was about to add to this already volatile situation.

The raptor came to a slow stop near Kishil. Her eyes met mine, and she bowed her head for a moment before chuffing at the man in question. A sense of pride swept through me. Storm was acknowledging me as someone deserving of her respect. After what had happened... that was progress.

"Make it stop! And stop moving!" He looked crazed, sweating in a heat he wasn't built for. His pale skin glowed red where the sun had punished him, only to reveal paler skin beneath the strange vest he wore as he moved.

"You've gone mad, Gunner," I told him, speaking in his own tongue now, grateful for the gift from the Mockingbird. "Your men abandoned you because they knew this path meant death for them. Look at your dragons." I held my arm out toward Talon. "They're going to rip you to shreds. If you harm that boy, I'll join them. Have you ever eaten human flesh?"

"What? You wouldn't—"

"I would. It's delicious if it's cooked right. My people have eaten their enemies for generations, it's why we don't have many."

"No."

I nodded, sidestepping toward Chayton, drawing the man's attention to me and away from the scalies. I shrugged, playing with the end of my braid.

"The trick is to carve the meat while your prey is still living, so that it's tender when you cook it. Humans toughen up so quickly." I licked my lips, now fully blocking Chayton from Gunner's bow.

Gunner cursed under his breath, turning toward Talon. He'd only managed a step or two toward the man before he spun around. Stealth wasn't on our side. Gunner was at the center of a large circle in the middle of the village, he could see everything.

Except behind him.

I peered over Gunner's shoulder and then quickly snapped my eyes back to his, taunting him as Kishil bent down to let his raptor take hold of his body. He grunted and Gunner turned, pointing his bow at a magnificent creature where a man had once stood.

"Get back, dragons!" he yelled at Kishil and Storm, as they lurched toward him then danced back. This looked like a game they had played a few times.

"Where are your men going?" I pressed. If we knew where they were heading, we could cut them off and stop them from telling their homeland about the scalies.

"To the ship, of course," Gunner spat, spinning around to point his bow at Talon, and finally Elu. Elu changed in an instant, morphing from a copper-skinned man to an almost yellow raptor. His scales were still moving into place when he struck for Gunner's arm.

The bow smacked him across the snout with a loud thud and he shook his head, circling the man with the other three raptors.

"Where is it? They might let you live if you tell me." Another lie. They were going to rip him limb from limb, and there was nothing I could or even wanted to do about it.

"Sage, what are you doing?" my father whispered. He must have snuck up behind me while I was focused on the drama unfolding before me. Chayton was nowhere to be found. "I can't understand what you're saying to him, it's bizarre. What can I do?"

"Nothing, they're only waiting for me to get this information and then he'll be—"

Talon surged forward and latched on to Gunner's arm, the one controlling the bow. The arrow loosed but skidded safely through the dirt at our feet. In seconds, Gunner was on the ground.

"Get it off of me!" he screamed.

Talon snarled, jerking on the arm. He was merely toying with him. That arm would have been torn from his body instantly if he'd wanted to do so. Kishil leapt on top of Gunner, burying his talons in his chest and abdomen. His screams grew higher and I winced. A glance around showed the people lingering in front of their homes turning away from the gruesome display.

Storm chirped happily as her snout closed over a femur.

"End this, Gunner," I whispered, kneeling near him and the nearly rabid scalies. "Tell me where they are."

"There's a beach—" He gasped between screams, his hands beating tirelessly against the raptors assaulting him. "S-s-southwest of here. Where the palms end," he groaned, his eyes searching out mine and begging for mercy.

I nodded before turning way. A final, torturous scream tore through the clearing and I looked for Elu. My yellow raptor was waiting, his eyes boring into me. "Go tell your people where they can find them, hurry, before they leave. If they make it back to their homeland with news that 'dragons' are men, we'll be overrun with these traders," I ordered.

Elu's head dipped, his tattoos visible as he bowed to me. He didn't wait for more words, instead he ran toward the woods, skirting past anyone in his way. The faint jingle of the alarm wire sounded only moments later.

"We will go to the beach, I think I know where he meant." Kishil's voice was rough, ragged. I turned to see him covered in blood from his mouth to his legs. I wouldn't look at the body on the ground. I didn't want to know how far they'd gone. It wasn't something I was comfortable with, not yet. This was a part of them, but it wasn't my norm.

"Are you okay?" Talon asked, his arm coming around my waist as Kishil pulled me into a hug.

Blood smeared against my clothes and I hugged them tight, trying to ignore the warm sticky sensation seeping through against my skin.

"Go. Stop them, I'll be here when you return," I whispered.

Kishil released me, as some emotion I didn't understand passed over his face, before his raptor exploded out of him. Talon shifted back and they ran through the village, heading to the beach the traders were using.

Storm waited for a moment—still in raptor form—until I met her eyes. Her bloody snout dipped again, for the second time in a short span. It wasn't lost on me that she took the time to show me respect, even in the absence of her new Alpha. Maybe Storm wouldn't always be a threat. Maybe she could accept me one day.

I held my chin high and turned to face my people as the song of a mockingbird rang through the village. I searched for the source of the sound, and found the Mockingbird himself sitting atop a chickee, ruffling his feathers with his beak.

"I'll take that as a 'good job,'" I muttered.

Chapter 22

Sage

I sank into the river, washing my arms and face with the oil my mother had given me. She'd said I needed to. I swallowed hard as I dipped down into the water, wetting my hair. I lathered my dark tresses as I went, rinsing the paint and dried blood from my body. I'd went into my chickee last night and rinsed myself off in the bowl I kept by my bed, but it wasn't nearly enough water to remove all the markings, hence my presence at the river.

I scrubbed until the last bits of white paint ran down my skin with the dripping water. Dunking beneath the surface to rinse off any remaining oil, I quickly broke through the surface again and made my way to the shore. My people tried to limit their time in the river, since gators were notorious and they didn't discriminate—matriarchs had fallen to them before.

"Watch your step, Clever Girl," a deep voice purred from the shadows of the trees. I leapt onto the shore, running toward Talon's voice. They were back! I'd expected them to be gone for a few days at least, and it had hardly been a whole day yet. I was happy to see him as he stepped on to the bank, his arms opened wide as I launched myself at him.

He caught me with ease, chuckling as he spun me around. I wrapped my arms around his neck, burying my face in his hair.

"Well, I think I like how you welcome me after I've been gone. Maybe we should stay gone more often. What do you think?"

"I think it's a terrible idea," Kishil muttered as he came up behind me. I was transferred into his arms and he cradled me against his chest, even though I was soaking wet.

"I'm getting you wet," I whispered.

"I think that's supposed to be our line," Elu murmured from the side. He came up and kissed me on the lips quickly before he darted away again. "Put her down! Her mother has something planned. I don't think we're supposed to have our claws all over her right now."

"What?" I blinked, trying to understand what he meant.

"Indeed, she *does* have something planned. No touching until the dance is over," my father called from the nearest chickee.

I blushed against Kishil's chest, and slid down to my feet. A snarl rattled through Talon and I pointed at him in warning. He stopped almost instantly.

"A dance?" Kishil asked. The grin on his face told me he already had a good idea of what it meant.

"Well... you told them I'm your mate. My people have a wedding dance. If you don't want to..." My toes drug through the soil. I suddenly felt very self-conscious. I hadn't been consulted about this either. My mother and father didn't know the details of how we'd come to be mated. When I didn't correct them—when I *decided* to allow this mating to stand—they must have gotten to work planning the ceremony to honor our traditions.

"Of course we want to," Kishil whispered. "Even if it is a silly human custom."

"We should go learn about this dance, while you go do whatever aspiring matriarchs are supposed to do." Talon grimaced. He didn't strike me as a dancer, so this should be interesting.

Someone swatted me on the ass and I rolled my eyes skyward. This life was going to be interesting, that was for sure.

I CLASPED THE COLORFUL CLOTH AROUND MY NECK. IT HUNG freely down the front, revealing the perfect amount of cleavage to tease my future husbands with. Were they husbands or mates? I guess it would depend on whom I was speaking to.

"What are you thinking?" Mom inquired, as she cinched the fabric just above the small of my back. She had repainted my symbols, adding some color where before it had all been white. The vast majority of my marks were still white, but the pops of color let me know that I'd done something right during all of this.

"I was trying to figure out if I should call them my mates or my husbands," I whispered.

"You don't have to call them either, you know that, don't you? If you're having second thoughts—"

I turned around, gripping her hands in my own. Her smile was slow and kind, warming her eyes.

"It's fast. I'll tell you all about how it happened one day, but just know that they feel like a part of my soul now." I sucked in a breath at how true that felt. They were a part of me. Whether it was some kind of magic the claiming marks had bewitched me with, or my own heart playing traitor, I belonged to them.

"My sweet, curious child," Mom cried, wrapping me in a tight hug. I leaned in to her embrace, soaking up her warmth. "Let's go then, they'll be ready."

I followed her out of the chickee and through the village until we reached the center. Torches had been lit and lined the area. Sacred symbols were drawn in the dirt. I swallowed, stepping around them carefully, until I reached the middle of the design. The dance had to be executed correctly, or the marriage was 'shunned by the Spirits.'

I glanced around at all of the familiar faces who were watching. Chayton sat with my father, holding drums in their laps. They'd play the beat that we were supposed to dance to. At the end, everyone should be in the center of the design, with none of the symbols disturbed. My mouth went dry as a series of chirping clicks reached my ears. I spun around, a smile on my lips, as I watched my mates step toward the circle in raptor form.

"Of course you would," I whispered, shaking my head.

They all three rose in unison, baying out. The drums began and I twirled through the center of the design, dancing between each symbol carefully. Elu was the first one I came to, my fingers grazed across the back of the yellow raptor and he began bobbing and weaving through the maze of symbols with me.

The drums picked up speed as I neared Talon—the wild, sweet hearted warrior. My hands loosely wrapped around his neck as I danced around him, and he made his way through the circle with me. I spun and ducked, weaving between my raptors as we approached Kishil.

He was bobbing back and forth on his feet, swaying with the beat.

The drums beat faster as I got near him, tracing my finger across his snout before I spun away. It was an invitation to chase me, and they did. I twirled and rolled my hips as I worked my way back to the center of the circle.

I came to a stop, turning around to see if they'd made it back with me, as the three of them leapt into the center of the circle.

Three raptors leaned forward, their chins sweeping above the dirt in a sort of bow as the drums came to a sudden stop. My chest rose and fell as I glanced around at the symbols, undisturbed by our dance. I raised my hands, yelling out a victory cry.

My husbands rose to their full height, clicking and chirping before they bayed out together. Several bays sounded in the woods and scalies began filing into the village in both raptor and human form. I covered my mouth, grinning wide. I hadn't expected that at all.

One by one the guys shifted back into their human form, and children came running up with pants for them to put on—no beads this time—with smiles on their faces.

"Elder Nova said you'd need these so the next matriarch doesn't feed her to the scalies," the little boy whispered with a smile, before he ran off. He was careful not to disturb the symbols on the ground, at least.

"Well, at least Nova is learning," I commented with a grin.

"That old woman is going to molest us one day," Kishil muttered. I pressed my lips to his, and then was turned around by Talon for a kiss of his own. Elu was next, and his lips were by far the softest between the three of them.

I stood there, in a wedding dress, in the middle of a village where scalies were mingling with my people like they were old friends, on my wedding night.

"Is it what you wanted?" Elu asked softly against my mouth. I shook my head, drawing concerned glances from the three of them.

"It's more," I whispered, looking skyward for the umpteenth time that day. The Mockingbird was nowhere to be found, but I hoped he knew how thankful I was.

"I love you all," I choked out.

Kishil tucked my hair behind my ear.

Talon grabbed my hand and led me toward the chickee that would be ours from now on.

I glanced over my shoulder one last time at my people—they were happy, whole, and surrounded by friends. I bit my lip, steeling myself before I let my loves pull me into our new home.

Elu chuckled as he pushed the tapestries apart to reveal the massive bed they must have moved from their pack house.

This was home.

ACKNOWLEDGMENTS

Thank you to everyone who took the time to look over this book when it was still a baby stuck in Google Docs. My alphas, betas, and editors helped shape this book into the story that it is. Each and every one if you is amazing and I appreciate all the hard work and time you spent with me on this project. Thank you Jess and Bri for your editing and proofreading!

This project wouldn't be what it is without Kendra Moreno. I had originally planned a stand alone about my raptors but thanks to our conversations and nerding out together, this idea grew into an entire series in a shared universe with one of the most amazing women I have ever met. Thank you so much for coming into my life and being such a joy and support. I love you, girl!

As always, my three-way + MalMal kept me sane while I wrote this in between family drama, moving, death, bills, and all the quiet things that can keep authors from putting out work. Thank you for always being there for me. Katie, Kendra, Mal, I honestly don't know if I'd be able to handle all the things without you and I appreciate you *so so much*. Never change.

And I want to thank you, the reader. Without you, this would just be an e-book floating around Amazon. You give my work life and I am so thankful you took a chance on a new style of book with me. You fucking rock.

ABOUT THE AUTHOR

Poppy Woods is a Paranormal and Urban Fantasy Romance author. When she isn't chasing her three year old hellion around their Georgia home or writing, she can usually be found with a drink in her and her nose in a book.

Just remember, if you catch a Poppy in the wild, cocktails and chocolate are a valid form of bribery!

ALSO BY POPPY WOODS